Slime Incorporated

Adam Graham

Great Detective Books
Boise, Idaho
© 2014 Adam Graham
All Rights Reserved

ISBN: 978-1496030528

Other Books by Adam Graham:

Tales of the Dim Knight (Splashdown Books)
Fly Another Day
Powerhouse Hard Pressed

Slander is the sum of all villainies
and the slanderer is the king of all villains
.-JB Cranfill

Chapter 1

"So would you put idiot or moron?"

Jerry Newton looked up at me from behind his gold-colored PC. "Ustick, neither is quite up to our professional standards."

The boss and I were seated in the office of Newton Investigations. We had eight peeling, artificial wood desks and eight mismatched office chairs in need of yet another reupholstering. My other six colleagues had all either gone home for the weekend or were out on assignment.

The sterile white walls bore only our business license and the first dollar the business ever collected. Both framed items hung behind the boss near the window. It gave a nice view of the traffic headed down River Street toward the library, which was cleverly named "Library!"

I swished around in my mouth my flavorless Juicy Fruit gum. "This has got to be the dumbest guy I've run into yet. I go to his house, and he's got a stack of these stolen computers—with the company lease numbers facing the windows, mind you. He copped out to the whole thing. And I got on to him just because of his shoes."

"How?" Newton asked as he picked lint off his navy sweater vest. He was chubby, but his afternoon snack was plain celery sticks, in a plastic baggie. They were on his desk beside his Idaho Medal of Honor for Law Enforcement certificate. He straightened it. "They were just a pair of tennis shoes."

"To the untrained eye, but I saw their label. Those shoes retail for $300 on Amazon. They're not available locally. Thirty bucks would be pricey for a pair of shoes on his pay."

Newton typed on his computer's keyboard. "You have too much faith in your own instincts, Ustick. If they'd been a gift from a rich friend, you would have cost the client two billable hours plus and ninety-six miles of gasoline."

"He lives in Homedale." I snorted. "If the people there had friends that gave them $300 shoes, they wouldn't live in Homedale."

"That's where you're wrong. Some of us don't want to spend our whole lives like rats trapped on a wheel."

I smirked. "Did we get transported to New York or Philly? Boise is only what? The 120th largest city in America?"

The boss stopped typing and glared at me. "104th, Ustick."

"Sorry, I didn't get the latest circular from the Chamber of Commerce."

He pointed a celery stick at me. "You can be wrong."

"Sure, I'm wrong twenty-five percent of the time. That's built into my salary. Otherwise, I'd be Sherlock Holmes, and you couldn't afford me. I'd be living the good life in Homedale."

The boss leaned forward. "You're playing with people's money and lives. Sometimes, it's like you're living out a boyhood fantasy."

"Nah. It was simply easier to get on here than to join the Power Rangers, and becoming a cowboy was impractical."

The boss sighed. "Never mind. Do you have anything else to do other than distract me?"

"I have to hit the save button on my Word document."

"Do Control S. It'll give me more time to work without you chattering."

A bald man in his thirties blustered through our door. The stranger wore a pin-striped suit, a red tie, wingtips, and the ghost of a permanent smirk, from the wrinkles around his mouth.

Time to live up to Newton's definition of professionalism. I turned my head away from the visitor, spit my used-up gum in a wrapper, and dropped it in the trash can under my desk.

The stranger was swaggering past me, smelling like a fifty-dollar bottle of Gucci cologne. He stopped by Newton's desk. "Hey, Fig."

The boss shuddered but shoved the celery in his desk and looked up with a standard issue, professional smile. "Are you talking to me, sir?"

"Sir?" Laughing, our guest slapped his leg. "That's no way to talk to the best power forward ever in the history of Mount Tacoma High. I certainly remember our respectable point guard."

Newton scrunched his eyebrows together and stood. "I'm sorry, I don't remember you. High school was more years ago than I'd like to admit."

"Fig, I'm surprised. You're a detective."

I rolled my eyes. *Not another joker who thinks detectives have Jedi powers.*

The smirk grew wider. "Okay, the old powers of deduction are allowed to be a little off at the end of a hard week. I'm Bart Bradley."

Newton eyed Bradley's chrome dome and inhaled, leaning away from him. "You've changed a lot."

"You haven't—aside from too many donuts." The jerk's smirk stretched into the proportions of a cheeky grin.

Gritting his teeth, Newton shook his hand and waved at the chair across from his desk. "Have a seat. What can I do for you?"

The chair creaked as Bradley lowered himself into it. "Fig, I need you to help with a background check on a job candidate."

I sighed. *Great. I'm the only operative available, so this will delay my weekend.*

Newton sat and pulled a yellow notepad from his desk drawer. "Who is the candidate?"

Bradley reached into his jacket's inside pocket, pulled a photo out, and slid it across Newton's desk.

The boss glanced at it, snarled, and flicked the photo back at Bradley like he'd wanted to stab him with it. "Go to the devil!"

I gaped at him. What had gotten into him?

Bradley raised a hand. "Fig—"

"And another thing." Newton jumped up and got in Bradley's face, his eyes blazing. "I hated that nickname in high school. If you use it again, I'll lay you out. You lied right off and said this was an employer background check. You want a smear job? Find yourself another boy, pally."

Bradley stood. "Opposition research is a legit field of investigation."

"Nice Orwellian euphemism."

"A lot of men look good until you find out who they really are."

"You can hire every bottom feeder in Boise, but they won't find anything on Ignacio Hernandez." Newton stabbed at finger at Bradley. "Get your rear out of my office before Mr. Ustick and I toss you out on it."

I stood. And here I'd thought I wouldn't have any fun at work before I went home.

Bradley shook his head and chuckled. "Too bad, Newton. Just wanted to send an old pal some business." He glanced around at our office. "Looks like you could use it."

With that, he strode out the door without closing it.

Party pooper. I flopped at my desk.

Newton strode to the door and slammed it.

The frame rattled.

He kicked over the empty trash can by his desk, straightened the can, and sat. "Ustick, get me that report, now!"

I bit back a comeback and emailed Newton the report. I poked my head out from behind my computer. "That was disappointing. It's been years since I've gotten to toss someone out on their rear."

Newton sighed. "I'm sorry. That was unprofessional."

I rolled my chair out into the aisle, so I was facing his desk. "Oh, I found it entertaining. You were so upset, I thought you might say fanny."

"But I did curse out a potential client."

In a way I consider worthy of being made fun of. "Two questions, boss."

Newton glowered. "What?"

"What kind of nickname is Fig?"

"Put the nickname and my last name together."

"Fig Newt—" I chuckled. "That's a good one. I'll have to remember it."

He grimaced. "Just don't repeat it."

"Second question. Why did you go nuts over exposing a politician?"

"Don't you have work to do?"

"Other than shutting down my computer? Nope. I'm ready to go home. So again, what set you off?"

Newton turned his chair towards me. "When I was in college, I worked part-time at Hernandez's corporate office. During my sophomore year, my dad died while stopping an armed robbery. I left school and sought a full-time job that could support my family. Hernandez found out. He helped my mom find work and took care of my undergraduate tuition as well as my brother's."

"Nice guy."

"And there's never been any publicity about it. He really took an interest in me, and I'm not the only one. He and his wife are good people. It boils my blood to think, because he wants to make the state better, they're going to be put through the ringer by the likes of Bart Bradley."

I leaned back. "Hernandez sounds like the type of guy I might vote for— if I voted."

Newton lifted his chin. "I never you took you for an idiot."

My cheeks grew hot. "What do you mean by that?"

Smiling, the boss leaned in. "In Ancient Greece, the word idiot referred to people who didn't vote."

I waved it aside. "In modern America, idiot means the guy who sits on pins and needles for two weeks on call waiting to see if our beloved county will summon him to jury duty. That won't happen to me."

"You'd be surprised. The registered voters list doesn't double as a jurors list in Idaho. You can still be called."

"I won't get called. Anyway, are you going to tell your kindly benefactor to watch his back?"

Newton shook his head. "Hernandez has been around long enough to know a gubernatorial campaign isn't going to be a breezy picnic. Even scum like Bradley deserve what happens in this office to be confidential."

I looked at my watch. "Now that my curiosity is satisfied, mind if I leave? I've already put in forty-four hours this week, and you have no client to bill for my overtime pay."

The boss waved me away. "Sure, see you on Monday."

I shut down my computer. I pulled my fine black hair out of its ponytail, retied it, and let it fall just below my shoulder blade to the middle of my back. I put on my scarlet fedora, and walked to the coat rack. I pulled my tan overcoat on over my scarlet suit, worn with a pair of red leather wingtips. Under my jacket, I carried a 9mm Glock in a shoulder holster.

After ambling out of the building, I walked down the stairs and onto the sidewalk. A little uneven pile of slush remained on a shadowed portion of the grass. The rest of the grass was wet with no slush. The sun was shining bright while a cold wind was blowing, as if nature wasn't quite sure what season it was. Typical for February in Boise.

I hopped into my pink 2005 Jaguar.

Across the parking lot, Newton's pal Bradley sat at the wheel of a late model silver Impala with rental car plates, hunched over a smartphone.

On second thought, my curiosity hasn't quite been satisfied. Where would you go to find a bottom-feeding private detective in Boise? I plugged my iPhone into the car's docking station and turned on my tunes. Beyonce's voice filled the cabin.

Three songs in, Bradley finished with the phone and started the Impala.

I waited for him to pull out before following him and merged into traffic two car lengths back. We drove down River Street, across 9th, past the library, and turned left onto Capitol.

Near the end of the boulevard, Bradley turned right onto Bannock and pulled into a parking lot of a two-story building. The wooden sign listed only one private investigator firm, Sheryl Thompson and Associates. Bradley parked and stomped to Thompson's office.

Well, that figured. I drove around the block three times before finding a metered parking space in front of a dentist's office half a block away, in sight of Bradley's car.

Time for the most exciting part of my job: waiting.

I fed the meter for half an hour's worth of parking and popped in a fresh stick of Juicy Fruit. I leaned back in my seat, savored the orange cream pop flavor and hunkered down with the Angry Birds on my iPhone.

After twenty minutes, Bradley came downstairs, got in the car, fiddled with his smartphone a bit, and drove away.

I followed him over to 9th and to Vista Avenue. About two miles down, he hung a left into the lot of the Holiday Inn Express.

Most likely, he was simply returning to his hotel room after having found his bottom feeder. Sheryl Thompson would turn down a paying job the day Donald Trump refused publicity.

Either way, it wasn't my case. I yawned. Time to head home.

A few minutes later, I parked outside my duplex's garage, picked up a stack of mail I'd grabbed from my box, and went inside the house.

The kitchen's gray tile stretched into the entryway. I headed to the left, onto the slate blue living room carpet.

Against one wall was a baby blue leather couch with matching recliner. I laid the mail on the end table by my recliner. To the right of it was my purple keyboard on a music stand with a brown chair borrowed from the dinette set. On the wall across from the couch was a stone shelf. There, I kept three food-flavored candles in jars and one lighter. I lit the butterscotch blondies candle and breathed in the "fresh out of the oven" smell without the fuss.

I slipped my phone into the high-end docking station and turned on the radio app. The Hip Hop station's tunes poured out of the station's speakers. I switched it to a reggae station, perfect for chilling on a Friday afternoon.

I settled into my recliner and smiled at my mural of the Vermillion rocks at Pariah Canyon. The ruddy, spiraled formations looked like they were from another world.

After a minute, I yawned and sorted the mail. Junk, circular, junk, junk.

Letter from Ada County.

Huh? What would the county want with me? Assessments shouldn't be out for a couple months.

I opened the letter and cursed.

A summons for jury duty.

Chapter 2

One month later, my colleague Wanda Parks was reading a letter at her desk and the boss was on the phone. I settled in at my computer. *I hope I didn't get a big attachment that clogged my inbox and put me in email jail while I was off work last week. It should all be spam, since my open cases were all reassigned to other investigators.* The boss hung up and looked over at me. "How'd jury duty go?"

I sighed. "Well, the trial was easy enough. Started Wednesday morning, and we should've been out on Thursday afternoon. It was clear the defendant had done the burglary. Unfortunately, one jerky juror wanted to play like it was *Twelve Angry Men.* He kept asking to see exhibits, getting testimony read back to us, reviewing every little point over and over again."

Wanda smacked her lips. "Refusing to meekly go along with the majority doesn't mean the guy was showboating. Man's got a right to his opinion."

"That possibility went out the window when he asked me if I were the defendant's executioner." I rolled my eyes. "Anyway, he pushed this thing into Friday and wanted us to be sequestered over the weekend, but the judge saw no reason for it. By today, our holdout was willing to listen to reason, and we got the verdict in. The whole shebang was settled just before lunch." I took a breath and aimed my chin at Newton. "You got anything for me?"

Newton shook his head. "A new client's coming in at three o'clock, but that's Wanda's assignment. Reed and Henson are supposed to report in at two. I'll find out if they could use your help on the Western Mutual investigation."

I yawned. "Okay, I'll sit here bored."

"I don't think so. Clean up your email inbox."

I grunted. Would the fun never stop?

An olive-skinned man opened the door and strode in our office like he was a motivational speaker here tell us we too could be millionaires. He looked to be approximately five-foot-six. Behind him came a pale, white-haired man about six-foot-one. He wore a gray Tommy Hilfiger suit, took long strides, and had a stern expression etched on his face. He had his hands behind his back. If he were an actor, I'd have cast him as a football coach or maybe a general.

Newton jumped up from his desk and extended his hand to the short motivational speaker. "Mr. Hernandez, it's good to see you."

Hernandez grinned and slapped Newton on the back. "It's good to see you, Jerry. Is business going well?"

"Can't complain."

That makes one of us. I frowned. Two short weeks ago, the boss had sat us all down and explained we wouldn't be getting raises this year.

The pale man spoke. "Mr. Newton, have you seen today's paper?"

"Not yet."

"We need help." Hernandez eyed Wanda and me. "It's confidential."

I arched my eyebrow. "So confidential that it was in today's paper?"

The pale man glowered at me. "This case is very confidential."

Newton swallowed. "Everyone in my office can be trusted, but we can step into the consultation room. Cole Ustick will be working on your case, so he'll need to be there."

"We want you on the case." The pale man said it like it was an order.

Newton drew a breath. "Sir, I don't believe I got your name."

"Marc Hearst. I'm Mr. Hernandez's campaign manager."

"This isn't a one-man office, Mr. Hearst. I supervise six people, and they do most of the investigative work. I help only as needed."

Hernandez nodded. "Of course, Jerry. You've got to run your business."

The boss grabbed a standard contract form from his desk.

The four of us shuffled into the consultation room. Seven mismatched office chairs surrounded a rectangular office table with a leather top.

The boss sat at the head of the table. I sat at his right. The clients sat on the left, with Hernandez by the boss.

I studied the two men. Hernandez was a chubby guy, though I assumed some of that was muscle, based on calluses on his hands. His nails had been clipped but had a few rough edges and were dry. He fidgeted in the chair.

Hearst was gaunt. He had well-manicured nails, and his surviving hairs were neatly combed.

The boss began. "What can we do for you?"

Hearst folded his hands on the table. "Today's paper has falsely accused Mr. Hernandez of sexual assaulting three women."

The boss and I exchanged glances. Hernandez was coming to the wrong place if he thought we'd help a criminal cover things up and escape justice.

Hernandez peered at the boss. "I would never mistreat a woman. I told you what I told every young man: treat women with respect because they're someone's wife, or sister, or—" He looked down. "—or someone's daughter."

Newton rested his hand on Hernandez's arm. "I know you wouldn't do such a thing."

I cleared my throat. "Who are the women? And when and where are they alleging this happened?"

Hearst clenched his jaw. "That's what we want you to find out."

"Excuse me?" I asked.

"The paper's sources are all anonymous. The only timeframe offered by the paper is between 2006 and 2010."

The boss rubbed his eyes. "So let me get this straight. The paper printed a story where anonymous people accused Hernandez of doing non-specific things at non-specific times. Were they specific about places?"

"Once, it was in a park. In two cases, it was in a car. According to them, he took them on a date and made unwanted sexual advances. Our lawyers have advised us those actions would constitute assault, if it were true. The park story alleges he jumped some random woman." Hearst stood, folded his arms, and stared down at us. "Gentlemen, we can't let these stories go, but we need to get specifics to respond well to this."

I asked, "And knowing when this happened will help?"

Hernandez nodded. "I use a day planner to keep track of my schedule, and I have my old ones in storage going back to the 1990s. You ask me where I was at a given time, and I can find out from, and probably also tell you who I was with."

The boss scratched his nose. "Let me see if I understand. Our job is to find these women and get specifics on their allegations."

Hearst nodded. "Precisely."

"Sir, we'll be glad to take the case." Newton unfolded the contract and handed it to Hernandez. "We'll do a standard contract. Our rate is forty-five dollars per hour plus expenses, and we require $2000 retainer."

Hernandez signed the document, pulled out a checkbook, and wrote a check for the retainer. "Here you go, Jerry."

"Thank you, sir." Newton turned to Hearst. "Who do you think cooked up this story?"

Hearst pursed his lips. "We see a number of possibilities. There's the governor, who we're leading by a solid margin according to the latest primary polls. There's the Democrats, who hate my candidate more than they hate the governor. In addition, the unions will lose big, if Mr. Hernandez gets elected and gets his tax reform package passed."

"Any personal or business enemies who just might have it out for you?"

Hernandez shook his head. "I have business rivals, not business enemies. There's probably a disgruntled employee or dissatisfied customer out there, but I can't think of anyone who'd stoop to this."

Newton pulled out a business card and handed it to Hernandez. "Fax us a list of anyone you can think of. In addition, I need a list of your campaign staffers and volunteers."

Hearst grimaced. "Why do you need a list of volunteers?"

"One of them may know something or have been bought. We have to check all the angles."

Hearst cleared his throat. "Our people are absolutely above suspicion."

I mustered my most professional smile. "Mr. Hearst, in any investigation, nobody is above suspicion. Are you an investigator?"

He huffed. "If I were, then I wouldn't be talking to a hippy private eye, now would I?"

I'd best let the dated insult pass. "If you're going to hire experts, you've got to let us do our job. Otherwise, find someone you will trust to use their judgment to do the investigation."

"I just want to be sure you don't cause problems around the campaign."

Oh please. Then don't hire investigators. You'll have a nice, happy, losing campaign.

The boss cleared his throat. "Don't worry. We'll be discreet."

I sighed. *I hate it when he promises what we can't deliver.*

First Hernandez rose, then Hearst. Hernandez patted Newton's shoulder like a father. "Jerry, I'd like to pray for you before we go."

I scrunched together my eyebrows. I'd never been offered God's help on a case before, or needed it, but I guess it couldn't hurt.

Newton bowed his head, and I followed his lead.

Hernandez touched both my back and Newton's. "Dear Lord, we thank you for Jerry. Lord, I pray you would be with him and his employee as they investigate this matter, and help them to uncover your truth. Keep them safe and bless their efforts. In Jesus' name, amen."

I raised my head. Hearst's cheeks were pink. *Apparently, political consultants find mixing prayer and business as awkward as some private detectives do.*

Hernandez tapped Newton's arm. "Thanks for your time. I do appreciate your help, and I'm sure you'll get to the bottom of this."

We walked them out. Wanda had left on an assignment.

Newton slumped at his desk and held his head in his hands.

I paced around the office. "Question. Did he do it?"

"No way." Newton straightened up, glared, and swatted in my direction like he would a fly. "Do you have any ideas where we should start?"

I shrugged. "I can get us a pretty good lead, but I will need some money from petty cash."

"How much?"

"Two hundred."

"What's it for?"

"Trust me."

The boss leaned back in his chair. "The only reason you're not telling me is you don't think I'll approve the expense."

I sighed. "Remember the jerk that came in right before I got called to jury duty? The one who wanted us to look into Hernandez?"

"Too well. What about him?"

"I followed him. He went straight to another detective agency. Based on how long he was in there, I think he found his bottom feeder."

"Okay, and what's the two hundred for?"

"Leah Brooks."

Bowing his head, the boss interlaced his middle fingers, ring fingers, and pinkies while touching his nose with his index fingers and resting his thumb under his chin.

I popped a stick of gum in my mouth. "Boss, we need a quick lead. The longer a thing like this drags on, the worse it is for the accused."

The boss sat another ten seconds before he pulled out a key, opened a locked desk drawer, and pulled out a ledger and the petty cash. He handed me a wad of twenty dollar bills. "I really don't like this."

"You will if we find the women."

I strode down a hall of vacant offices until I reached a dark brown door. Between the glass and the blinds of the window was a sign that read, "Rock-Star Network Solutions."

As I entered, a dragon roared from the speaker above the door.

Leah Brooks sat at her black marble desk, which had a fireball painted on it. Her pixie cut was half bleach blonde and half Superman blue. She wore a lip ring and a light blue t-shirt with a unicorn flying over a rainbow. She'd told me she was five months pregnant, but she still wasn't showing. Behind her was a mural of a unicorn flying over a rainbow.

Leah stopped typing but kept her eyes on her monitor. "Ustick, what can I do for you?"

"I need you to peek inside a computer system."

"Whose?" Leah continued to focus on her machine.

"Sheryl Thompson and Associates."

She chuckled. "First find me Osama bin Laden's family Bible."

"Are you saying Sheryl Thompson doesn't have a computer system?"

"Give the man a prize." Leah grinned at me, clapping. "Thompson is Boise's biggest Luddite. She makes her employees prepare their reports on Brother Word Processors. There's one computer that they use for Internet searches, but if they want to print anything, it comes off a dot matrix printer."

"Dot matrix?"

"Yeah. Like this." She reached into a drawer and pulled out a piece of paper with a series of holes on either side.

"What are the holes for?"

"In theory, it keeps the printer paper straight. In practice, I learned my best swear words when my mother was dealing with paper jams."

Stay on topic. "So, what about their files?"

She snorted. "Oh come on, Sherlock. You not had enough coffee today? Where do you think they keep their files? The most unhackable system in the world—a filing cabinet."

I sighed. "Thanks."

"No problem." Her fingers flew across her keyboard.

At eight that night, I stood outside the office of Sheryl Thompson and Associates. I was dressed in black dress pants and a black turtleneck sweater. My gun was at home, where it couldn't get me a longer prison sentence if I got caught. I counted off five twenty dollar bills and handed them to the janitor.

The janitor put the money into his coveralls packet. "Remember, you got just an hour. When I'm done cleaning, you're out of here."

It shouldn't take that long. I nodded.

The janitor left. I slipped into the office. Hopefully, we'd get a lead. *It couldn't do worse than three hours of the boss's boring, ineffective "old-fashioned legwork."*

I turned on my flashlight.

The walls were baby blue. A reception desk half as wide as our office blocked off most of the room. I circled my light around the desk until I found a gap. I scanned ahead. A dozen cubicles lay at the end of the hall. I shone the flashlight to the right.

A name plate said, "Sheryl Thompson, Chief Investigator."

Sounds like she's working for a congress, not two-bit divorce attorneys. I turned my light to the left. It highlighted a padlocked room marked, "Filing."

I grinned. Picking this one would take twenty seconds. I knelt and pulled a lock picking tool from my pants pockets, along with my iPhone. I pulled up the stopwatch. "Name that tune."

I started the stopwatch, picked the padlock, and pressed the stop button on the stopwatch. The display reported my time as 18.9 seconds. I slipped my phone in my pocket and walked in.

Three gray filing cabinets lay ahead. I dashed to the first filing cabinet and knelt by the fourth drawer. It was listed as Bo-Bu. I pulled on the drawer. Locked.

Here we go again. I pulled out my stopwatch and went to work.

Fourteen seconds later, the lock came open. I pulled the drawer out and flipped through the files. Bode . . . Bolen . . . Bradford . . . Bradley. Make that Aaron Bradley. I moved on to the next file. Bart Bradley.

Bingo. I clutched the prize file.

The light in the filing room came on.

Uh oh.

"Partner, hands in the air!"

I straightened up and turned around, hands raised.

The man in the doorway wore a purple and brown cowboy shirt, a cowboy hat, and cowboy boots. His goatee made him look like a country music star. He smelled of Stetson cologne.

"Whatdya think you're doing in here?" The cowboy's accent was as New York as Rockefeller Plaza.

"The janitor let me in."

Brooklyn Cowboy looked me over. "Who do you work for?"

"Work? Entering offices after hours is my hobby."

"Fool, when somebody's got a gun on you, you don't crack wise. Kick that file and your wallet over to me."

I put the file on the ground, kicked it over, and reached for my wallet.

Brooklyn Cowboy waved the gun. "Pull the wallet, nice and slow. This thing's got a hair trigger, and I wouldn't want to get too excited."

"You've been getting your daily supply of clichés, I see." I removed my wallet and kicked it over.

While still keeping an eye on me, he picked up my wallet and opened it. He glanced at my ID. "Cole Ustick. What is a fancy dresser like you doing in black? I didn't recognize you."

"Didn't you hear? All black is the latest thing. Every burglar in Milan is wearing it."

Brooklyn Cowboy smirked. "I'll bet. You ought to try dressing normal."

"You first, Buffalo Bob."

Brooklyn Cowboy snarled. "What'd I tell you about cracking wise? Don't you work for an ex-cop? Does he know you're breaking and entering?"

"No, and my mother doesn't know either."

Brooklyn Cowboy snatched up the file and opened it. "Oh, this guy." He growled. "Has that Bradley jerk hired you to reinvestigate the case?"

"We didn't think you'd let us look at your file on him, after the slipshod job you did."

"Slipshod? Please, Bradley told you wrong. This way."

17

The cowboy waved his gun, led me out to the cubicle area, and pointed at a chair. "Siddown, partner."

I lowered myself down carefully.

He put the file in my hand. "Read that."

I opened and noted the name of the client, Bradley and Associates in Seattle. The invoice was for $20,000 for 400 hours of work plus $10,000 in expenses. I skimmed the expense page. A couple airline flights, hotel rooms, taxi cabs, copies, and a couple thousand for miscellaneous expenses. I turned to the summary.

They'd tailed Hernandez for several days, interviewed people who knew him from all over the country, visited the cities he frequented, and greased dozens of palms to get confidential information: personnel files, library lending reports, military records. Their result: Hernandez was as clean as an OCD patient's apartment. The Vatican would've started the canonization process, if he weren't both alive and a protestant former Assistant Pastor.

I closed the file, put it on the table, and eyed Brooklyn Cowboy. "So you have nothing on the women accusing him of sexual assault?"

He smirked. "Bradley raised a big stink over paying so much for a clean background check."

"Yeah." Laughing, I reopened the file. "He paid you on February 20th."

"If that's what the file says."

I clucked my tongue. "So any theory as to how you missed it?"

"Missed what?" Brooklyn Cowboy glared, his eyes bloodshot. He jabbed me in the chest. "The story's fake. If it were real, we would've found it."

I bit my lip. "Your methods of investigation wouldn't necessarily turn up some women he randomly met and assaulted."

"Maybe not, but it revealed what type of guy he was. We obtained his credit card statements. No porn subscriptions. Not even any visits to Victoria's Secrets. It doesn't fit."

"That's a good point," I said, rising from the chair. "Well, I'll be going."

"Not so fast. I got a gun on you."

"So? Rule number one of pulling a gun on someone: never do it unless you're prepared to actually shoot them. When you first saw me in here, you were prepared." I walked out from behind the desk. "Now, you know I'm not a burglar. I'm a fellow private investigator out for some professional courtesy, for which I thank you."

"You looked at confidential files."

"And you guys looked at confidential credit card statements." I laughed and held my hands out. "Think about this. You kill me, and you're going to have to either call the cops and explain why, or you're going to have to find somewhere to hide my body."

He twitched. "I could call the cops on you."

"For what? The janitor let me in. You let me read the file. Though, the cops might be interested in some of your tactics. Bribing a city librarian is still bribing a public official. If you involve the cops, I doubt Sheryl Thompson will be too happy with you."

Brooklyn Cowboy grunted and jerked his thumb at the door. "Hit the road, partner."

I tipped my hat. "It was a pleasure doing business with you."

Chapter 3

I strode into the office the next morning. I wore a plum-colored suit and a matching fedora with a white shirt and a gray tie.

The boss was reading over my report. "Ustick, come on over."

I rolled my chair to Newton's desk and had a seat. "Yeah, Boss?"

"So all you learned last night is who didn't find these women."

I leaned back in my chair. "Don't forget, the client also got a character reference from a wannabe cowboy from Brooklyn."

Newton blinked. "Ustick, stick to trying to find out who these women are. The client's innocence isn't in question."

Biased much? That's always in question. I leaned back. "Sure, he's a great guy by all accounts, but so was Durand. You know what he did."

Newton closed his eyes. "Ustick, often the person you suspect least of being an abuser turns out to be one, but it's not true with Hernandez. He was very respectful to every woman in our office. He's devoted to his wife. This whole story put out by the paper, it's not in his nature."

My sister's vacant-eyed face rose in my mind. My jaw tightened and my fists clenched as I glared at the boss. "A woman wouldn't lie about this."

"Most wouldn't, like most people wouldn't jump in front of a car to get an insurance settlement, but we've investigated cases where that's happened."

"Whatever. He's still most likely guilty, statistically."

Newton cleared his throat. "We need to narrow the field of suspects. Who benefits from Mr. Hernandez falling in the polls? I have a few answers.

First, there are his primary opponents, the governor and Teddy Starr. Second, there's the opposing party. That's a good place to start. Try taking the direct approach, ask some questions. Let's see if we can get someone rattled."

"What about Bart Bradley?"

"Look into him, too, and check around the campaign headquarters and see if they have any information."

Fall Out Boy was playing on my iPhone as I drove past Nampa on the freeway. I entered the shrinking stretch of countryside that lay between the last suburb and the next suburb.

The boss' number flashed on my caller ID. I pressed the button on the hand's free device clipped to my ear. "Ustick."

"Go ahead and cross Teddy Starr off your list. I did some research. He's a fringe candidate who wouldn't have the sophistication for a smear like this."

I growled. "You might have done the research before sending me."

The boss swallowed. "Sorry, but at least we saved you an interview."

"I'll head early to my interview of the Director of the Idaho Democratic Party." I took the next exit. The putrid odor of the Simplot plant assaulted me. Thank God I had the windows up. Simplot made a steel mill smell like a dozen roses on Valentine's Day.

I got back on the freeway headed in the opposite direction, back toward Meridian. Once there, I parked in front of Wingers and checked the time on my iPhone. I was forty minutes early, so I had time to connect my phone to the web and do some research on Bart Bradley.

Other than the address of the office of Bart Bradley and Associates in downtown Seattle, the man didn't exist. Yet, he'd dropped tens of thousands of dollars into Sheryl Thompson's office. Maybe his picture existed.

My image search produced three pictures taken by weekly newspapers in New York, Boston, and Indianapolis. The shots were all from election night parties and were candid. He was looking away from the camera, talking with other people. The best image was from Indianapolis. I saved the picture on my phone and then used a photo editing app to crop the picture, so a full view of Bradley's face was shown. I saved the picture and opened up my Baccarat app.

My phone rang. I paused my game. "Ustick."

"Hey, it's Michelle."

"Are we still on for tonight?"

"No. That's why I called. I've met a guy, and I've agreed to pursue an exclusive relationship with him."

I shrugged. "Who's the guy?"

"Dennis Faraday."

I tapped my finger on the dash. "I've met him. He's not too crazy. I hope everything works out for you."

"That's it?"

Oh yeah, there was a practical part of this. "I'll check my place and see if you left anything that you need back. Is there anything of mine over there?"

"We dated for nine months, and you just want to be sure you didn't leave a pair of socks?"

"What should I want?"

"I thought that maybe we meant something to each other!"

Why did women do this? I shook my head. "Michelle, I told you a year ago what my terms are. We'd go on dates whenever it was convenient for us: no emotional hassle or hang ups. We were free to date other people, never had to do anything we didn't want to do, and could leave with no hard feelings at any time. This wasn't a lifelong commitment. It was a week-to-week lease."

Dead air buzzed before she said quietly, "I'd hoped that, over the past few months, you'd begun to feel for me what I feel for you."

"I'm sorry."

"Have you ever been in love, Ustick?"

"I love women and love being around them."

"That's not what I asked."

"If you mean, has my heart ever beaten like a drum, and I not been able to sleep for thinking about my lady love, the answer's no."

"Maybe you can't fall in love. Maybe that's why you couldn't fall in love with me. That makes sense."

"Sure, if that works for you."

"Well, I'm in love with Dennis, and we're gonna be pure magic. It's your loss." She hung up.

It'd be magic, all right. She'd only committed to Dennis as a wedge to get at me. I opened the note on my phone with my girlfriend waiting list on it. The top two names were Ella and Jenna, both twenty-one. No, it was the younger ones that pulled Michelle's folly. Best to stop seeing college-age women. Third on the list was Darlene. I shook my head. She was twenty-nine, which wasn't a problem, but my other girlfriends were twenty-six, twenty-seven, and thirty-one. If I started dating another older woman, it'd look like I had a mother complex. I'd save Darlene for when one of the older ones moved on.

Fourth on my waiting list was Journey. She was twenty-three. Last time we'd talked, she didn't have a steady boyfriend, but she was going to Miami on vacation this week, so that was still out for a date this week. I had a couple good prospects at number six and seven, but I'd better wait until Journey got back. She deserved a chance, since I'd known her the longest.

I glance at my phone. It was ten till noon. I got out of the car and went into Wingers.

The waitress said, "Just one?"

"No, two. The other person's not here yet."

The waitress led me back. "Anything for you to drink?"

"Pina Colada." I took my hat off.

The waitress returned with my drink. I opened the menu.

I sipped intermittently for the next twenty minutes while I waited for my lunch guest.

At 12:10, a guy about my age walked over dressed in a green and blue button-down shirt and a pair of Dockers. He wore glasses with light plastic frames. His nails were trimmed neatly. He asked, "Are you Mr. Ustick?"

I stood. "Yes, and you must be Jason Mathers."

"Yes, sir." He extended his hand.

I shook his hand. "Good to meet you. Have a seat."

Mathers sat in front of the menu the waitress had left for him.

I asked, "You want a daiquiri or a margarita? They're top notch here."

"No, I don't drink this early."

I nodded. It would've been nice to loosen him up a bit, but maybe he'd be honest with me anyway.

The waitress came by and looked at my empty Pina Colada. "Would you like another?"

I shook my head. "Just water, thanks."

"Not a problem." The waitress eyed us like a quiz show host waiting for our answer to a million dollar question.

Mathers caught my gaze. "What are you having?"

"The double sauce burger."

"Okay, I'll get the Winger Burger."

The waitress wrote on her order pad and left.

Mathers said, "I came to this meeting out of curiosity. I've never met a private detective before."

I grinned. "I've never met a state executive director of the Democratic Party before."

"Would you mind answering a few questions?"

"If you'll answer some of mine."

"If I can. I gather you're investigating the allegations against Hernandez in the gubernatorial race. I don't know anything beyond what's in the papers."

"We'll see. We have to justify this meal on the client's expense account."

He grinned. "Fair enough, if I'm going to be fed by a Republican, they should get something. I was kind of surprised by your clothing. Why do you dress like that?"

"I don't like to wear boring colors. For your other questions, this can probably answer those." I pulled a piece of paper out of my inside coat pocket and unfolded it. "My FAQ."

He blinked.

I raised the paper. "My Frequently Asked Questions. You know, like they have on websites?"

"Go ahead." He laughed.

I began to read. "Do we work on murder cases, or follow husbands and wives? The answer is no to both. Murder cases are investigated by the police, and the boss doesn't do domestic cases except for missing kids. Mostly, we do insurance work and security checks."

He chuckled. "Have you ever killed a man in the line of duty?"

I dropped the FAQ and grimaced. "Last year. My boss confronted our client with evidence that our client was a child molester. The client tried to strangle my boss. I came in on it and shot him."

Because the slimeball had molested my sister.

The waitress brought us glasses of water.

Mathers eyed me. "Wow, I was kidding. That must've been tough to do."

"It had to be done. The story got a lot of media coverage. Everywhere I went for a solid month, people were buying me drinks, paying for meals."

"Doesn't sound like that was a good thing."

I downed my water. "So let me ask the common questions for state party bosses. You ever kill a man in the line of duty?"

He smirked. "Ustick, you have excellent avoidance techniques."

"If you're a shrink, I can't afford your rates."

"I majored in Psychology, but I don't have a Master's degree."

"What's a guy with a Psych degree doing in politics?"

He leaned forward and rested his forearms on the table. "Knowledge of the human mind and psychology is a great asset in politics, not a common one, either, with all of the business and law degrees in politics. I decided I wanted to make a difference. I helped out in the College Democrats and made some connections."

"How did you get the job here?"

"Really, it was a great opportunity. Most other job offers I had placed me under someone else's thumb. Most political folks have control issues, so my psychological approach to politics was pretty much ignored on the previous campaigns I worked on. I was a dreg."

"So, you got to try your psychology? How did it work out?"

Mathers glared at me. "Come on, drop the sarcasm."

"What sarcasm? I don't pay attention to the news."

"Unfortunately, this state is so messed up, people were unresponsive. I could go on for hours about this state's emotional and mental problems."

I mentally squirmed as he ranted for a good twenty minutes while the waitress bought the food. We started to eat. Why had he decided I was a safe guy to vent to? Maybe, because I didn't watch the news.

I had to get the conversation back on track. I cleared my throat. "So, if you can't beat 'em, psychoanalyze 'em."

He laughed. "That is one luxury my degree affords me, but my job has many challenges."

"Any of these have to do with the race for governor?"

He glanced over at the nearby tables. "Two candidates are running in our primary. Either would improve the lives of working families across Idaho."

"Do you think they can beat the Republican candidate?"

"Is this just between the two of us?"

"I don't work for a newspaper."

Mathers leaned in towards me and whispered, "Both of our candidates have no chance of winning in Idaho. Only the unions' help would even keep the loss under twenty points."

I whispered back, "And they won't?"

He shook his head. "Not if the governor wins re-nomination."

"Why not?"

"The governor has been an opponent of organized labor throughout his career, but he's moderating a bit. He's signed some executive orders that have helped them out." Jason sipped his water, swished it in his mouth like it was wine and then swallowed like it'd been vinegar. "In exchange for these bread crumbs, they're lending him their support."

"And you don't approve."

"I believe in loyalty and principle. The only books some politicians ever read were written by Machiavelli."

"You're a decent guy." I raised my glass. "You don't belong in politics." I reached in my pocket and pulled out a business card. "If you hear anything, please call me."

"Thanks." Mathers put the card in his pocket and slid his own to me.

I took it and we talked and ate for another few minutes.

He scarfed down the remainder of his French fries. "I've got another appointment. It's been a pleasure meeting you."

"Likewise." I stood and shook his hand.

After I'd returned to Boise, I parked downtown on a public garage's first level, walked two blocks down to Bannock, and stopped in front of an office with a window full of green and white "Re-elect Flanagan" signs.

A bell gonged as I entered the governor's campaign headquarters.

A college kid ran over smelling of Brute cologne. "Can I help you, sir?"

"I'm here to see Mr. Wexler, the campaign manager. I was told he'd be here today."

"He's on a conference call. He'll be out in a few minutes. Take a seat."

I put my card on the reception desk, grabbed a campaign brochure, and leafed through it.

Clichés and non-specific promises filled every brochure page except the one with two photos. One was of the governor and his family, and the other showed a picture of the governor wearing jeans as he rode a horse. *That's Idaho for you.* I opened up my Kindle app on my phone and pulled up *The People of the Mist* by H. Rider Haggard.

I got through a couple chapters before a guy with salt and pepper hair and matching goatee emerged from his office. I slid my phone into my pocket and looked up.

The college kid handed the guy my card. "A Mr. Ustick's here to see you, Mr. Wexler."

"I know who he is." Wexler scowled at me. "You're a private detective who wants to harass me about our opponent's indiscretions."

I leaned against the wall. "Well, I wouldn't put it that way, but could we have a moment?"

Wexler folded his arms. "I don't know anything about the Hernandez scandal that hasn't been in the newspaper."

"Yes, you do."

"Are you calling me a liar?"

I stared into his big gray eyes. "Yes, sir."

The man took a step back as if pushed. "That's outrageous!"

"I never said I wanted to talk to you about the Hernandez case."

"What else would you be here about?"

"My card says, 'Newton Security and Investigations.' I could have been here to offer our services. I could have been doing a background check on someone who once worked for you."

"I don't have time for this nonsense. Get out."

"Good afternoon." I adjusted my hat, left, and strolled down the city street. Outside of Newton's office and the Hernandez campaign, no one other than Jason Mathers had known what I was investigating, and Mathers wasn't the type to warn the opposition I was coming.

That meant a leak in the Hernandez campaign.

I dashed two blocks up and one block over to the Hernandez campaign's headquarters. It had blue and orange signs, apparently meant to play to BSU fans. I entered.

A woman a couple years younger than me was hanging a sign on the wall. Her layered, dark red hair fell to the neck of her tan and light green patterned blouse. She completed the ensemble with a light brown ankle-length, A-line skirt and brown Mary Jane flats.

She turned and smiled warmly. "Hello, how may I help you, sir?"

I removed my hat. "Miss, I'm Ustick, a private investigator working for Mr. Hernandez."

She extended her hand. "Good to know you, Mr. Ustick. I'm Tara Burke, the deputy communications director."

I took her soft hand and shook it. "A pleasure to meet you, Tara."

She winced. "Do I know you from somewhere?"

"I don't think so." I would have remembered her.

She shrugged. "It's just unexpected familiarity."

"Familiarity?"

"At one time, first names were only used between people who knew each other well. It was a sign of trust and a close relationship when someone's first name was used. Now everyone presumes familiarity without even asking."

I smiled. "Can I call you Tara?"

She sighed heavily, nodding. "If you called me Ms. Burke, you'd be the only one other than Mr. Hernandez." She bit her lip. "I think I have seen you somewhere. Perhaps at mass. Have you ever been to St. Mary's?"

"My mom and I attend."

"Of course!" Tara snapped her fingers. "You're Calandra Ustick's son. She's a wonderful lady. I don't think I've seen you in a while."

I hadn't been since Christmas, and it was easy not to notice everyone at mass. "I'm going to do my best to make it to mass on Easter."

"Well, let me show you around the office. We're still getting moved in, so things are a bit of a mess." She led me over to a tall blonde who wore a gray pants suit, matching heels, and fire engine red nail polish. "Denise, I want you to meet Mr. Ustick."

Denise shook my hand firmly. "I'm Denise Waters, Deputy Campaign Manager. I swear, if it were up to Tara, we'd be using Mister and Miss So-and-So more than a British department store. Mr. Ustick, what's your first name?"

I tensed. Only in Boise had being named Cole Andrew Ustick ever made me the butt of jokes. "It's just Ustick, thanks."

Denise smiled. "I used to live on Ustick Road. What's the connection?"

"None. I'm a Philly boy, lived there until I was fifteen."

"I see. Ustick, a staff meeting is starting any minute. Your boss is waiting for you in the conference room."

I raised my eyebrows. What was Newton doing here?

Denise sashayed into a brown carpeted hallway.

Tara and I followed.

Nearly a dozen people sat around the room with Hernandez. It had rows of folding chairs set up and a podium.

My boss was off to one side, chewing on a Kit Kat.

He shouted, "Ustick! Over here."

Uh-oh. Broken diet? Something was wrong.

I strolled over. "What are you doing here?"

"Special meeting."

"Is this about the job?" I asked.

The boss took a bite of his Kit Kat, chewed, and swallowed it. "We may not have a job after this meeting."

Chapter 4

The boss stuffed the empty Kit Kat wrapper in his left jacket pocket as we stood in the Hernandez campaign's bustling conference room. Newton stomped over to the vending machine and fed it a dollar bill. "There are two more stories on the newspaper's website."

I leaned in towards Newton and whispered, "Have you ever heard the old saying that where there's smoke, there's fire?"

The boss pressed the key combination for M&M's. "In this case, where there's smoke, there's someone blowing a lot of it."

The M&M's dropped to the bottom of the vending machine, and the boss grabbed them out. "Hernandez's wife, his siblings, even his nephew is getting grief over it. The word on the internet is that he's going to drop out."

That's the best way to ensure everyone think you're guilty. "Who are the other guests at this gala?"

The boss popped half a dozen M&M's in his mouth, chewed angrily, and swallowed. He pointed to a muscular, tanned man about my age who had short brown hair and was six foot two. His short sleeves showed off biceps covered with tattoos. "That's Jared Bach, the campaign's communications director."

I stared at Bach. "Running back for BSU, right?"

"Yeah, he had that big run against Nevada."

"I remember. Three hundred yards, four touchdowns. Last one won it with only five seconds on the clock." I frowned. He was also the guy my mom made clear that I should've been like. He and his blushing bride had made a big deal about avoiding even kissing before marriage.

The boss pointed to a middle-aged lady dressed in a campaign t-shirt and jeans. "That's Melanie Keen, the state field director." The boss tossed another handful of M&Ms into his mouth. After chewing them, he pointed towards a balding white guy in a blue suit. "That's Boris Rollins, the finance chairman."

"And everyone else?"

The boss shrugged. "From what I gather, they're the campaign's major supporters."

"Are they suspects?"

"Would you write a check to a campaign and then sabotage it?" The boss finished off the M&Ms and fed another dollar to the vending machine.

I marched off toward where the members of the staff were sitting, in the front row of a series of folding chairs. I took a seat behind Tara and Denise.

Hernandez walked in dressed in a black suit and stood before the mic at the front of the room. "Friends, as I've previously told you and the press, the allegations against me are false. However, this taken a toll on my friends and my family, especially my lovely wife, Liu. This creates stress for her and she has a heart condition. She doesn't need this. I've got to put my family first."

I scanned the room. People's heads were downcast. I'd look at the boss, but no doubt by now he was eating a giant Nestle Crunch bar.

Tara whispered, "Come, Holy Spirit."

Hernandez continued. "I ran for governor to fix our education system and help get good jobs into Idaho. For the past two weeks, all we've been able to discuss is the latest bogus rumor. We can't change our state this way. We've become a distraction."

Tara rose from her seat. "Mr. Hernandez, could I say something?"

What the heck? I gaped. Even I knew a campaign staffer didn't interrupt a candidate's big speech, particularly a swan song. Ms. Burke had some nerve, if nothing else.

Glaring, Hearst jumped up like a lawyer on TV. "Young lady, sit down. You have no business interrupting the candidate."

Mr. Hernandez smiled at her. "Ms. Burke, I think we should hear from you after I'm done."

"Please let me speak before you commit yourself." She looked around the room.

Hearst flushed red. "Sit down!"

Hernandez positioned himself in between Tara and Hearst. "Leave her alone. She's taken a year off from law school to help our state and deserves treated with the utmost respect." Hernandez sent a final glare at Hearst before turning to Tara. He gave a slight bow. "Ms. Burke, the floor is yours."

"Thank you, Mr. Hernandez," she said.

He sat by his wife, Liu. She was a petite, thin, middle-aged woman with chin-length, jet black hair.

Tara went to the mic and looked Hernandez in the eye. "No one here can know the pain you and your family have been through." She scanned the audience. "I understand entirely why you would want to leave the race and take that white light of publicity off of them. You've worked hard and deserve rest and peace. This won't get you that.

"Every time you enter a room, someone will be gossiping about if you're the man who groped all those women. The roaring wind of media gossip will die down, but only to a foul breeze, one that will still impact your family and everyone who loves you. If you quit, it will be a victory for slander. It will be surrender to an insidious evil."

Tara stared at Hernandez. "The Republic was built upon the blood and sweat of men who gave the best of their lives so we could all be free. We both know people who have given all in that fight, but then there are powerbrokers. They seek to destroy anyone who stands in their way. Slander, dirty tricks, no tactic is too low, and the press is a willing accomplice, selling their souls to sell papers or get ratings. Ladies and gentlemen, they are Slime Incorporated."

She scanned the room. "They are a corrosive acid that is eating away our Republic. Slime Incorporated thrives on fear. Thousands of people across the country would run for public office, if it weren't for the media, who threaten to destroy their reputations and families. What we're left with as alternatives all too often are well-meaning people so unfit for public office, no responsible voter could support them." She glanced back at Mr. Hernandez. "You wanted to inspire business people to get involved in politics. What message will you be sending to them if you drop out?"

Hernandez waved it aside. "This isn't about me. No matter what happens to this campaign, the fight to change the state can continue."

"Sir, we're a little more than two months away from the primary. If you drop out, you'll hand the governor a fifth term. We'd talk about changing the state. We'd add yet another ineffectual, conservative political committee to the half-dozen already in existence, get condescended to by the establishment, and pat ourselves on the head for a job well done. We can either do that, or we can gird ourselves for battle and storm the strongholds of the establishment, giving no quarter to hell's libel. I plead with you. Fight, sir, by God, fight, or everything we have sacrificed will have been for nothing."

The room burst into applause. Several people stood to their feet.

I whistled. *If I ever get in trouble, I want her as my lawyer.*

Hernandez stood. "You know, I'm tempted to endorse Tara."

The room erupted into laughter and more applause.

"Ignacio," Mrs. Hernandez said.

Hernandez turned to his wife. "Yes, dear?"

"It's okay."

"But, dear, your heart."

"I'm a big girl. We both know she's right."

"Indeed." Hernandez cleared his throat and nodded. "Then it's business as usual. We'll work hard, do our best, and talk about the issues that matter to our state as much as possible, so we can defeat . . . Slime Incorporated, yeah I like that. Slime incorporated will not defeat us."

The audience once again applauded.

"All right, everyone. Back to work."

My boss walked over to me, smiling. "Ustick, how'd your morning go?"

I filled him in on the events of the afternoon, prior to the big meeting.

The boss nodded. "See what you can learn here. I'll talk with Melanie Keen on my way out, since she's heading up to the Panhandle. Get your report on my desk before you quit for the day."

The boss strode towards Melanie. I scanned the room for Jared Bach. I found him standing in the corner on his cell phone.

Bach was saying into his phone, "Dora, we deny that anything like this ever happened. We don't know why anyone would make such allegations." He listened another minute then sneered at the phone. "Our stance remains that no number of false allegations makes a true one. No, we have no plans to slow down in our efforts to offer a better future to the people of Idaho. You're welcome." He hung up and looked at me earnestly. "May I help you?"

"Cole Ustick. I'm an investigator hired by Mr. Hernandez to look into these allegations."

He grinned wide. "Man, I could hug you. This thing has been driving me crazy. I've fielding questions on this thing forever it seems like."

"They've asked you to respond to allegations, but they've not given you any names?"

"Yeah, the latest story claims he groped a woman who worked for him sometime between 2003 and 2006. It took half an hour to get Gordon Thomas to even tell me which business this lady was supposed to work at. Hernandez has owned several."

"Gordon Thomas has been breaking all these stories?"

"Yep. The rest of the media's been playing follow the leader."

"Do you know why these women might go to Thomas?"

Bach ran his hands through his hair. "He's been reporting so long, if he reports it, folks think its gospel, particularly other reporters." Bach glanced at his watch. "I've got to talk to our webmaster and get a press release up on this latest story. Anything else?"

I made a few notes on my smart phone. "Thank you for your time."

He handed me my card. "You can call my cell number any time, day or night if you need any help. I'll do anything to get this monkey off my back."

If I needed an ex-jock Communications Major at three in the morning, I'd be sure to give him a call. "Thanks."

I shook my head. Time to write a report detailing the nothing I'd learned. On my way out, I passed Tara at her desk. She had her eyes closed as she whispered too low for me to make out what she was saying.

She looked up and blinked. "Mr. Ustick. You haven't been here long, have you?"

"Just got here. Were you praying?"

"Yes. I've got to drive to the printer's to pick up campaign supplies."

"What does prayer have to do with office supplies?"

"It makes me feel better whenever I have to travel anywhere."

I'd have to remember that next time I drove down Eagle Road.

She stood, leaned over, grabbed her blue windbreaker off the back of her chair, and when she did strands of red hair brushed against her cheek.

I said, "I can help you with that?"

"Thank you," she said.

I held her jacket for her as she put it on. I said, "There you go."

She smiled. "That's very kind of you." Her smile was genuine and her eyes were vibrant and bright as a spring day at Lucky Peak.

"After the great speech you gave today, they're having you run out to get office supplies?"

"My title may be the deputy communications director, but in such a small campaign office, everyone has to do their part." She headed to the door.

So she was all that and she wasn't conceited about it. I definitely wanted to get better acquainted. "Tara, could we have dinner tonight?"

She blinked at me. "I don't go out alone with men I don't know."

The last time I'd been shot down so quickly, I'd been ten years old and playing *Wing Commander* for the first time. *How are you going to get to know me if you don't go out with me?* I grimaced. *That line's pathetic, and pathetic will not get you a date.*

Instead, I smiled. "Well, maybe another time."

She returned my smile and trotted away.

"So, you're available tonight?"

Who said that? I turned.

Denise was looking me over while holding a zebra-striped handbag. "I'm free tonight, too. Would you like to get dinner?"

I grinned. There was always another woman waiting. "Sure. Seven okay?"

She grabbed a pen off her desk and scribbled down the address for her apartment and ran her cool soft hand across my cheek. "I'll be waiting."

Just before seven, I was in the lobby of Denise Waters' high rise apartment. I was wearing my gold suit with matching wingtips, a black shirt, and a gold-patterned tie. I popped a stick of Juicy Fruit in my mouth.

She sauntered out of the elevator at six fifty-eight. She carried a black handbag and wore a black strapless dress that went down to the middle of her thigh with black heels.

I ditched the gum in the wrapper and stuck it in my pocket.

She smiled. "You look even sharper than in the afternoon."

I smiled. "You're not bad yourself."

"So where are we going?"

I was thinking the RAM Restaurant and Brewery, but that dress earns you a posh upgrade. "The Black Feather."

We got in my Jaguar, parked in an all-night garage, and walked over to Eighth Street to the Black Feather Lounge. After a couple minutes, we were shown to a table that seated two. I pulled out her chair. She sat and scooted herself in to the table. I took my seat facing the door.

The waitress came over. "Can I start you off with something to drink?"

"Amber ale," I said.

"I'll get a Manhattan," Denise said.

The waitress wrote down our orders. "Do you need a few minutes?"

Denise said, "I'm ready. What about you?"

I scanned the menu. "I'll get the Eggplant Lasagna."

"I'll take the Butterleaf salad," Denise said.

The waitress smiled. "Your drinks will be out in a moment."

I made eye contact with Denise. "So, how long have you lived here?"

She smiled. "You ask questions all day. I don't want interrogated."

"Fair enough. You can ask the questions."

Denise asked, "What's with the suits?"

"I'd always liked bright colors growing up. Then, in college, I visited a friend's church back in Philly, and the pastor was wearing an orange suit and he had an orange microphone. This guy had sixteen different microphone heads off to the side. My friend said every time this guy preached, he matched his microphone head to his suit. I figured, if he can do it, I can do it. With a little adjustment here and there, I found my style."

"Other than being a private eye, what do you do?"

"Swimming, laser tag, and listen to music."

"What type of music are you into?"

"Most kinds. From Gregorian chants to country, top 40 hits, rhythm and blues, reggae, and heavy metal."

"That's quite a wide range." Denise smiled. "I listen to folk music, square dancing, and country."

That was the type of musical tastes that would land you at the geek table in Philly. "I wouldn't have pegged you as the type."

"Oh, I'm not, but I've learned to love it. That's a good political skill."

I laughed. "So you don't really care for it but pretend to?"

"No, I choose to. It's like the old arranged marriages. The women didn't always end up miserable, most ended up happy. Some of them got the type of political power a modern woman can still only get if she spends twenty years kissing up to men."

"So you're making the case for arranged marriage."

"I'm making the case for making practical choices to get what you want in less than ideal cultural circumstances. I know what I want, and I know what I have to do to get it, so I learn to love what I have to do."

"So that's all you listen to?"

The waitress brought our drinks.

Denise took a sip. "What a woman actually keeps on her MP3 player is her own affair. So tell me about your work as a private detective."

Would that it were appropriate to hand out my F.A.Q. on dates.

After both dinner and her third Manhattan had arrived, I said, "Boy, that was some speech today."

"It was definitely interesting."

"You don't seem happy with a speech that saved your job."

Her cheeks reddened. "It kept Mr. Hernandez in the race, but America can survive some yellow journalism, if you ask me. The alarmist, 'the future of our Republic is at stake' stuff was a very Tara thing to say, though."

"What do you mean?"

Denise chuckled. "Tara takes everything so seriously. A couple days ago, she posted an alleged Teddy Roosevelt quote on her Facebook wall. 'We stand at Armageddon and we battle for the Lord.' Over a campaign for governor! Really? Can you believe that tripe?"

I sipped a glass of amber ale. "You don't seem to like her much."

"Oh, I wouldn't say that."

"I would."

"We're simply very different, Ustick." Denise took another sip from her Manhattan. "She's nice enough, for a self-righteous fanatic."

"What makes you say that?"

She grimaced. "You're here on a date with me! Why talk about her the whole time?"

Easy, I'd rather be on a date with her. I put up my hands. "I'm just curious. That's why I'm a private investigator. When I understand what you're saying, we'll move on to something else."

"Fair enough." Denise leaned back in her chair. "It's the little things. She carries a rosary in her purse. I came back from lunch one day and found her with it at her desk running her fingers through the beads."

I grimaced. "You know I'm Catholic, too."

"Do you carry a rosary with you?"

"No."

"When was the last time you've been to church?"

"Christmas."

"And when will you be back?"

"Easter."

"There you go." Denise laughed and finished off the Manhattan. "You've got religion in its right place. She lets it dominate her entire life. I think it's a combination of her being ultra-Catholic and homeschooled. Bad combination. I mean, she barely even drinks. The only time I've seen her have a drink was at Mr. Hernandez's New Year's Eve party. She had one glass of champagne, and I bet she went to confession over it the next day."

"I doubt it." I took a sip of ale. "That's not a sin."

She shook her head. "Oh, right. Catholics aren't the ones who have a problem with drinking. That's the Mormons. I get confused because you both have a lot of kids."

Are you trying to be offensive or is that just too many Manhattans talking? "How can you actually know how much she drinks outside of work unless you hang out socially?"

"Come on. She wouldn't have much opportunity for social drinking. She goes to church more than some of the priests."

Given priests attended mass every day, I doubted that. "You two have many fights?"

Denise laughed. "We've never spoken a single harsh word to each other. We even exchanged Christmas presents."

"But you despise her."

"That's a harsh word. Besides, it's politics. In politics, you pretend to like not only individuals, but whole groups of people who you really loathe. The last thing any campaign needs is dissention in the ranks, and the last thing I need on my political record is causing it."

"So, why did you get involved in politics?"

She took a bite of salad. "When I was a child, we stayed in this rundown shack. If the rent was one day late, our landlord would be by with a friendly reminder and he would be back every day until it was paid. We moved when Mother got a better job. Through years of hard work, she became important in the Minnesota Republican Party. One day, I came home from school, and I heard a man pleading with her to help him with a business venture. I looked in the living room, and it was our old landlord."

"So did she help him?"

"What matters is that she had the power to either help him or let him be broken. Right then, I decided that I wanted to be in politics."

I swallowed a bite of eggplant lasagna. *Give me a Catholic and homeschooled woman over a hot and power-mad one any day.* "How does working for an insurgent gubernatorial campaign play into your plans for world domination?"

Denise wiped her mouth. "World domination is a bit too ambitious. At this time, my goal is to become a U.S. Senator before I'm forty. Of course, first once one of our fossils in Washington must head back to Idaho. That said, I've only backed Hernandez because Hearst did. We worked for the governor until Hearst decided the governor had gotten complacent, resigned, and started his own consulting firm, rehiring me there. When Hernandez made noises about running for Governor, Hearst encouraged him and agreed to come on board."

"So why follow the same man through the whole thing?"

"You've got to have some loyalty, if you're going to get anywhere."

"So that's the only reason you're working for Hernandez?"

Denise nodded. "Most primary campaigns are very high school, really. In this campaign, for example, the governor and Hernandez only disagree on a half-dozen things. It comes down to style and those age-old battles. The rich kid versus the poor kid. The smart kid versus the jock."

At least she's honest. "Campaigns also run on gossip like in high school?"

She chuckled. "I did very well in high school. That's why I'll do very well in politics."

The waitress came by. "Would you like dessert?"

Denise shook her head. "No, thank you."

"I'm good."

The waitress nodded.

She returned a few minutes later with our check.

Denise and I walked back toward the parking garage. We reached the car. She got in and dropped her handbag behind her seat. I drove her back to her apartment and pulled into a space up front.

I turned toward her. "Well, here's your stop."

"Indeed." Her gray, smoky eyes sparkled in the moonlight. She inched towards me. "I had a good time, Ustick." She touched my hand and ran it up my arm. "Are you Latino?"

"No. My mother's family is Italian."

She ran her hand across my cheek and stared into my eyes. "Italian, very nice." Her perfume was an intriguing lilac scent. "I love Italians."

I could inhale this all day.

She stroked my hand.

My heart raced. *She's good.*

She stroked my cheek and then my neck.

I put my arm on her shoulder. "I love that scent."

She slid closer until her face was a couple inches from mine.

I pulled her into a kiss. *She's very good.*

She reached over and untied my tie and my top two shirt buttons.

My watched beeped. It was nine o'clock.

I pushed her away. "I've got an appointment."

"Oh, it can wait." She stroked my cheek. "Come upstairs. It'll only be for a minute. I've got a lovely view from my terrace."

I reached for the door.

Stop and think, Ustick. You know the game she's playing.

Swallowing, I shook my head. "No, I'd rather not play tonight."

She wrinkled her nose, her apparent attempt at looking innocent. "What are you talking about?"

"We met seven short hours ago, and you're all over me? You're on the hunt. You've got a blank spot in your trophy case for a private investigator."

"Why are you so shy?"

"I made a New Years resolution."

She stroked my chin. "Those are made to be broken. It's March."

Last year, I'd made it to at least April. I brushed her hand away. "No."

She scowled but it morphed into a half smile. Her eyes gleamed like a wildcat eying a mouse. "Good luck, Mr. Ustick and good bye."

Denise slammed the car door behind her.

I drove off, getting on State Street. *Sadly, she'll go far in politics that way.*

After I arrived home, I checked my watch. It was 9:22 in Boise, and 8:22 in Seattle. It was early. I changed into my Broncos blue and orange pajamas.

My cell phone rang.

I picked it up.

"Hi, Dad." My son's voice came over the line.

"Hey, kid. You're early." I walked into his bedroom at my place. One wall featured a mural of his favorite superhero, Powerhouse, who allegedly was real and lived in Seattle. "You in your pajamas?"

"Yep."

"Got your toys put away?"

"Yep."

"Did you brush your teeth?"

"Um, hold on." He placed the phone down with a thud.

I sat and waited.

A few minutes later, his voice came on. "Yep."

I chuckled. "Okay, now get in bed, turn the phone on speaker, and turn off the lights."

More noise came over the line. "Done, Dad."

"Okay," I said, grabbing my Kindle from off the nightstand. "What would you like tonight? Dr. Seuss?"

"No. Cyclone Pedia Brown."

I laughed. "Remember, it's En-Cyclo-pedia Brown. You always fall asleep before he solves the case. It's a little advanced for you."

"But Mom says you can't come live with us because you're a grown-up Encyclopedia Brown."

Ugh. His mother and I agreed on one thing.
It reeked to answer questions like the one that got that answer. It didn't
make any sense, but I couldn't fault her there. *How do you explain to a four-year-old
why his parents don't live together, in our situation? The only reason Jenson is on Earth is
strangers had sex first and then discovered they couldn't stand each other.*

Chapter 5

I finished off my Dutch Brother's coffee while leaning back in my desk chair at Newton Investigations.

The boss asked, "So, is there anything else I should know?"

I threw away my paper cup and shrugged. "Denise Waters has money coming from outside of the campaign."

"How do you know?"

"According to my research, the campaign pays her $2400 a month. At her apartment building, the rent runs $1300 a month. She's got a Subaru BRZ in her name, and its payment has got to be nearly $300 a month. Then there's taxes, insurance for the car, plus at least $105 a month for manicures alone."

The boss raised his eyebrows. "How did you arrive at $105 a month?"

"One of my girlfriends worked at a high-end salon that charged $35 for manicures. They're the exclusive distributor of Denise's shade of nail polish."

"She could have bought it on the Internet."

I frowned. "I've checked the pictures she's posted on Facebook. In all of them, she's wearing colors from that line. Based on the pictures, she gets her nails done professionally a lot."

"Could be a wealthy boyfriend."

"Why would she risk offending a sugar daddy by being seen with me?"

"Could be she's hitting up her mom."

"Could be someone's giving her a nice payoff."

Newton shook his head. "I don't think so, but we'll keep it on the table."

I looked at my watch. "Mind if I get some water?"

"Sure. I think I've got a good picture of what's going on."

"After an hour, I hope so." I strolled over to the water cooler and put my purple sports bottle under the spigot.

Sixteen ounces of filtered water slurped out.

Newton said, "Let's run through this one more time."

The door swung open and Hearst stomped in.

"Good morning," I said, grinning.

Hearst stood over the boss's desk and stared down at him. "Newton, you promised a discreet investigation! And what do I hear? You people went to Governor Flanagan's headquarters and accused his campaign of dirty tricks."

The boss stood, leveling his gaze at Hearst. "We're asking questions to get at the truth."

"You can't question the governor's campaign like they're criminals!"

I shrugged. *Politician? Criminal? Is there some difference?*

The boss said, "We're trying to find out who started this rumor."

"That's not what you're being paid to do. Never mind that. Just find the women slandering Hernandez."

"If the story's planted, if we find who planted it, we'll find the women."

"When Ignacio gets into office, he'll have enough challenges healing the wounds from the election cycle without your colorful operative accusing his opponent's campaign of fraud."

I glared. "I'm sitting right here, Hearst. Did you teach Wexler how to bluster? He does it just like you, and I gathered from my research that he was your protégé."

"This isn't about protecting Wexler. I'm trying to protect this campaign."

Who'd said anything about protecting Wexler? I raised my eyebrows, staring. "Are you sure?"

Hearst glared at me. "What do you mean by that, Ustick?"

Newton said, "He didn't mean—"

Hearst lashed his palm out at Newton. "I asked him, not you. What does the punk mean?"

I stood. "This punk did some research last night on your distinguished career. You worked for the governor for thirty-six years, right up from the State Senate."

"That's no secret."

"Yeah, but I also discovered people were calling for the governor's head right after he got re-elected. A lot of people in his party were angry at him."

Hearst turned his hand over. "It's only the right wing that's always unhappy. They've never come up with anything but a fringe candidate."

I leaned on my desk. "Yeah, but suppose someone, we'll call this person X, knew the governor was in trouble. X loves the governor, worked for him a long time, so X campaigns for Hernandez only to set him up for the big fall.

Thus X destroys the Hernandez campaign to save the governor. X has a lot of media connections, so it's no problem for X to make it happen."

Hearst glared. "You dare accuse me of such a betrayal?"

I put up my right hand. "I didn't say anything about you, and it wouldn't be personal if I did. At this point, everyone on the Hernandez campaign is a possible suspect, albeit some will be quicker to eliminate than others."

Newton cleared his throat. "Gentlemen, we've all gotten off-track. The point is, we have to get to the source of the accusation."

Hearst leaned over the desk. "Newton, I've been in politics for almost forty years. There's so much gossip, you'll never untangle it. We came up with a new strategy at campaign headquarters. If you want to learn something, tail the reporter that's been writing these stories."

Uh-huh. Denise Waters' fingerprints were all over this dumb change of orders. I rolled my eyes and whispered, "Hell hath no fury."

Hearst glanced at me before returning his gaze at Newton.

Newton leaned back. "With all due respect, that's a passive approach. We don't even know if Thomas is going to make contact with anyone else."

"Only one way to find out." Hearst sneered at us. "You'll do it."

Newton blinked. "Is this what Mr. Hernandez wants?"

"He agrees with me."

I pursed my lips. This was going to end our short relationship with the Hernandez campaign. Newton would certainly not have a client telling us how to do our job. *So what's next for me? An insurance investigation?*

Newton sighed heavily. "Have it your way. We'll put a tail on him around the clock."

"That's fine." Hearst shot me a smirk that would have gotten his teeth knocked out if he were twenty-five years younger and not a client.

Hearst strutted from the office.

I glowered at the boss. "Since when have we let some amateur dictate a strategy that won't work? Are we going to follow Thomas until the primary?"

The boss put out his right hand. "I like Hernandez. He needs help. First, it's possible this plan could work."

I shrugged. "If it does, I'll buy winning Powerball tickets this week, too. I'll be on the lucky streak of my life."

Newton leaned forward. "After a week or so, if we've done our best to do it their way and gotten no results, I'll be able to persuade them to do it our way. The important thing is to do your best not to be passive-aggressive."

"Don't worry, Boss. I'll leave that to you."

"For the record, your interaction with Hearst was inappropriate and hot-headed."

I shrugged. "For the record, you have my apologies, even though he's an arrogant pain in the butt."

The boss nodded. "Understood. Ustick, go home and plan on working tonight from 6 p.m. to 3 a.m. and the next two nights from 5 p.m. to 3 a.m. Call Wanda before you leave for your shift, and she'll let you know where she's at. This is a 24-hour tail job. Be sure to wear appropriate tailing clothes and drive an unmarked company car."

As much as my shift sucks, it could be worse. I snickered. "What poor sucker are you going to get to come out and relieve me at three in the morning?"

The boss glared. "I am that poor sucker."

I stared out the car window at the newspaperman's darkened house. An old Garth Brooks CD was playing softly. I yawned. The boss pulled up behind me in his Suburban. I looked at my dash clock. It read 2:55 and was the only light around other than a street lamp.

The boss got out of his SUV and walked over to the passenger door of the black Ford Taurus. I unlocked the power lock and turned off the CD.

He slid into the passenger seat. "How was tonight?"

"Oh, it was very fascinating. Thomas met a woman."

"Really?"

"Yeah, she was fourteen years old and evidently his daughter."

"Ustick."

"Oh, they went to see the latest popular paranormal romance flick. So I got to see it for the sixth time, thanks to my mom and girlfriends."

"Okay."

"They ate dinner at the Fish Shack and spent the rest of their evening quietly at home, going to bed at eleven o'clock. Though, at twenty minutes after one, I saw Thomas walk past the window, but I believe he was headed for the restroom."

Newton raised his hands. "I get it."

"I don't think you do." I adjusted my BSU sweatshirt. "The movies all lied. Reporters' lives are boring. After three nights, the most interesting thing he's done is attend a public hearing at a mosquito district. This stupid stunt cramped my style, which I'd never complain about if there were a point."

The boss looked me over. "That sweatshirt doesn't fit you right."

"I borrowed it from an ex-girlfriend."

The boss raised an eyebrow. "It's a woman's sweatshirt?"

"Nah, she borrowed it from an ex-boyfriend and forgot to give it back when they broke up. Then again, maybe he borrowed it from an old girlfriend in the first place, but you're off topic."

The boss sighed. "I understand your frustration, but tedium is often part of the job. I remember a lot of long stakeouts back when I was a cop."

"But this isn't going to lead anywhere."

"Ustick, you have a three-day weekend coming up so you can relax."

"Wrong. I'm going to use it to get a grasp of this case."

"Suit yourself. I've got three extra operatives I've hired to help with the tail job this weekend, and they'll also be helping out during the week, so you'll be back to eight hours. Your shift next week will be three to eleven, Tuesday through Saturday."

"Fantastic," I said, annunciating each syllable.

He slapped me on the shoulder. "I'll try and get you off this after next week one, way or another. I'll either get the campaign to drop this absurdity, or I'll find you another case. Now get back to the office, write up your report, and get some rest."

Didn't he get it? I didn't want off the case. I wanted to learn something about it. This weekend, I was going to at least get a few answers.

I wore an orange suit as I stepped through the Hernandez campaign's front door.

Tara glanced up at me but remained seated. "Hello, Mr. Ustick. How is your investigation going?"

"As well as could be expected, but I'm not here about that. I'm here to volunteer. On the website, you said you were having an envelope stuffing party at ten this morning."

"Yes." She checked her silver analog wrist watch. "It's time to start, so I guess it's just the two of us." She led me to a table. "Have a seat, Mr. Ustick. I'll go get the supplies."

A few moments later, she returned with a box of envelopes and a stack of fundraising letters. She placed the items in front of me and sat across from me. "Each letter is personalized and is matched to a label. Fold the letter, put it in the envelope, and apply the label."

"Sounds easy enough."

We began folding envelopes.

After my tenth envelope, I glanced up at her. "So what do you think of Gordon Thomas?"

She sealed an envelope. "He's just another reporter with an agenda."

"So he doesn't have anything personally against Hernandez?"

"Other than Thomas being a liberal, he has no reason to be angry with us." She put the envelope she was working on down. "Why are you asking me about that?"

"I just figured, since you were the Deputy Communications Director, that you worked with the press and knew them."

She shook her head. "No, sorry. I send out press releases. I've answered a few emails, but I've never even talked to the man."

"I see." After a few minutes, I said, "Not much of a party."

"It's hard to get anyone out here on a Saturday morning."

"Particularly with a sexual assault scandal going on."

She raised her left eyebrow. "That doesn't help. No."

"Do you think it's possible the story came from inside the campaign? Most of the other staff isn't here. Doesn't seem like they're too loyal."

She frowned. "Most of the staff is off doing other important work."

"And the Deputy Communications Director has nothing better to do?"

"On this campaign, it's just a title. We all do what we can."

"Right, and what Denise can do on Saturday morning is sleep in late to recover from Friday night."

Tara stopped stuffing. "She is my friend. I won't gossip about her. Quite frankly, I think she did the right thing with you."

"Huh?" I blinked. "Excuse me?"

Tara folded her arms. "Yes, Denise told me about how you acted like you're God's gift to women. It's like what my mother told me."

"A lot of women act like I'm God's gift to them, but I always act like a gentleman."

"That's not how I heard it."

Glowering, I folded another envelope. "So you have no compunction about gossiping about me."

She shook her head. "It wasn't gossip. Denise was really upset, and your mother and my mother are friends and they pray together. I know how you treat women, and I'm not interested in being in your harem."

"I'm always a—"

"What is your definition of a gentleman?" She laughed mirthlessly. "Let me guess. You're clear upfront that they're not the only ones you're with, and you're honest about what you want."

"Well, yeah."

She curled her lip and shook her head. "Ustick, it doesn't matter how many women consent to being mistreated. You have no business talking badly about Denise. She was baptized Lutheran but never confirmed, and grew up in an irreligious home. However, you ought to know better, Ustick. Your mother raised you in the Church, which taught you that women aren't here to dispense favors to men but were created for higher things. You treat women like we're convenience stores." She gestured flippantly with her right hand. "Oh, the Stinker station's not open. I'll go to Jackson's. Sorry, Ustick, I'm not interested in being one of your sexual service stations."

She returned to stuffing envelopes.

I stared at the letters and the envelopes between us. My cheek burned. "I never suggested anything like that. I only asked you on a date."

"I know how your kind operate, Mr. Ustick. Understand this: I'm on a mission. My mission is to do my part to save this state's political system from the indifference and the corruption that are undermining it. I don't need a distraction, let alone a stumbling block."

Glad to know she's too holy for me. "It must be lonely to be on a mission from God."

"This isn't the *Blues Brothers*, Mr. Ustick. I'm not lonely. I have a lot of friends." She eyed the envelopes and letters. "You only came here to talk to me. I can finish these."

"No, I am a gentleman, even if you don't believe it." I shook my head. Sheesh, I'd struck out previously, but not before coming up to bat.

Chapter 6

"What's that song?"

At Leah Brooks' question, I looked up from the keys of the grand piano that had captured my fingers. Leah reclined on a rainbow-colored couch in her living room. Her tapping bare feet had a pedicure with black nail polish. She asked again, "What are you playing?"

"Hmm, let me see." I hummed the tune I was playing a moment before I sang, "Streaks on the china never mattered before. Who cares." I rested my fingers on the ivory. "The theme to *Mr. Belvedere.*"

She laughed. "How can you not know what you're playing?"

"I wasn't playing the piano. It was playing me."

She curled her lip. "Is that a Zen thing?"

"I mean I let my mind go and have no idea where that came from."

"Well, I recognized the Beethoven, just not the Belvedere."

I continued playing the song.

After a minute, she said, "I got the lyrics off my phone. Can I sing it?"

I chuckled. "You want to do an alternative rock version of Belvedere?"

"No, a normal version. We could make it a duet."

"I don't sing."

"You just did a few minutes ago."

"I made an exception. My singing career ended when my voice changed."

"Come on. Do a mother-to-be a favor."

"Fine." I played.

We sang the song, if you call what I did singing. I got more into it as we finished the final line. "And we might live a good life yet."

I struck the last note.

Leah clapped. "You're a blast. Come over here on the couch. Did you bring any of the sparkling grape juice?"

I nodded. "Yeah, it's in the fridge. You like that stuff?"

"No, but I'd rather pretend I'm drinking weak, really bad wine rather than have to admit I'm not allowed wine at all."

"One moment while I go get it." I strode into the hall. It was adorned with an eclectic mix of Charlie Russell prints and punk rock bands. Across the entrance to the kitchen was a white banner with fiery letters. "Abandon hope, all ye who enter here."

She's only joking. I shuddered anyway and turned on the light. Her fridge featured a photo collage. It included dozens of people, from Barack Obama and Ellen DeGeneres to random musicians. A few photos featured Leah with her friends and her own band. I opened the fridge and pulled out the bottle sparking grape juice. I went to the hand-carved Celtic knotwork cupboard and grabbed a couple wine glasses with dragons on them.

I brought the bottle in to the living room.

She peered at the second glass. "You having one with me."

I unwrapped the foil around the bottleneck. "I was thinking about it, but I don't know." I smirked. "I'm driving."

"You think it's bad for your image, don't you? A tough private detective having sparking grape juice."

"The bottle's mislabeled." I fished my Swiss Army knife out of pocket and popped the top off with a bottle opener. "It's prenatal wine, and it's not right to ask a lady to drink alone." I joined her on the couch and poured each of us a glass. I took mine and sipped.

She took her glass and sipped. "You know, Ustick. I wish you'd been my kid's father."

I swallowed. What made her say that? I'd kept her on my girlfriends list, but only because she was too much fun to officially downgrade her to just a friend. "I thought we'd decided we weren't right for each other as a couple."

"Oh, we're not right as a couple." She took another sip. "It would've been a business transaction with a bigger payoff than usual. I wanted someone very intelligent as the father. I just realized that the way you play is genius."

"My genes are flattered."

"Don't get me wrong." Leah stroked her stomach. "My Johanna has a wonderful father. He's very athletic, and he teaches at BSU."

"You're not talking about a father. You're talking about a sperm donor."

She chuckled. "That's Patrick. He doesn't care."

"He knows?"

"I ran into him at Albertsons on Broadway, and he asked how I was. I told him I was going to have a baby in July. All he said was, 'That's nice.'"

"But you didn't tell him the child was his."

She rolled her eyes. "Ustick, the guy has a doctorate in Chemistry. He can do the math. We were together from September to November. He just doesn't care."

"He doesn't know that he's a father."

She furrowed her brow. "I'm not a slut. I only have one man at a time." I put up a hand. "What I meant is that he didn't make the connection."

"It's obvious. I don't know why guys need us to draw a diagram. Besides, I don't need him to raise a child. My mom raised me without my sperm donor, as you put it."

"You're an amazing woman. So is my mom, and I'm sure your mom is too. But I remember when my dad was alive, and I miss him."

She grimaced. "I don't need a man's help."

"Mom has been fond of the saying, 'Mother knows best,' ever since Dad died." I swallowed hard. In recent years, she'd gotten fond of finishing that saying with " . . . because Father is too immature." Especially while she was twisting my arm into letting my son's mother have full custody.

Leah shoved me in the shoulder. "Hey, tell me about your investigation."

"Hey, I'm in the middle of a three-day weekend."

"Uh-huh." She folded her arms.

Sighing, I looked around the room. She'd always liked to hear about my cases, and she had better thing to do than blab around town. She was a good one to bounce ideas off. "I got a lot of info, but nothing adds up." I told her first of my trip to campaign headquarters and finished with, "So, between the two of us, Tara and I got all the envelopes folded in an hour and a half."

"Spent in stone cold silence?"

"No, she turned on some music and she thanked me at the end."

"You like her." Leah turned her nose up. "Too bad she's a frigid prig."

Best to leave that topic alone. I took another sip of prenatal wine. "Next I met a political blogger named Doug Witherley over at Applebee's on Vista."

"You learn anything."

"Too much." I pulled out my yellow notepad and scanned the pages I'd already written on. "With the exceptions of Denise, Tara, and Hearst, everyone on the campaign are political novices. Except for Hearst, they were all brought in at cheap salaries because they believe in Hernandez."

"Or at least they act like it."

"They're not the likeliest suspects. Before the scandal, polls shows the governor losing badly to Hernandez. The way Witherley tells it, hundreds of political cronies will lose big if the governor goes down, and tons of businesses have sweetheart tax loopholes for everything from nail salons to gold bouillon. Hernandez wants to clean up the tax code and get it to a simple rate. Plus, the governor's promised to create a couple hundred union jobs."

Leah glowered, grunting. "What if all these women are telling the truth about Hernandez?"

"Then why would he hire us?"

"Publicity, what else?" She sneered, her lip ring coming to a point. "He can say he's doing everything he can do to disprove the allegations and find 'the truth' this way."

"Yeah, but he's not put any publicity out on this."

"He could intend to buy the women off or threaten them to back off."

"Newton vouches for Hernandez. That's enough for me—for now."

"A lot of sickos manage to get good people to vouch for them."

Something I'd rather not think about. "Point taken."

"Just be careful. I know you wouldn't want to help a creep."

"So far, I've not been much help to anyone." I cleared my throat. "Other than gathering motives, only thing I did was gather background checks on everyone I'd met on the case."

"Anything interesting?"

"First, I found out the governor's campaign manager has won races in ugly ways: last minute sex scandals and one election where it coincidentally came out that his client's opponent was married to a recovering drug addict. Wexler's client came back and won the election, and the opponent's wife committed suicide on election night."

Leah gripped her glass. "Any proof the campaign manager was in on it?"

"There never is, with his sort. If Tara's right about Slime Incorporated, then Wexler is the CEO."

"What else did you learn?"

"Tara graduated first in her class at University of Idaho. She was second runner up in the national spelling bee when she was eleven. She was President of the College Republicans and of the College Right-to-Life. She volunteers at St. Vincent De Paul and her stepfather's big in the Knights of Columbus. She likes *Passion of the Christ*, *Mythbusters*, Saint Margaret, and Pope John Paul II. There's a picture of her meeting John Paul when she was a little girl."

Leah raised an eyebrow. "What does that have to do with the case?"

"Nothing, but it's interesting."

She tossed a pillow at me. "Cyberstalker."

I laughed. "Hi, Detective. This is Hacker. You're nosy."

My cell phone began to play "Puttin' on the Ritz."

"Sorry." I checked the phone. The caller ID had a local 208 number. *I wonder who that is? Can't be my son or his mom or grandma. This is an Idaho number.*

I answered the call. "Ustick."

"Hello, this is Jason Mathers of the Idaho Democratic Party."

I smiled. "How are you doing, man?"

"Good, Ustick. Did I tell you I'm a Unitarian?"

"Nah, I don't ask people if they're Unitarians when I'm on a case."

"Gordon Thomas goes to my church. He said someone was tailing him."

"Do tell." I gritted my teeth.

"I'm glad you're not in on something like this. Tailing a reporter would have to be the dumbest thing a campaign could do. A reporter will get ticked off at the campaign. It would probably be a PR black eye for the agency. If I knew a private eye who was in on that sort of dumb stunt, I'd tell him to cut it out for his own sake. I trust my meaning is clear."

"It is. You're a decent guy."

"Yep, that's why I'll never make a good executive director." He hung up. I placed my half finished glass on the end table. "I'm sorry. I got to go."

"But I thought you had one more day in your three-day weekend."

"So did I. This is an emergency." I stood. "Take care of yourself, Leah."

"You too, Ustick. Let me know how it goes."

I dashed out of her apartment onto the concrete landing and trudged down the steps. I could tell the boss, and he could tell the campaign that their hotshot campaign manager's bright idea was about to blow up their faces, but the geniuses at the Hernandez campaign might put us on an equally asinine task and still earn both themselves and Newton Investigations the worst type of publicity possible.

If only the reporter could get some big problems of his own that would keep him off our backs. Maybe something that would hurt his credibility.

I stopped on the second story landing. A woman with layered red hair and a floral print skirt exited the apartment. Tara?

She got closer.

No, it wasn't her. This woman was older, and her complexion wasn't as clear as Tara's. I smiled. If I could be fooled a second, couldn't Thomas? All I needed was someone who could impersonate Tara and put Thomas on the wrong trail. I got in my car, open my address book on my phone and dialed the number of Fontaine Ford.

She picked up the phone. "Ustick, it's been ages since we've talked. I'd hoped you'd get to see me before my play closed."

"LA is a little out of my way. Are you doing anything?"

"Only looking for my next part, darling. I've got twenty days before my finances run out and I have to take a case."

"You remember that favor you owe me?"

Dead air buzzed for a moment. Fontaine's voice came back. "Yes."

"I'm collecting. I've got a job for you. Catch the next plane out here."

"For a free job? Sorry, but I can't afford it."

"I'll pay your airfare and give you a hundred bucks for this. It's only a three hour job."

"You also need to pay my rent for a day here."

"How much is it?"

"One day? Let's see, that's two hundred dollars."

I blinked. "The rent's that high in LA?"

"It is if you need to reassure agents that you're a star, not a green actress without experience or connections."

Eight weeks as a secondary lead in a play, and she's gone Hollywood on me. "Yeah, I know, you're ready for your close up, but I can't afford to pay that on top of what I've already offered. So how about I pay your hotel, meals, and trip out?"

"I take it that Mr. Newton doesn't know about this."

"If my boss knew what I was planning, I'd be looking for a new job. Of course, the same could be said for San Diego." Meaning the time the trail of an insurance scam took me clear out there, and I turned up that another client had hired Fontaine's agency to investigate the same perp. "Then, I believe you were the detective asking me to help you without advising your boss of actions that would've gotten you fired."

"You don't need to remind me, Ustick. I pay my debts. But will the cops mind that I'm not a licensed detective in your state?"

"We don't license private detectives in Idaho. Even if we did, this is an acting job. I need you because I know you can pull off any character."

Fontaine chuckled. "That you're right about."

"I mean, you even managed to be convincing when you pretended to find me repulsive."

"Who said I was acting?"

"You better start practicing for your Tony acceptance speech."

"I'll be there in a few hours. I've got to pack." She hung up.

I put the phone back in my pocket. *You always have to have the last word.*

A sour feeling hit my stomach. I had nothing to feel guilty about. This might make Tara look bad for a little while, but it'd make Thomas look worse. If it got Hernandez cleared in the eyes of the public, she would thank me for it, if I ever told her. Besides, she could learn a lesson in humility, something she was going to need if she was going to be a saint.

I sat at the airport in an orange plastic chair. Across the terminal, dozens of passengers streamed through airport security, the only entertainment handy. I peered at the time on my watch, ten fifteen. Fontaine's plane had been on the ground for five minutes. I yawned.

Fontaine strode through the terminal. Her form-fitting, sleeveless olive top showed off her well-toned, well-tanned arms and accentuated her chest. Her black camo mini-skirt came to the middle of her thigh, revealing legs that matched her arms.

She moved in close to me and smiled. Her perfume was Euphoria from Calvin Klein.

I grinned. "You look hot."

"You should see what I packed for bedtime." She winked flirtatiously.

New Year's resolution, Ustick. Stick to business. I cleared my throat. "Actually, being hot is a detriment for this job."

She blinked and slapped her hips. "'Scuse me?"

"This role requires sweet, innocent femininity with a quiet strength."

"I can do that."

"We have to start practicing tonight."

Fontaine curled her lip. "I'd hoped we could pick up where we left off."

"I believe where we left off was you laughing and calling me names when I didn't want to move away from my mother and quit my job to be your live-in boyfriend in New York."

"Sorry, I didn't appreciate it then, but I do now. I've changed."

"So have I. It's useless to talk about picking up as if we haven't. We'd have to start from the beginning, and we don't have time for that."

"Maybe next time, when I come to Boise or you go to Los Angeles."

No need to hurt her feelings. "Let's talk about the job."

I sat in my Jaguar outside the Super 8 the next morning at eleven o'clock.

Fontaine exited the lobby. Her skin had been lightened a shade. She wore a mid-calf olive dress with a beige purse. She had on a red wig and walked like an office professional.

She opened the car door.

I clucked my tongue. "You're still the mistress of disguise."

Fontaine nodded. "It's been quite a challenge. I only had two hours to observe her while volunteering at the campaign office."

"I don't think her friends could tell you apart until you spoke."

"Do you want me to mimic her voice?"

"No. I want him to realize his error as soon as he hears her voice. I bet it won't be until after he runs the story." I pulled a small shopping bag from Reilly's out of my jacket. "Here, put this on."

Fontaine reached into the bag and pulled out a silver-plated crucifix. She stared at it and ran her hand across it.

I pulled out of the parking lot, turned left on to Elder, and got into the left lane.

Fontaine said, "You know, she's pretty nice."

"Yeah." I took a left on to Vista.

"You're not her type, Ustick."

I chuckled. "What makes you think I have any special interest in her?"

"Oh, I don't know. All those little coaching tips about how I should play the part." She clasped her hands together. "Remember, every movement has to embody innocence and virtue, and every word has to drip with conviction."

"That's who she is."

Fontaine rolled her eyes. "I hope what you're planning doesn't hurt her."

"She won't like what we do, but she'll like what it does for her boss." I took a left at the end of Vista on to Capitol.

"Why won't she like it?"

"It's dishonest and underhanded. She'd never go for it, I'm sure."

"Then should we do it?"

I grinned. "The only way kind and honest people accomplish anything is if sneaky people lend them a hand."

"True that." Fontaine slipped the crucifix around her neck.

"Okay, it's show time." I took a left into Ann Morrison and parked in the shadow of a sycamore tree. "Mr. Thomas will be waiting for you. Remember to tell the story with Tara ordering steak."

She waved this away. "Don't worry, I know my lines. Gordon Thomas will get a performance he won't soon forget."

Chapter 7

I grabbed a copy of the Idaho Herald newspaper and a donut at the Texaco Station and took them to the counter. I was wearing my hair loose and had on a black mock turtleneck with a matching pair of black slacks.

The middle-aged, blond clerk rang up my items and glanced me over, her brows knit. "You want a Powerball ticket?"

"I never buy when it's under $100 million, Barbara."

She laughed. "Yeah, you wouldn't want to settle for a mere sixty million."

I handed over my credit card.

She finished processing my order. "You're kind of subdued today."

Not in the mood for small talk, that's for sure.

I read the front page's headline article:

Hernandez Staffer Alleges Sexual Assault
By Gordon Thomas
Tara Burke has been an impassioned proponent of the campaign of Republican Gubernatorial Candidate Ignacio Hernandez. According to Burke, she recently found herself on the defense. She claims, on March 5th, she ate with Hernandez at a Boise steakhouse. After she ordered her steak, Burke alleges that Hernandez reached under the table and placed his hand under her skirt.

"I told him it was inappropriate," said Burke, "but he wouldn't stop until I threatened to cry out. It's really disappointing. I've believed in his campaign."

I smiled. *Nicely done, Fontaine.* If Thomas had known the significance of the day, he wouldn't have printed the story. Of course, I had to double check the date of Ash Wednesday on Google before giving Fontaine her lines.

The clerk asked, "Why aren't you wearing any colors?"

"Black's a color." *In this context anyway.*

Barbara sighed. "I like your bright colors. Most men don't wear anything so interesting."

"So I've heard." I grabbed my donut and paper and walked to the door. I drove down to the campaign office and found a gaggle of press people seated there. Gordon Thomas had his back to me.

I grinned. This time, he was going to lead me on something more than a wild goose chase.

The Communications Director stood by a water tank off to the left of the podium. Jared Bach's face was set like dried concrete. It was the expression Broncos had gotten used to seeing when he was waiting to play. I joined him.

He blinked. "Ustick?"

"Yeah."

"I wasn't sure. You look, uh, different."

"Any word from Tara?"

"She called at 6:15, said the story was false, to call a press conference for her at eleven. She said she'd be at adoration in three hours, whatever that is."

I chuckled. "It's a Catholic church service. She must be coming here straight from St. Mark's."

Tara entered the office, peeled off a black coat, revealing her bright blue ankle length dress. She stood at the podium, reached into her purse, and pulled out a prepared report. "Good morning, everyone. My name is Tara Burke. I'm the Deputy Communications Director for Hernandez for Governor, and I am here to respond to the story appearing in today's paper." Tara raised her hand to the reporters. "The leftwing press downplays the proven abusive behavior of leftwing politicians. With conservative politicians, you report even unproven rumors of scandals as if they were fact. This is an outrageous inequity."

Thomas blinked and his lips formed a frown.

"One reporter has written several pieces using anonymous sources to back up his slanderous claims. Now he says he has a source: me." She stared at Thomas. "Mr. Thomas, please stand."

Everyone glanced at Thomas.

He stood, looking like the toughest teacher in school had called on him.

She glared at him. "Mr. Thomas, I have never before spoken to you. I have never dined alone with Mr. Hernandez. He has never behaved toward me in any way that was inconsistent with the conduct of a gentleman. In addition, the date in your article was Ash Wednesday, which marks the beginning of the season of Lent. I didn't even eat dinner that night."

Thomas turned red then green, shifting his feet like a guilty school boy. She stared at him. "One question, Mr. Thomas. Have you ever spoken to me before?"

Another reporter stood, scowling. "The person calling a press conference doesn't get to interrogate the press."

Tara waved. "You'll want to know how this ended up in the paper. Well, so do I. Mr. Thomas, if you'd rather not answer my last question, offer any defense you'd like."

He looked at Tara and pointed his fingers. "You set me up!"

"That adds slander to libel. Are you saying you've spoken to me before?"

Thomas dashed towards the exit.

Bach pushed the stop button on the digital camcorder and pumped his fist like he did when Boise State had beaten Miami in his last game. "Man, they're going to love this on Facebook."

I sped off after Thomas. Wanda sat in her 1994 Ford Excursion. I tapped on the window.

Wanda rolled down the car window a quarter of an inch and peered at me with her black eyes. "Ustick, that you?"

"Yeah."

She unlocked the door. "What are you doing? You're not on until three."

I hopped in beside her. "Boss told me to help with the tail."

"No, he didn't. He never lets you wear your hair loose on the job."

"Okay, it's a hunch."

A few yards ahead of us, Thomas drove away.

Wanda pulled out and followed Thomas' car from six car lengths behind him. "It's more than a hunch. You've put in more unpaid hours than anyone I know. You need a hobby."

"This is my hobby."

A few minutes later, we followed Thomas into the lot of an apartment complex near the Greenbelt on the Boise River across from BSU. Thomas got out of the car and trotted up the outdoors' staircase to the third floor.

I hopped out of Wanda's car. "If I'm not back by the time he leaves, go without me."

She rolled her eyes. "I will, bossy."

I ran to the apartment building's mail lockbox and peered up at the room Thomas had entered. The white numbers read, "314." I looked at the mailbox and found 314. The name plate read, "Katrina Robles." I clambered up the stairs to the third floor and dashed to the door that Thomas had gone into.

Thomas shouted, "She punked me!"

I put my ear to the door.

"Not my problem," a woman's voice said faintly.

"If I'm forced to retract this, no one's going to believe your story."

"So? I did my duty. It was your job to take care of telling our stories, and you blew it by being a tool. Now get out."

I dashed to the vending machine in the hall and put a crisp dollar bill in. I looked up and down the machine.

Thomas pounded past me to the stairwell.

I checked my pocket. I only had two sticks of Juicy Fruit left. I pressed H5, grabbed a package of Juicy Fruit, and shoved it in my pocket. I took my current piece out of my mouth, wadded it up, and tossed it in the trash.

The gum stuck to the lid.

I peeled it off and dropped it directly in the trash bag. I turned on the voice recorder on my cell phone. I marched over to room 314 and knocked.

The woman's voice said, "Who are you?"

"Ms. Robles, I'd like to talk to you."

"You didn't answer my question."

"I'm a man who will return with Ignacio Hernandez and the press if you turn me away."

The door opened, and the doorway was empty. I entered.

A firm fist knocked me into the wall.

I slumped to the floor and looked up.

A muscular woman stood over me. She looked around, grabbed a soft-ball bat from beside the sofa, and wielded the bat like it was a club.

If I'd come in a couple seconds later, I could have gotten the business end of the bat rather than her ferocious jab. I flinched. "Stop!"

"Say please." She laughed.

I rolled my eyes. Dull pain shot through them. "Okay, please stop."

"Now, this is a reversal." She lowered the bat to her side. "Sit still, and I'll be back with some ice for that eye. I'd hate to see your pretty face ruined."

After she left, I glanced around. A sectional couch took up a third of the room. A gray standing lamp was badly spray painted teal. A small end table had a cordless phone on it that was painted teal with nail polish. Taped to the phone was a business card with a crown logo on it. Exercise weights and the kitchen dominated the rest of the room.

She returned in maybe twenty seconds and placed a wash cloth and a first aid ice pack over my left eye. "There you go. When you're done, go tell your boss to not send any more goons to threaten me."

I eyed her. She had a beautiful, smooth complexion, and her long blonde hair flowed over shoulders. She wore a teal bikini top and exercise shorts. Only two things might be off-putting to some men: she was over six feet tall and had well-toned muscles on every visible part of her body. Her fingers and toes were neatly trimmed and her toes were painted teal.

I rose and extended my hands, palms out. "I didn't come here to fight you. And even if I had, I would've changed my mind. I'm a private detective."

She giggled. "Who says please."

"Look, I'm working for Hernandez and have been assigned to find you."

She folded her arms. "So what are you going to do with me, big boy?"

"That depends on whether I believe you. I don't want to help a creep get away with abusing women." Bile burned my mouth. "My sister was abused. So I'm sensitive. To be honest, it's kind of hard to imagine—"

"Any man wanting me?" She sneered.

I shook my head. "Not at all. I was going to say I can't imagine any guy whose not on WrestleMania trying to attack you."

She waved. "Three years ago, I was thin, weak, and awkward. After that incident, I realized I needed to change myself, if I were going to survive. I'm still not much to look at, but no one's going to mess with me."

I grimaced. "Lady, I hate it when women put their looks down. You're usually wrong, and I can't set you straight without being taken wrong."

"Are you trying to get out alive or desperate for a girlfriend?"

"That question illustrates my point. The women I know all assume any man who compliments you has an angle."

"How should I take you?"

"As an observer of feminine beauty. I can say without any agenda that you've got a beautiful face and that you're—"

"All natural." She flexed her toned bicep.

I grinned. "More than I can say for the lady body builder I dated. So you were saying the incident occurred three years ago. Do you remember when?"

She slapped her head. "Vaguely. I believe it was summer."

I frowned. I'd have to narrow it down. "Morning or Evening?"

She closed her eyes. "Evening. I remember it was dark out. It was close to eleven."

"Where were you?"

"The depot. I was outside the restroom."

"Did you often hang around the city parks after dark? They close after sundown."

She shook her head. "I never go there when it's closed."

"Must have been a special occasion then."

She snapped her fingers. "Fireworks. I was there to see fireworks."

"So, the Fourth of July?"

"Yeah, it had to be." She rubbed her chin. "I don't know why I couldn't remember it."

"Tell me what happened."

She bit her lip. "I don't think so."

"Come on, I'm trying to help here."

She swallowed. "I was leaving the ladies room, and I heard a noise, and then all the sudden these arms were around me, with his hands on my breasts."

Tears gushed down her reddening cheeks. "I turned around and saw the monster's shirt. He towered over me. I could barely see the face of the man." *Someone hurt her.* I said softly, "What happened then?"

"He started to pull me back toward the men's room. I was screaming and crying. A female cop shouted at him. Hernandez took off. The police officer pursued him but didn't catch him." She wiped her eyes. "Do you believe me?"

I stared. She was sincere, but Hernandez was too short, and he couldn't evade a cop on foot. "You're not lying about being sexually assaulted."

She smiled.

I cleared my throat. "However, Hernandez can't be your attacker."

She glared, her eyes hard. "Can you prove that?"

"Fairly certain."

"So now you're going to make me a spectacle."

"I'd rather not. I'll figure out what to do."

"You think I'm going to let you leave?"

"One of my colleagues dropped me off. We both saw Thomas come in here. If I don't show up for work at three, my boss is going to be here with a gun. Right now, I'm the only friend you've got, Katrina. I'll do what I can."

Glowering, she clinched her fist but then relaxed it. "Fine."

"One question. Why'd you go to Gordon Thomas with this and insist on anonymity?"

She spoke in a monotone. "It allowed me to safeguard my privacy while helping protect other women from becoming the next victims."

I raised my left eyebrow. That sounded like something someone had told her to say. "I'll try and talk to you before anything appears in public. Do you work tonight?"

"Yeah, from three to eleven thirty. I'm a waitress at Dugan's."

"I probably won't figure out how to help my client without harming you until after you go to work. You want me to come by tomorrow?"

She nodded. "Come by after nine. I want to get my morning workout done. Between you and Thomas, my afternoon workout is shot."

"Okay." I headed for the door.

She called after me "What's your name?"

"Ustick."

"What makes you think it couldn't have been Hernandez?"

I smiled. "I'll show you, shortly, if you don't figure out what I mean by shortly first."

I strolled into Newton Investigations. I'd changed into an olive green suit with a gold shirt, black tie, and olive colored fedora and had tied my hair back.

Newton looked up from his computer screen. "You're forty-five minutes early, and you're supposed to call Wanda and find out where she is."

I waved, grinning. "Give Wanda the rest of the day off. I've found one of Thomas' sources."

Newton peered up at me. "Tell me about it."

"First, I need to call the client."

The boss sighed, picked up his desk's phone, and dialed a number. He waited a few seconds. "Hi, this is Jerry Newton. We need to get in touch with you as soon as you can. Please call Mr. Ustick's phone. It's on the card he left with your office."

I sat at my desk and checked my work email for the next six minutes. My cell phone rang. I picked up. "Ustick."

A voice came over the phone. "This is Mark Hearst."

I sighed. I hadn't asked to speak to him. "Is Mr. Hernandez there?"

"He's here. We're on speaker phone."

"Anyone else in the room?"

"No."

I fingered a forbidden stick of Juicy Fruit. "I've got a date for one of the allegations. Its from thirty-four months ago."

Hernandez's voice came over the line. "I'll need to have you call my personal assistant, Denny Brewster. The information on my Blackberry only goes back two years."

"Maybe you'd remember. It was on the Fourth of July."

"Yes, that I would." Hernandez sounded like he was smiling. "The last few years, I've been heading back east with my wife Liu to some of the cities that were prominent in the Revolution. Now let me see . . . yeah, that year was Philadelphia."

"Do you have any proof?" I asked.

Hearst demanded, "Do you doubt Mr. Hernandez's word?"

"I don't, but I'm not sure the media will go on the honor system."

Sighing, Hernandez said, "I'll dig up the airline tickets. My wife also has a lot of pictures from each trip on Facebook."

"That's fine. One other thing. Do you jog any?"

"I've had arthritis in my knee for five years. Walking half a mile is about all I can handle. Any parades I'm in, I have to ride in."

We'd about earned our fee. I put my hand over my cell phone's speaker and whispered to Newton, "Boss, you free for a phone call?"

The boss typed a little more and stopped. "At your earliest convenience."

I returned to the cell phone call. "Mr. Hernandez, let me get Newton on here. Just one moment." I pressed the button to call the boss and conferenced him in. "Gentlemen, I've found one of the women behind Thomas' stories. I can prove her story's false."

Hearst said, "We can call a press conference for this afternoon."

"Hold it, speedy. She accused the wrong man, but this really happened to her. I can tell."

"How?"

"I've been in this business for four years. I know how to spot a liar. What I think happened here was transference. She was the second woman featured. Some man hurt her, but she didn't see who it was. She needed to know who to be scared of, and who to punish, so she transferred the blame in her mind to Hernandez, so somebody would pay."

"That's preposterous."

On my computer, a chat window popped up from Newton. "Glad that Psychology course I paid for at CWI didn't go to waste."

Yay for the College of Western Idaho, but chat windows while talking on the phone were distracting. I locked the computer by pressing three keys on the keyboard. "She clearly did misidentify her unknown but real assailant. I promised her we wouldn't do anything until I talked to her tomorrow."

"Who are you to agree to that? You're working for us."

"Ustick's right." The boss's voice echoed. "If she's lying, and you hound her, she'll come up with another story and deny everything Ustick says. If we confront her with the evidence, she'll know she underestimated us, and she'll be glad to get out of this without a lawsuit."

I said, "Plus, if I'm right, and she's been hurt, we could push her over the edge if we expose her to public humiliation."

Hearst growled. "That she's unstable is something we should use against Thomas. If she kills herself or something, it'll be on his head, not ours."

I grimaced. "No, sir, it'll be on my head."

Hernandez's voice came on the line. "Ustick, you gave the woman your word. Keep it."

Hearst started, "But, Ignacio—"

"Mark, if the only way I win this election by destroying people, I'd rather lose. Now, Ustick, what do you need?"

"I need any proof you can get of your Philadelphia trip as well as your medical records on my desk by eight o'clock tomorrow morning."

"Excellent. I'll have my office get that to you immediately."

Newton's voice echoed as he spoke over the phone while in the same room as me. "Mr. Hernandez, can I cancel the tail on Mr. Thomas? It's costing you a thousand dollars a day."

"Please do so. All right, Gentlemen, if there's nothing else, we've got a fundraiser to get back to. Good day." Hernandez hung up.

Newton put his phone down and turned to me. "Get your report ready on your conversation with this woman with all the details, send copies to me, Hernandez, and Hearst. Then go home."

I said, "But I haven't been here half an hour."

The boss waved. "If I know you, Cole, you spent more than eight hours on this case this weekend. If the Department of Labor ever gets wind of how much you work off the clock, I could get in trouble for allowing it."

"What do you want me to put on my timecard?"

"Seven thirty to four."

"I got up at nine, so you'll be paying me for sleeping."

"I'll call Wanda and send her home, too. I'll find something else for her to do tomorrow. One of the temps, Mr. Roark, will still do the eleven to seven shift. I hate letting people go without notice."

"I wouldn't press our luck. A reliable source told me Thomas is catching on to the tail."

"But he led us right to his source."

"Yeah, but he still suspects. Somebody made a mistake. I know it wasn't me, and I'll bet you it wasn't Wanda. It was one of the temps."

Newton sighed and lowered his head. "I'll let Roark know his services are no longer be needed."

The next morning, I ambled to my desk. It had a manila file folder laying on it. I picked the folder up and leafed through the contents: Three pictures of Hernandez and his wife in Philadelphia, plane ticket stubs dated July 2nd with return ticket stubs marked for July 6th, a doctor's report diagnosing him with arthritis in his knees, and an unsigned affidavit acknowledging Katrina Robles as a source of Thomas stories and renouncing the story as "false and the result of mental distress."

The boss spoke up. "Haven't seen the teal suit in a while."

I glanced over at him. "It appeared to be her favorite color. Had it on the rugs, the couch, her clothes, and even her nails. I figure it'll soften the blow."

"You're about to tell her that she's delusional and made a false allegation in the largest newspaper in the state. But it'll be okay because you're wearing her favorite color."

"Couldn't hurt."

"You're too much." The boss shook his head. "Let me know if you run into any problems."

I nodded. "I'm headed over there now."

At five till nine, I carried the campaign's folder as I strolled up the stairs of Katrina's apartment complex. Blaring alternative rock music accompanied me to the door marked 314. I knocked on it. "Miss Robles!"

Only her sound system answered, with its guitars, pounding drums, and the screams of a no-talent lead vocalist.

"Miss Robles!"

Still only the crappy band could be heard.

I checked the door.

It opened.

I pulled my gun from my shoulder holster, set my phone to record, and put it in my left front pocket. I stuffed the folder in the huge inner pocket of my suit jacket. I crept in and scanned the room.

The lamp was gone. The air smelled of potpourri.

Two restaurant shoes rose from behind the couch. It sat three feet from the window. I ran around the couch and peered behind it from the side.

Katrina Robles lay on her back. Her feet were propped up on the couch at an odd angle. Dried blood stained her white dress shirt.

Oh no. I dashed to her, knelt, and checked her clammy wrist for a pulse. I made the sign of the cross.

Chapter 8

I used my handkerchief to turn off what Katherine Robles had called music, backed out of her apartment, and called my boss.

Newton sighed. "Hello, Ustick. Police there yet?"

"Nope."

"The cops who show up before the detectives might ruin evidence."

"What makes you say that?"

"Curious cops are the worst for ruining crime scenes."

"Good to know." As if I could do anything about it. "Did you get the video I attached to my text message?"

"Yeah. The only thing I saw was that crime scene's been tampered with. But this isn't our case. Your job is to answer the police's questions and get back to the office to regroup."

"So you think it's just coincidence that I came here to ask questions, and she's dead?"

"Possible. She could've had a disagreement with an ex-boyfriend, or it could've been a robbery. Anything missing?"

I peeked in the open front door. "The only thing I'm certain is missing is a $25 standing lamp, and that isn't something you'd break in for. There was also a softball bat, but it could be in a closet or something."

"Let's focus on the investigation we've been assigned—uh, hired for. Don't poke into the murder investigation even on your own time."

"Boss, that is the last thing I want to do, but I got a hunch that we will be looking into it soon enough."

The boss tisked. "You and your hunches."

Two police officers entered the room wearing latex gloves. I glanced at their name tags, Rudolph and Gutierrez. Rudolph was thin, baby-faced, and wide-eyed. Gutierrez was short, stout, and had a brown mustache.

Gutierrez nodded to me. "Cole Ustick, I presume? We got your dead body report over the radio."

Rudolph clutched his notepad. "Can you tell how long she's been dead?"

I blinked. *Kid, if you were any greener, you'd be on the produce aisle.* "The body felt kind of lukewarm when I checked it."

Gutierrez sighed at his partner. "Let's walk through the apartment."

They went inside the apartment, headed in the direction I remembered the kitchen being.

Gutierrez said faintly, "Back door's open."

Detective Charlie Weston jogged up the stairs and joined me outside the apartment. The nearly bald, middle-aged detective wore a pair of paper booties over his shoes and a pair of latex gloves over his hands. He carried a clipboard and a box of what looked like tissues. He deposited the tissues by the door.

I smiled. "Detective."

He frowned. "Ustick, who else is here?"

"Officers Gutierrez and Rudolph. I think they're in the kitchen."

Weston sighed. "I've got to get this crime scene under my control, and then I'll talk to you. When did you get here?"

"Right about nine. I can show you the video from when I first came in."

"Later." He waved and held out the clipboard. "Sign here."

I signed his crime scene log and handed it back to him.

He put it by the stereo and pulled a role of tape out of his coat pocket. After he'd cordoned off the crime scene, he walked through the living room, making observations into a digital voice recorder. Half a dozen other officers came and went, signing the crime scene log.

Weston returned holding a small notebook.

I checked the time on my watch. Nine forty-five.

He frowned at me. "Did you touch anything?"

"I checked the body for a pulse and used a handkerchief to turn off the stereo. That's all."

"Did you notice the floor had been vacuumed and shampooed?"

"If that's why I smelled potpourri, yes." I peeked inside the apartment's door. "Are you saying it was done after the murder?"

"It's too clean. Do you see anything missing?"

"Yesterday, there was a standing lamp and a softball bat."

"The lamp must have broken in the struggle." Weston wrote in his notebook. "What were you doing here?"

I told him everything, except my little charade with Gordon Thomas.

Weston narrowed his eyes at me like he thought I might be lying. "Where were you last night?"

I grimaced. Yes, I did need an alibi. Good thing I had a solid one. "I picked up a girlfriend at nine and we were together until a quarter after one."

"What was her name and where did you go?"

"Her name is Jenae Lord. I took her to the Edwards theater near the Wal-Mart on Overland. We saw *Living Again*. That started at about nine thirty. Let me check the stub." I pulled out my wallet and retrieved the stub. "The movie was at nine forty, and it let out at about eleven forty. We went to Gino's in Meridian for a cocktail, and I dropped her off at her place at about one."

Weston nodded, closed his notebook, and handed me a form. "Please put everything you've just told me on this statement form and include contact information for Ms. Lord. Now, I've got a crime scene to process."

I turned towards the door.

"Sir, I found this," a cop called as he came out holding a stick vac in his gloved hand.

Weston coughed. "That wasn't used. It's covered in dust. I doubt it even works." He glared at me. "Was there something I could do for you,. Ustick?"

"No, sir."

"Then go fill that statement out by the vending machines."

While seated at my desk at Newton Investigations, I marked the report for my boss as "Complete."

The office's landline rang. I picked it up. "Ustick."

Steve Reed's voice came over the line. "Is the boss there?"

"No, Newton is out with a client. He left me in charge."

"Our allegedly disabled security guard just bench pressed 160 pounds at Gold's Gym."

I pulled up the report on Reed's case file on my computer. "Dr. Gordon will have to explain why he told the insurance company our friend couldn't lift anything heavier than a coffee cup. If you've got enough to prove fraud, come on in and write your report."

"You got anything else for me?"

"Let me see." I used my mouse to double-click the computer icon for the available case folder, opening it. "You're in luck. We got three insurance cases. None urgent. Once you write your report, check the Feldman file."

"Will do, Ustick."

I change the filename for the Feldman file to include SR to mark it for Reed. I would probably move on to one of the other two cases soon enough.

My cell phone rang. I answered it. "Ustick."

"Sir, this is Detective Weston. We need you to come to headquarters and identify the lamp."

"You got it down in the morgue, or do you want me to pick it out of a line up?"

"No, it's in the evidence room, and there's only one to identify."

I rolled my eyes. Was sarcasm wasted on this guy or what? "I can't leave the office. The boss is out, and we're between receptionists."

"Hmm. Tell you what, I can bring it down to your office."

"That's fine. You know where it's at?"

"Yes, I'll be there in six minutes."

Precisely six minutes later, Detective Weston strolled in carrying a black trash bag and wearing latex gloves. He opened the bag and pulled out a lamp base that was spray-painted teal.

I got up from my chair and peered at the lamp's paint job. "Yep, that's the lamp. It's like what they say about families. Every well-painted lamp is the same, but every poorly painted lamp is poorly painted in its own way."

"Thanks for the philosophy." Weston pressed his lips together. "One last question, Mr. Ustick. Was there any flaw in the lampshade?"

"What do you mean?"

"Like a chip or gap."

I shrugged. "Not that I could see, but I only saw one side of it."

"Thank you for your time." Weston shoved the lamp back in the black plastic bag and marched out.

The office phone rang again.

I picked it up. "Ustick."

The boss growled in my ear. "How many times have I told you not to answer the office phone that way? If it's a client, they may think they have the wrong number, particularly with your surname. There are businesses on Ustick that are named after the street they're located on."

So he's not happy about something and taking it out on me. "It's too bad I don't have a surname that wouldn't have that problem, like Franklin, Jefferson, or Overland." All were names of Boise streets.

"Ustick, I'm not in the mood today."

"Mea culpa, my lord. A thousand pardons. I won't let it happen again."

"I'm not going to be back for a while. Close up at five and take an hour off for dinner."

"But I get off at five."

"You got a date?"

"For seven. I'm meeting a girlfriend out at Texas Roadhouse."

"Better make it seven thirty. We have a conference with Hernandez and his staff at our office scheduled for six. Whatever you work over, just come in later tomorrow by that much."

"What's the conference about?"

"Our continued employment with the campaign."

"They calling off the investigation?"

"Not sure, but they're scared stiff. The police had Hernandez, Hearst, and me in for questioning for about half an hour each. And they just grabbed Denise Waters for a session."

"How was yours with your buddy Weston?"

"His new partner, Detective French, questioned me. She went way too far. She demanded detailed reports on everything we did for Hernandez. I was ready to call our lawyer until Hernandez offered a compromise. We're to hand over all files related to Katrina Robles and tailing Gordon Thomas."

"That'll be our revenge because some cop will have to read the reports. That's punishment enough."

Newton chuckled. "You always manage to look on the bright side. But get the information together and send it to Detective French. I sent you an email with her contact information."

"Will do, boss."

I leaned back as I sat at the conference table in Newton Investigations' consultation room. I used my phone to text Angelica Solterbeck. *Sorry. Boss is making me work til 8. Rain check?*

Hearst continued his filibuster, shaking his fist at me. "You people were supposed to make things better. Now look what you did."

I scanned the room. Newton's head was sagging. Hernandez was staring at the table. Jared Bach fixed his gaze straight at Hearst. Tara and Denise were seated beside each other. Denise stared to the head of the table and was taking copious notes. Tara sat still, eyes closed.

My phone delivered Angie's reply. *;(It's okay. Call me l8er.*

I texted back. *Will do.*

"Ustick!" Hearst shouted. "Are you paying attention to me?"

I looked up. "Yes, sir. I was just letting my girlfriend know I'm not going to be able to make our dinner date. It's a new-fangled thing called texting."

"Watch your tone."

The boss stood and glared at Hearst. "Try following your own advice, Mr. Hearst."

Hernandez raised his hands. "Gentlemen, please. Mr. Ustick, even before the texting, you hadn't said anything. Is that because you have nothing to say?"

"Nothing I'd like to share."

Hernandez glanced me over. "Are you just frustrated, or do you have something important to add?"

"I do, but do you want to hear it?"

"Yes, please. Mark, have a seat."

I looked around the table. "For the last forty-five minutes, I've borne it as you guys have expressed frustrations with the police and with the way the investigation has progressed."

Hearst snorted. "We wouldn't be in this mess, if we'd gone to the press with the info right away. She would've been forced to make a public retraction. That would've helped the campaign immensely. Who knows? She might even be still alive, if it weren't for you."

I smiled as sweetly as I could. *You'd love me to get angry back. One, two, three, four, five, six, . . .*

Hernandez swallowed hard. "Mark, the young woman is dead. That's the primary thing, not this campaign."

Hearst snarled. "You've got to stop thinking like that. Politics is war by other means, and she was an enemy combatant."

"Excuse me?" I leaned forward in my chair and scowled at Hearst. "No, she wasn't an enemy combatant. She was a constituent who'd been abused, not by Mr. Hernandez, but by somebody. She was confused, God knows why, but she was a good person. She didn't deserve killed, either in the press or literally. Though maybe you thought differently. Maybe you killed the enemy."

"Shut your mouth!" Hearst shook his fist as he added a slur that would be wrong even if he hadn't misjudged my sexual orientation.

The only sound was the old baseboard heater buzzing in the corner.

Everyone but Denise frowned at Hearst. She shot me a crooked smile.

Wow. I'd heard about spurned women spreading such rumors. Never seen it before.

Hernandez said, "Mark, that was uncalled for. I'm getting sick of the way you treat people. That's not how I do business."

Hearst sneered at me. "You want an official apology, Ustick?"

I grinned. "Nice try, but I know your game. You want to gain power over me by getting me on the defensive. Not gonna happen. Further, a guy who plays that dirty is addicted to drama. You've spent a ton of time screaming at people who aren't screaming back. You need to rile me, both to relieve your itch for drama, and so you won't look so ridiculous."

"Don't you dare presume to psychoanalyze me, twerp."

I cleared my throat. "Back to what I was saying. You all have lousy alibis for the murder night. You were alone in separate motel rooms in Caldwell, where no one minds what car is coming or going. I follow my gut and I follow the facts. Except for Tara, everyone here had gotten a copy of my report with Katrina's name and address in it. Most likely, one of the people at this table is responsible for her murder, and you used me as your finger man."

Everyone other than the boss and Hernandez gasped.

Hearst sputtered, red-faced. His scowl deepened. "That's preposterous."

"Like you said, politics is war. One of you is a double agent. I don't know who it is, and neither do the police."

Tara cupped her hands. "Mr. Ustick, it could've been Mr. Thomas who murdered a woman. The death has gotten his false story out of the headlines."

I rolled my eyes. "No dice. I followed this guy for days. He went to an NRA meeting to talk to a congressman. You should've seen his face. Believe me, he's not a gun person. I know it'd fit into your neat ideological view, but I'll shave my head if he's the guy."

She bit her lip and eyed my hair like she was trying to imagine me bald. The buzzer overhead sounded.

"I'll get it." Newton left the room.

Once the buzzing had stopped, Hernandez said, "Our question isn't, 'whodunit?' Whoever is behind this murder needs to be caught, but the police will handle that. Our question is whether we want to continue to investigate these women."

Bach raised his hand. "If, as Ustick said, Thomas was getting on to our investigation, I don't think it's wise to continue it, in light of the murder of Ms. Robles. We have enough to deal with already in terms of the rumors that the campaign was somehow involved."

Denise stopped taking notes. "I can't imagine them thinking Hernandez is involved."

I swallowed. "I can."

Hearst said, "How? According to your tape, we were going to prove her a filthy liar."

"If her real story would've been even more damaging, Hernandez would have a motive for murder. I don't buy it, but the police might."

"Really, you must be hard up for business." Hearst laughed and waved dismissively. "We no longer need a private investigator at present. The case is no longer of interest to us."

Tara frowned and raised her index finger. "I don't see how that can be, given the campaign's dedication to the sanctity of life. If all men matter, then all murders matter."

I added, "And what God has so mysteriously created, we must not suffer to be mysteriously destroyed."

Tara blinked. "You know Chesterton?"

"Yes." I grinned at her. "Mom had me read every one of his books over three summers."

Denise cleared her throat.

Tara said, "Truth be told, that passage was arguing for a justification of police. I just think we want to be careful not to—"

"You can't do this!" Newton said as he and Weston rushed in.

Weston replied, "I'm sorry, Jerry. It's out of my hands."

"Let him come in and surrender in the morning."

"Sorry, the captain won't allow it." Detective Weston stormed around the conference table. "Ignacio Hernandez, you're under arrest for the murder of Katrina Robles."

I shot a glance at Hearst and pursed my lips. Hernandez had gotten his wish. Justice's interests were being served by the police.

Chapter 9

On Friday, I strode into the office, whistling. "Good morning, Boss." I plopped at my desk, popped a stick of Juicy Fruit into my mouth, and waited for Newton to say something.

Instead, he sat staring at his computer screen.

I asked, "You curious at all how Mendelson case went last night?"

"Oh yeah." Newton glanced up from his computer. "How'd it go?"

"I got into Mendelson's card game as a waiter. All I had to do was put on a white tux. I served Dr. Mendelson his subpoena along with his Chardonnay, but our client doesn't have to go ahead with the lawsuit to get the back child support and alimony."

"Why not?"

"I threatened to call the police and report the illegal, high-stakes poker game and get it shut down. Mendelson decided he'd rather give me the money with a receipt." I sauntered to the safe in the corner, worked the combination, and pulled a suitcase out. I opened it on Newton's desk to reveal the suitcase contained $50,000 cash. "I also got him to sign a release requiring his employer to garnish his wages for child support and alimony."

The boss nodded. "Take that down to the bank and have them give you a cashier's check to send our client."

What's with you? I put up my right hand. "Don't gush. You wouldn't me to become an egomaniac."

The boss rubbed his eyes. "Sorry, Ustick. I'm just distracted."

Newton grabbed the pen in front of him and doodled on his notepad for a second. "What you described came too close to extortion. You should have just served the paper and gotten out of there with the information, so the lawyer could take care of this."

"So his kids could spend another five or six months in that rat trap trailer park while the lawyers fought it out? I was careful not to commit any crime in how I worded my threat."

"Some day, you're going to step over the line."

Sorry for not doing it your way, Mr. Ex-Cop. "It's not exactly an enthusiastic congratulations, but at least this time you responded."

Newton shook his head. "It's just this whole Hernandez case."

"Boss, we don't have a Hernandez case anymore. The guy's moved from refuting sexual assault allegations to trying to avoiding the needle."

The boss scowled and gritted his teeth. "That prosecutor is a total clown. Back when I was on the force, we had a guy dead to rights for beating a kid to death and torturing him. The prosecutor didn't pursue the death penalty. Yet, the office is 'not ruling it out' against Hernandez."

"The difference is this was premeditated, coldly planned murder."

The boss stood, clenching his fists. "He didn't do it. We need to find out who did."

I shook my head. "No."

"What do you mean?"

"It would ruin everything. Do you know how many people I've had to tell, 'No, we don't investigate murders'? That's something the police do. All we do is—'"

"Ustick—"

"—is investigate insurance scams and trace folks who skipped town, such as deadbeat parents who owe child support.' You've said the same thing."

The boss put up his hand. "Ustick—"

"We've worked tirelessly to ensure people don't confuse fact and fiction. If we go and start investigating murders, it'd be impossible to convince them we aren't straight out of some private eye film. People already think I'm like Archie Goodwin."

The boss gazed down at his stomach. "Oh come on. I've only put on a few pounds."

Self-conscious much? I cleared my throat. "I'm a real private investigator, not a movie role. Thanks to that sleaze Durand, I already can't say that I've never shot anybody. And now I can't tell people that I've never found a stiff. I'm not hunting for murderers. I'll never have a moment's peace at any party I go to."

"Those are selfish, shallow reasons to refuse to aid an innocent man."

"Who says he's innocent?"

"I do." Newton stuck out his chin.

Uh, really? I laughed. "You've told me time and time again that the cops are always right."

"Almost always."

"Which means Hernandez probably did it."

The boss pounded his desk. "Don't listen to what I told you! Listen to what I'm telling you."

I chuckled. "Oo-kay."

"He's innocent. Would you be willing to help me prove it?"

I grimaced like the boss had made me drink a tall glass of lukewarm, raw, unsweetened, undiluted lemon juice. "As of Tuesday night, I've had my fill of political clients for a lifetime. If I ever have to work for a politician again, it'll be too soon."

"Hernandez is a business man, not a politician."

"Every time I see a politician on TV, they say they're not one. Look it up in the dictionary. If you're running for office, you're a politician."

The boss growled. "How many hours you got in this week?"

"Including the hours you let me take on Monday, I'm up to thirty-eight."

"After you get the cashier's check for Mrs. Mendelson, write your report. Omit your persuasive suggestions to Dr. Mendelson. Then go home."

"That'll leave me at just forty hours."

"Which will avoid unnecessary overtime. I'll call you sometime between eight and nine on Saturday morning."

"Okay, then I'm off to the bank." I grabbed the briefcase of money.

I grabbed a red tray and walked up to the fast food restaurant counter. A plastic, giant, grinning fish hung above the cash register. The cartoon bubble coming out of its mouth said, "Welcome to the Fish Shack."

The smiling twenty-something female cashier said, "Welcome to Fish Shack. What can I get for you?"

"Thanks. I'll take a Fish Shack Platter and a Caesar Salad." I gave her a ten and a five to pay for my meal.

She gave me my change, pulled a ready-made salad out of a refrigerator, and placed my salad and a plastic table number card on my tray. "I'll be right out with your platter."

I nodded and ambled to a blue table. I sat and got to work on the salad.

A few minutes later, the counter girl arrived with a plastic basket with a mix of fish, scallops, clams, and chips in it.

"Mr. Ustick?" a girl asked behind me.

I glanced over my shoulder.

Tara stood a few feet away, dressed in a soft blue sleeveless sun dress with gold seahorses on it. She was carrying one-handed a tray with a salad on it as she waved at me with her free hand. "Do you mind if I join you?"

My heart skipped a beat. "Sure, have a seat."

She slid her tray onto the table then lowered herself across from me and swept her skirt under her. Her bodice showed her shoulders, save only for the dress's three-quarter inch strap. Her nails were painted turquoise.

She prayed over her salad and opened a package of croutons.

I started on the scallops. "So you come here often?"

"Nearly every Friday when I'm not busy with the campaign."

"Is the campaign running?"

Tara swallowed. "Mr. Hernandez let us go for the weekend. Before the murder, the weirdest call I got was some woman asking about his height. Now, I've spent all day taking calls from people playing judge, jury, and executioner, armchair quarterback style. The paper's feeding them with all the rumors and innuendo coming out of the prosecutor's office." She shook her head. "They can talk to the machine for a while. Mr. Hernandez said he'll recalibrate."

Translation: The old boy was thinking about calling it quits.

She raised her arm to bring her soda to her lips. On her upper arm was an image of Christ falling beneath the cross on the road to Jerusalem.

I blinked. "Is that a tattoo?"

"Of the Third Station of the Cross." Tara took another bite of her salad and finished it before speaking again. "It's airbrushed. I just added a new one."

"Never took you as a tattoo sort."

"I prefer to think of mine as body art I redo as often and as easily as I redo my nails. Though, what I put on my arms is far more meaningful than my nail color." She sipped from her cup. "I felt so bad for you on Tuesday night. Mr. Hearst is a little high strung. He gets nasty when things don't go his way."

"Does Hernandez like him?"

Tara smiled. "Mr. Hernandez likes everyone he meets, even the reporters. Plus Mr. Hearst is really a genius at political strategy and organization."

"He was operating outside his genius. I never told him how to organize his precincts."

"Mr. Hearst doesn't know his limits. What he said to you was wrong, but he'll apologize."

I chuckled. "When?"

"June or maybe December."

"You're kidding."

Tara shook her head. "Eight years ago, on another campaign, I messed up a shipment with a thousand yard signs. Mr. Hearst cursed at me in front of the entire staff. I went home bawling."

I squeezed my glass. "What happened?"

"That was in September. He came out to my home around Thanksgiving, apologized profusely, and gave me a half-dozen Phyllis Schafly books."

Which doesn't make him being an abusive jerk okay. "Nice guy. I won't hold my breath for an apology."

"Does what he said bother you?"

I shrugged. "I don't need to win any elections, so I can be myself. Most people who give me that type of crap are plain ignorant. In Hearst's case, he just doesn't like me."

"Yeah." Tara brought her fork to her mouth to take a bite of salad. "He said the nastiest thing about you on Wednesday. He accused you of not being a Republican."

"I'm not."

She dropped her fork. It slipped off the edge of the table. She stared like I'd declared I was a Satanist. "You're a Democrat?"

I put up a hand. "Look, not everyone is on one side or the other of your political war. I don't care about the stakes, so I don't vote. I let smart people like you have your say on how to run the country."

"Oh." She grimaced and pushed her salad around the plate with her fork.

I swallowed a bite of my clams. "Ms. Burke, now that you can no longer be construed in any way as my client, I did have one thing I wanted to ask. Would you accept a friend request on Facebook?"

She smiled. "I've never been asked that outside of a computer notice."

"I just wanted to be sure it was okay."

"If it wasn't, I'd just ignore it, but yes, I'll be happy to accept."

I returned her smile. "Thanks."

She took a couple bites of her salad. "Mr. Ustick, I hate to do this to you at dinner. My father was a plumber, and people would come up to him and ask unappetizing questions at horrible times when I was very little."

I kept my gaze on my food. "You have a professional issue for me?"

Tara replied, "Yes, do you mind?"

"Go ahead. I'll eat while you talk."

"It's about the libel issue with Mr. Thomas. I met this afternoon with my lawyer and the paper's lawyers."

"Are they settling?"

"They're threatening a counterclaim for extortion and fraud if I don't drop the matter."

I looked up from my platter. "Huh?"

"They claim Mr. Thomas met with someone. He claims a source at the campaign verified that I was the person he met with, based on the description provided. That source also said I was a credible source." She took a sip from her water cup. "The paper implied that, if this went to trial, they would prove I colluded with the perpetrators of this hoax."

I felt queasy. "But whoever impersonated you was making it up to hurt Hernandez."

"According to the paper's lawyers, the story was made up so it wouldn't be believed."

I adjusted my tie. "What do you mean?"

She stuck her fork into a piece of salmon. "During Lent, I only order fish or vegetarian meals. The newspaper article intentionally mentioned having a steak on Ash Wednesday, of all days. The only reason the imposter would give this information was to immediately sink the credibility of the story, counting on Thomas to allow it to sneak into print."

"So what if the imposter was trying to help Hernandez? No way can the paper actually connect it to you. It's a bluff to scare you."

She put her fork down. "Ustick, I don't like being caught in a web of lies, particularly when I don't know who is spinning it. This might appear to help Hernandez initially, but it could be part of a long-term plan to destroy him and me. I need to find out who put me in this position and why. That's why I'm thinking I could hire a detective."

I adjusted my tie. "To do what?"

"Thomas indicated he met the imposter at Ann Morrison Park. He didn't say when, but it was probably on Monday, or maybe over the weekend. Maybe a detective could find out who was in Ann Morrison."

"You want to know everybody who went into Ann Morrison over the weekend and on Monday? Even at this time of year, the answer is hundreds, maybe thousands. As long as Thomas isn't willing to narrow down the time, there's not a whole lot you can do." *Thank God.*

Tara spread her hands on the table. "I could put $2,000 on it. Though, I'd been hoping to use that to live on when I got back to law school."

"Keep your money. That might pay for fifty man-hours of work, and all you're likely to get out of it is a receipt."

"So I have to narrow down what we're looking for myself first." Tara blew out her breath and pursed her lips. "Maybe one of the front desk people would have noticed. Or you could find out if anyone was on a photography project and happened to take a picture."

I swallowed. *Or someone tailing Thomas was taking pictures of everyone he met. I'd bet one of those substitute detectives took pictures, and they're in the file at work.* "Don't worry about finding the right angle now. You don't have a fortune, and there's no need to borrow trouble. Most likely, there's no next step in this situation."

She sighed. "Maybe, I'll hold off for now."

I stood. "Well, I better get going."

"But you still have a lot of fish and chips left, even some scallops."

"They always serve way too much food here. I've got to get over to the Morrison Center. I'm meeting a friend. We're going to see a play."

Tara stood and shook my hand. "Have a good time, it was nice talking to you, Mr. Ustick."

Wish I could say the same to you.

I parked outside a local university's theater. The clock on my Jaguar's dash gave the time as six thirty-five. I pulled my cell phone out of my pocket and dialed the number at my son's house.

"Carter residence. Michaels speaking."

Apparently, even with her money, Jensen's grandmother couldn't afford a butler named Jeeves. "This is Cole Ustick. Is Jenson available?"

"Yes, sir. I'll get him for you."

A moment later, Jenson's voice came on the line. "Hey, Dad."

"Hey, son. Calling early because a friend and I are going to see a play."

"Like Peter Pan? Grandma took me to see that a while ago."

"Nothing that good." It should be a crime to move *Hamlet* to the twenty-third century, but I wouldn't share that opinion with Janae, either. "What are you doing, son?"

"I got my first recital tomorrow."

"On the piano?"

"My teacher says I'm a pro-tea-gee."

I smiled. "It's prodigy, and I'm proud of you."

"Really?"

The way my son said "really" sliced a dagger through my heart. "I wish I could be there to prove how proud I am. Will your mom be there?"

"No, she's spending the weekend with her friend Hank. But Grandma will be there."

Why on Earth had that woman taken my son away from me so she could be either working or partying all of the time?

I shook myself. *Don't be such a selfish jerk, Ustick. Your son's getting more from his grandma than you could ever give him.* "Son, have Grandma make a video of your performance, and I'll watch it."

"Okay."

"So anything else today?"

"Grandma and I watched *Pinocchio*." My son spent the next five minutes on a blow-by-blow recap of the movie. "And you know what, Dad?"

"What?"

"Every time Pinocchio told a lie, his nose grew longer!"

"Really? Cool." I touched my nose and peered in the rear view mirror.

"Yeah! And the more lies that Pinocchio told, the longer and longer his nose grew. Finally it sprouted into a tree."

My head ached. "Son, I've got to go. I'll call you back real soon, so stay near the phone."

"You okay, Daddy?"

"No, my nose hurts." I groaned, face warming. "I mean, my head hurts. I'll call right back."

I hung up, grabbed an aspirin from the glove compartment and dashed to the car's trunk. Inside it was a case of bottled water.

After taking my aspirin, I carried my half-drank water back to the driver's seat. I felt my nose again and called my son back.

Hopefully he's done talking about Pinocchio.

Chapter 10

"Burning Down the House" echoed from the '80s station on my phone. I frowned as I stared at the image on my office computer's monitor. Terrific. The image was out of focus, but it was still possible to ID Fontaine Ford as the woman who had impersonated Tara.

I pulled up a slideshow of the photos in the folder this one had come from. A good thirty pictures flashed by, all of them of Fontaine.

So the temp agency detective liked her. I stared at the last image. It was blurry, but it included the front of my Jaguar, license plate and all.

I let out a curse. *Maybe Tara won't hire us. Or maybe she'll hire another agency. Jerk. How could I even consider letting her blow two grand when I know what happened?*

My cell phone rang.

I turned off the music and took the call. "Ustick."

The boss was on the line. "I didn't wake you, did I?"

"Not at all. I'm at the office. We must've just missed each other. Where are you?"

"Oh, well, let me give you the directions."

"Just text me the address. GPS will get me there."

"Will do."

"See you in fifteen minutes."

After locking up the office and getting in my car, I ended up clear out past downtown, headed east towards Table Rock, a mountain pillar. I turned off Warm Springs into a hillside residential area.

Half way up the hill, I found my destination: a spacious Spanish Colonial style house. It looked like it was auditioning for the cover of Better Homes and Gardens. I parked behind a red 2014 Bug outside the four-car garage. Conifer trees were on either side of the path leading to the house.

I walked up the path and took a deep breath. The crisp air was as clean as an obsessive compulsive's bathroom.

I reached the door and knocked. Fiddle music wafted out toward me.

Mrs. Hernandez opened the door. She smiled. "Ignacio's on the phone. Please come in."

"Uh, thanks." I entered the foyer, biting my lip. *Hernandez's place? What's this about?*

His wife asked, "May I take your coat and hat?"

"Sure." I gave them to her.

She opened the hall closet. Inside were two purses. One was Tara's black monogrammed shoulder bag. The other was Denise's giraffe-print handbag with a red handle.

Mrs. Hernandez led me across the hardwood floor to the living room area. It was painted a creamy gold color. It had two brown leather couches that could seat three people each, two blue love seats, and two recliners that faced the love seats and the couches. A half a dozen paintings adorned the walls, including one of Christ, and oriental and Spanish landscapes.

Tara and Denise were standing near the couch across from the piano. Tara wore an ankle-length vermillion skirt and a white blouse. Its sleeves were short enough that the third station of the cross was fully visible on her upper arm. Denise wore a pair of fashion jeans with a dragon embroidered on each leg. She'd paired them with a BSU t-shirt and a gray fedora and a pair of gray sneakers. She held a fiddle and bow.

"That was some fine fiddle playing," I said.

She smirked. "Learned from one of my mom's boyfriends. He was the best fiddle player in South Eastern Idaho, or that's what he said."

Mrs. Hernandez beamed. "You might be now, dearest. Thank you. It's been so long since we had music in the house."

I moseyed over to the grand piano in the far corner. "This is beautiful. Who plays?"

Mrs. Hernandez bit her lip. "My daughter Cynthia. Do you?"

"A little." I ran my hand across the top. "Never on anything this nice."

Mrs. Hernandez pointed open-handed towards the piano. "Please try it "

"I would love to, but I'm supposed to meet Mr. Newton for work, not for pleasure."

"Please grace us. My husband and Jerry are on a conference call with a lawyer. Those things are interminable."

I lowered myself onto the piano bench and played "Ode to Joy" followed by "Ave Maria."

Mrs. Hernandez sat on the edge of the couch and grinned. "Could you and Denise possibly play together?"

Denise nodded. "I'm game."

Mrs. Hernandez said, "Ustick, there's a song book in the stand. Could you get it? Play, 'I Saw the Light.'"

I got off the piano bench, opened the seat's secret compartment, and pulled out a spiral bound, beaten up paperback titled *Old Time Gospel Songs.* The cover was half-torn off. I handed the book to Denise. "Here. I play by ear."

Denise nodded and played a few notes of the song.

I put up a hand. "Okay, good enough."

Denise, Tara, and Mrs. Hernandez stood together. Tara held Denise's book for her while I played the piano. Tara sang soprano and Mrs. Hernandez attempted alto.

Tara said, "Ustick, could you play 'Healer of My Soul' for us?"

"Sing a little, and I can play pretty much anything."

Tara turned to Denise. "This one isn't a fiddle song. You could sit with Ms. Hernandez and maybe play something later."

Denise waved before she glanced at me then back to Tara. "Don't worry, dear. There's no song that the right fiddler can't handle."

I smiled. *Probably one of the more civil cat fights women have had over me.*

Tara hummed the tune for me. I started playing. Tara sang. Denise came in on the second verse with some soft fiddling. Tara would never cut a CD, but her voice was pretty.

After the song, Mrs. Hernandez swept over to me, beaming. "That was wonderful." She stroked the piano's top. "Mr. Ustick, do you like it?"

I played a few chords from memory. "It's fantastic."

"It's yours."

What? I stopped playing. "I wish I could accept, but my house is way too small. Plus Mr. Newton limits gifts from clients to $25 or less."

She patted my shoulder. "Come by and play any time you want."

The boss's voice came behind me. "Ustick!"

"On my way." I turned.

The boss stood by an interior door with Mr. Hernandez. The boss wore a red sweater with a dress shirt and tie underneath. Mr. Hernandez was in a green cowboy shirt and a pair of jeans.

I turned to the ladies. "Sorry, duty calls."

Mrs. Hernandez nodded. "I was about to go help make lunch."

I ambled over to the boss and Mr. Hernandez.

"Let's talk inside my office." Hernandez opened the door we stood by and led us inside.

The home office's right, left, and back walls were covered with pictures, trophies, and medals.

I said, "I hope you didn't mind the little performance."

"Not at all. It's been a long time since the piano's been played."

"Was that why your wife offered to give me the piano?"

"No." He walked behind a mahogany desk took a seat in a black leather chair and gestured for us to sit in two matching chairs

The boss and I settled into them.

Hernandez looked at me. "We lost both our daughters within a year of each other. Cynthia died in the army in Afghanistan. Maria died while serving as a missionary in India. It was so hard on us. Liu kept their rooms exactly as they had left them, as shrines." He looked past me.

I glanced up at a family portrait of the proud papa and mama and their two beautiful daughters. Hernandez looked about fifteen years younger in the picture with his hair almost jet black. Yet based on the style of the gray dress the one girl wore, it couldn't have been more than six years ago.

Hernandez heaved a sigh. "Then one day, Liu came to me and said God wanted us to dismantle the shrines. She gave away nearly everything that didn't have some sentimental value. With the things the girls loved, she wouldn't let those go until she found someone who would enjoy them as much as the girls had. It's been four years since she started this, and the piano is the last item."

And here I was cracking wise about her giving away the furniture. They've been through a lot. I bit my lip. "I'm sorry to hear about your loss. I lost my father on U.S.S. Cole when I was thirteen, so I can imagine what it was like."

Hernandez nodded. "That must have been very hard."

"I have a good mother, but I still miss him." Would he have been proud of me? Would he have known some way I could get out of this mess with Tara and the paper? He always had good answers.

"Mr. Ustick?"

I blinked. "I'm sorry. My mind wandered."

"That's quite all right. I got a little personal." Hernandez put his hands together under his chin a moment before returning his hands to his lap. "Jerry has explained you object to working for a politician. I did look politician up the dictionary, and you're right. One of the definitions of politician is someone running for office. I'll try and stop saying I'm not a politician in my speeches."

Could it be that he was actually a human being? I nodded. "Okay."

He looked into my eyes with his deep set brown eyes. "What I meant was that I'm not a professional politician. I spent forty years of my life in business. If I lose, I'll go back to that life. When I got in, I believed that if I lost, I could still say my life was a success."

"And you couldn't now? Why?"

Hernandez pointed behind him to a picture on the wall of a grizzled, brown-skinned man and a tired-looking woman. "My mother and father came to this country in the 1940s from Guatemala. They had nothing but the clothes on their backs and their integrity." He folded his arms and met my gaze. "My father taught me, 'Ignacio, whatever work you do, so long as you have a good reputation, you will be wealthy.' By that measure, I've been bankrupted."

Silence buzzed.

Hernandez continued. "I've been asked not to volunteer at a Summer Youth Camp at our church. I've taken part in it for the past twenty-six years, but now parents have stated they would be uncomfortable having me around. My wife can't go out among 'friends' without them asking her if it's true. I haven't even been indicted yet and the paper—" Hernandez grimaced. "The paper has convicted me with its selected leaks from the prosecutor's office."

I said, "Do you think you're in danger of actually being convicted?"

Hernandez shook his head. "I have a friend in the County Prosecutor's office. According to him, they don't have enough evidence to convict me, and the county prosecutor knows it. A few months after the primary, the case will be dropped due to lack of evidence." He slammed his fist on the desk. "I will go free, but the true murderer will never be brought to justice."

Newton nodded and stared hard at me. "And public opinion will forever condemn Ignacio Hernandez as a killer who got off scot-free."

And it'd be forever established that I had been the idiot who pointed the killer to his target and let him get away with it.

Hernandez tightened his fist. "I can accept losing the election, but I can't live my entire life under a cloud of suspicion. I'm asking you not as a politician, but as a man, to restore my reputation."

I leaned back in my leather chair and tapped my fingers together. "Is that campaign manager of yours going to tell us how to do our jobs?"

"No, you're being hired by me, not the campaign. You report to me."

"Will we have full access to your staff?"

"Yes."

"I don't know." I stood and paced. This whole Norman Rockwell 'just folks' routine of his could be an act. "I'd like to believe you, but the evidence seems pretty strong."

The boss snorted. "What evidence? All we—all the police have on him are newspaper reports. We know half the reports are exaggerated, and the rest of them are lies. It's no secret the prosecutor supports the governor, and it looks like a lot of his assistants are eager to impress him by leaking damaging information to the press."

"So what are the unexaggerated facts?"

"The murderer used Mr. Hernandez's Lincoln Town Car. The police have impounded it and won't return it until after the trial. I went down to the impound lot yesterday to examine it with Detective Weston present and checked the mileage book. Mr. Hernandez filled up right before he checked into the motel and then drove it to downtown Caldwell to deliver a speech. When he found out about the murder, he went straight back to the office."

"And?"

Newton said, "By my calculation, there's eighty extra miles on the car. The car was spotted at the murder scene because that neighborhood doesn't see many Lincoln Town Cars. In addition, Hernandez's wife, Liu, saw the police removing a small triangular piece of plastic from the trunk when they searched the car here before they took it away. With your identification of the lamp and them asking about a hole in a shade, it looks like they found a piece of the lamp in the back of the car."

If this went to trial, I'd be a star witness for lamp identification. "Was there any sign that either the locks or the ignition had been tampered with?"

"No." Newton shook his head. "To the best of my knowledge, the only other evidence the police have is a businessman who checked into the motel room next door to Hernandez's room at 11:00 on the night of the murder. He has told police the car was gone."

I turned to Hernandez. "Who had keys to the Lincoln?"

"Me, my wife, Jared Bach, and Mark Hearst."

"And Hearst was in the same motel as you?"

"Right. My wife was over in Twin Falls. Jared Bach was at home with his wife in Boise."

I turned back to the boss. "The paper says Hernandez made the murder gun himself. Is that an exaggeration?"

The boss and Hernandez exchanged glances.

Hernandez said, "Maybe I should show him the gun collection."

The boss nodded. Hernandez stood. The boss and I followed him out into the hallway and up a flight of stairs.

As we walked, I asked, "What about the time of death?"

Newton said, "The coroner puts it between midnight and one. I'd bet no later than 12:30 as she was found in her work clothes."

Hernandez turned the doorknob and escorted us into the place where good NRA members went when they died.

I gaped at the vast array of weaponry in the twenty by twenty room At the front of the room was every sort of modern gun I'd ever seen: pistols, revolvers, hunting rifles, assault rifles, and shotguns. There was enough heat packed in here to hold off a small army.

I whistled. "How many guns do you have in here?"

"Four hundred and fifty, but what I want to show you is towards the back." Hernandez led us about two thirds of the way through the room.

The modern guns gave way to World War Two rifles, Old West six-shooters, Revolutionary War muskets, and everything in between. They were all lined up two by two like animals on Noah's Ark. We reached a display missing one gun. Its widow was a tiny, two-barreled, metal pistol.

I pointed to the small pistol. "Where's her mate?"

Hernandez said, "At the crime lab. They took it from the house when they were doing the search." He walked over to a cabinet in the corner. "They asked me for the ammunition, too."

"Ammunition?" I blinked. "For these antiques?"

"One of my hobbies is gunsmithing." Hernandez pointed to the antique gun. "I prefer to make working replicas, including my own ammo. Though, I order it when I have to." He strode to the padlocked cabinet at the back of the room and pulled out a key with a blue ring and opened the padlock. "When the police took the ammo for the derringer, there were two rounds missing."

I took a few notes on my phone. "So the murder weapon was a replica of a 19th century gun? Anyone else have keys to the cabinet?"

"The only other key to the cabinet is in the safe inside my study. It hadn't been disturbed, and the lock hadn't been tampered with. Also, the door to this room is locked when I'm not home."

Newton added, "There's no sign of forced entry anywhere."

I said, "So, your car was used in the murder, which was committed with a gun and bullets that you personally crafted."

Hernandez nodded and sighed.

"So how's the alibi situation set?"

Newton shook his head. "Mr. Hernandez went to bed at 9:30 and sent no text messages and made no calls until the next morning. Three incoming cell calls went unanswered."

Hernandez rubbed his eyes. "I must have been dead tired. A cell phone call usually wakes me."

"Terrific." I reached inside my suit jacket, pulled out my yellow notepad, and scribbled on it. "All they're missing is an eyewitness."

Hernandez put a hand on my shoulder. "Now you know the situation. Come on, we'll be having lunch in twenty minutes."

"I don't think I'll have an appetite."

"Nonsense. You need your strength." He cleared his throat. "Gentlemen, I have to go help with the tamales. I'll see you at lunch."

After Hernandez walked away, the boss paced and pointed. "Take a look at this room. Imagine you're Ignacio Hernandez and you're going to commit a murder. Which handgun are you going to choose?" The boss pointed to more modern handguns. "You could have your pick of revolvers, small guns, big guns, semi-automatics. Why would you take a nineteenth century replica you crafted yourself and use it in commission of a felony?"

I grimaced. "The only advantage would be if the victim knew the killer and he could hide the gun and get close enough to surprise the victim, but there are .25s here that'd work just as well and not be nearly as traceable. Plus we know that the victim didn't know her killer. The lock was busted and there was a struggle. There was only one reason this gun was used."

Newton nodded. "I don't know how the murderer did it, but he stole this gun solely to implicate Hernandez. Are you in?"

I leaned back against the wall. Katrina Robles was dead because of me. If Hernandez didn't do it, then I needed to find out who did. Of course, it was possible Hernandez had done it and intentionally sought to make it so obvious he was guilty that everyone would think he was framed.

Either way, I had to know.

Chapter 11

On Wednesday, I sat in my car outside the single-story Canyon County Motel in Caldwell. I was holding my cell phone to my ear. The line was ringing. The line clicked. "Newton Investigations. Jerry Newton speaking."

"It's Ustick, boss. Did you read my report?"

"Yeah, the idea that somebody had made copies of Hernandez's keys in Parma was always a bit of a long shot, but thanks for checking."

"Thank the client. He underwrote it." I sighed. Two days of looking into this, and what did we have? Nada. "How does our list of suspects stand?"

"We have no serious suspects. Simply potential suspects who need to be ruled out."

"What about me? I knew more about Katrina Robles than anyone."

"You had no knowledge of Hernandez's home or habit. Further, you had an alibi for the night of the murder."

"Glad to know I've been crossed off the list." I cleared my throat. "After I interview the day desk clerk and the maid, I'll play it by ear."

"Sounds like a plan. Talk to you later." The boss hung up the phone.

I tossed my phone in the pocket of my lilac-colored suit, got out of my car, and entered the glass doors of the motel office. Behind the desk sat a well-tanned, middle-aged man wearing a red stripped shirt and jeans.

The man said, "Hello, sir. How may I help you?"

"Jaime Ramirez?" I asked.

He nodded. "You're looking at him."

I slid my card across. "Cole Ustick. I'm a private investigator."

"Like Jim Rockford?"

Cheeks warming, I glanced at the television. It had a *Rockford Files* rerun playing on it. "I'm here investigating the murder of Katrina Robles."

Ramirez said, "I've already told the police everything. According to the night clerk, party checked in and each person was given two keys. That was the last we saw until checkout. There's no way we'd know if someone left. There are three different exits from the parking lot."

I nodded. "I got that from the night clerk, Mr. Ramirez. I wanted to ask you about the reservation. You took that?"

He nodded. "Yes."

"Who placed the reservation?"

"The woman, Denise Waters. I reserved rooms 16 and 17 for herself and Mr. Hearst and then room 26 for Mr. Hernandez."

"Why was Hernandez so far from their rooms?"

Ramirez smiled. "It's funny you should ask. I had Room 15 available and offered it to them, but Ms. Waters said Hernandez wanted to be further away from the highway."

"Have they stayed here before?"

"I can't really tell you that. Privacy regulations."

Anticipated. I reached into my overcoat. "Here's an authorization from Mr. Hernandez to release any information."

The clerk blinked. "It'll take a while to look that up. It probably won't be until afternoon. I have a lot of guests checking out."

"Call me when you have something. Number's on the card."

The clerk clutched the card, glanced it, and then put it in his pocket.

I asked, "Is the maid here yet?"

The clerk nodded. "Yes, but she doesn't speak much English."

"What's her first language?"

"Spanish. She's from Nicaragua."

Glad she's not from Thailand. "I can speak enough Spanish." I adjusted my fedora. "Thank you for your time."

He nodded. "She should be halfway through the units."

I left the motel office and jogged around to the rooms on the back of the building. I spotted a cleaning cart outside room twenty-two. A pretty, young, olive-skinned woman was putting dirty towels onto it. She had wavy black hair and was wearing a red blouse and jeans.

I said in Spanish, "Hello, miss. May I please speak to you?"

She stared at me, blinking, then burst into a bright smile and replied in Spanish, "Hello, sir. How may I help you?"

"I'm Cole Ustick. I'm a private detective. I am investigating the murder of Katrina Robles. May I ask you a few questions, miss?"

"I told the police. They were in their rooms when I came here at seven. They left at eight in one car. That's all I know."

You may know something you don't think you know. "Thank you, Miss. Could you help me practice my Spanish, please?"

She glanced sideways at me. "I have to work."

"I can help a little."

"One thing, sir. Do not make the bed. Only I make the bed."

I nodded. "I won't touch it."

She sighed. "Very well."

I took off my jacket and hung it on the lamp outside the door. "What are you called, miss?"

"My name is Marcella Vaca."

Twenty minutes and four cleaned rooms later, Marcella was chattering at me rapidly in Spanish.

In my head, Newton's voice was saying, *"Ustick, you're wasting the client's time and money. Ignacio Hernandez isn't paying you to flirt with a maid. Stay on task and stop running off with your crazy hunches."*

I loaded dirty towels onto the maid's cart. *Shut up, conscience. Newton will be happy with the results if it goes somewhere. If it doesn't, we're not much worse off.* "So what brought you to America, Marcella?"

"I want to become an electrical engineer."

"That's a very good goal."

"You haven't spoken much, sir. I don't think you really need practice."

"I know Spanish very well, but I have few opportunities to use it. If I don't, I will lose it."

"How did you learn it?"

"I studied Spanish for four years in high school and two years in college. I also spent ten weeks living in Columbia." In high school, before God and I had a falling out over him letting my sister self-destruct.

"Are you Latino?"

"No, miss. My mother was Italian."

"Do you speak Italian?"

"Yes, my mother insisted I learn it in case we go to the old country. For Italian practice, I depend on movies and phone calls to my mother."

"Does your mother live around here?"

"Yes. She's a manager at Micron."

"Ah, and her son helps maids clean rooms."

I smiled. That'd be how Newton would see it. "My mother worked as a maid for two years after my father died, but she advanced to better positions."

"Like I will."

"Yes, like you will, miss." I emptied an ash tray into the trash can. "I was wondering. When you cleaned the rooms of the people here the night of the murder, did you notice anything unusual? Were they really messy?"

She laughed. "The person in room sixteen didn't even sleep in his bed."

If I'd understood the clerks, that was actually Denise Waters' room. My eyes widened, and I glanced to the pocket holding my phone.

"Was that important?"

I smiled. "Very important. It could change everything."

"Would you like to talk about it at dinner? I get out of class at seven."

Wow. I pick up women even when I'm not trying. Well, mining her for information and not sharing dinner wouldn't be right. "We can talk more at dinner, yes. Where do you want to go?"

"I'll take you." She smiled and batted her lashes at me flirtatiously. "I'm a modern woman. Meet me at McDonalds."

"Sure." *I'll have to remember to bring Tums.* I handed her my card. "Write down your number for me, and I'll call you if anything comes up."

She stowed my card in her jeans pocket and ripped a piece of paper off a hotel notepad she had on the cart and handed it to me. "Here, and tonight I'll practice my English with you."

"As you wish, miss." I headed for the car. Once there, I dialed Denise Waters' number. "Ustick here. Are you at campaign headquarters?"

Denise said, "Yes. Why?"

"I have some follow-up questions. Are you available in half an hour?"

"Make it forty minutes." She was typing, based on the soft clicking. "I have a conference call."

"Sounds good. I'll talk to you then." I hung up and headed back to Boise.

Thirty minutes later, I entered the deserted campaign office and surveyed the desks in this area. I meandered to Tara's unoccupied desk. It was decorated with pictures of her with various friends, as well a picture of Ronald Reagan and Pope John Paul II together.

Behind me, Denise cleared her throat. I spun.

Denise stood by one of the doors at the back. She carried a tan handbag and wore a gray sweater, a cream-colored skirt that went to mid-thigh, and tan pumps. "You wanted to see me."

"Can we speak in a private room?"

She led me in her door, into a conference room decorated with campaign posters. "Make this quick, I have a campaign to save. Between your office and the cops, I've gone over every detail of that night a dozen times."

"Make it a baker's dozen." I smiled and pressed the record button on the voice recorder in my pocket.

She perched on the edge of the table, crossed her legs, and set her purse beside her. "Let me guess your questions by answering them. Yes, I made the hotel reservations. We arrived in Caldwell a little bit before nine and checked in to our rooms. Hearst and I walked down to Mr. Hernandez's room, and I made us cocoa in the microwave. We talked about the campaign and headed our separate ways at nine fifteen. I posted a good night note on Facebook at nine twenty-five. I changed and went to bed at nine thirty. Anything else?"

"Did you sleep well?"

"Like a lamb, Ustick."

"That place is what, thirty-five dollars a night? Those beds must be pretty uncomfortable. I can't imagine a lady of your graces sleeping through the night there comfortably."

She grimaced. "Ustick, when you work for Ignacio Hernandez, you learn to sleep on cheap motel beds and like it. Sometimes, I wish he'd realize he's a multimillionaire, not the struggling son of a poor immigrant, but I've never let anything interfere with my sleep."

I smiled. "If you slept comfortably that night, Denise, you didn't do it in that bed."

She blinked. "What are you talking about?"

"I had a chat with the maid. She says you didn't sleep in your bed."

She waved it away. "Nonsense. My mother worked in hospitality and insisted I always make my bed when staying at a hotel. That's been my habit throughout life, and it'll continue even when I'm elected to the US Senate."

I shook my head. "She's an artist. She would know whether she made a bed as surely as Michelangelo would know the difference between his work and a reproduction of it."

"Give me a break." Denise laughed. "That doesn't prove a thing."

"True, but I could prove something, if I looked hard enough. We could go over to your apartment and find if your bed would pass muster in a motel. I could check with people who stayed with you in motels and see if you always make the bed. Better yet, I could hand the matter over to Detective Weston, and he'd go through the tedium for me."

Denise frowned.

I smiled. "Or you could be a good sport. Admit I caught you in a lie and tell me the truth. If it's not relevant to the investigation, I'll be discrete."

"Can I go talk to someone?"

"You're free to do as you like, but if you leave before I want you to, I'll be talking to Detective Weston. Truth doesn't require a conspiracy."

She cursed. "Mind if I text someone who can come and explain this?"

"By all means." I watched her.

She sent two texts, received two replies, and looked up. "Ten minutes. So I guess I'm your prisoner until then."

"Hey, I said you have the freedom to choose to leave. I'll simply choose to call Weston if you do. I have a pack of cards, if you want to pass the time."

"What's the stakes?"

I bit my lip. "I don't know. Maybe a dollar a game."

"No thanks. Gambling is no fun when the stakes are low. The higher the risk, the higher rewards, and the more thrilling it is. Twenty could be fun, but a dollar? I don't play with pikers." She wrinkled her nose, shook her head, and pulled out her smart phone.

And I never play cards with anyone who belongs in Gambler's Anonymous. I pulled out my phone and played Angry Birds.

Twelve minutes later, Hearst entered, scowling. "So what's happened?"

Denise scraped her hand through her hair. "Mark, he knows I didn't sleep in my bed on the night of the murder."

Hearst grunted and cursed at me. He paced a minute before he sat in the seat at the head of the table. "She fell asleep in my arms. We're lovers."

Ew. Of all the reasons for her not to be in her bed, why did it have to be that she was sleeping with a guy old enough to be her grandfather? I bit my tongue. "How long has this been going on?"

"Two years," Denise replied.

Hearst flinched. "Let me be clear. This isn't some dirty little affair."

Denise nodded. "What we have is—"

"Listen." I thrust out my hand. "My agency doesn't handle domestic cases, and I've already heard more than enough single, attractive young women explaining how their affairs with married, wrinkled, gray-haired old are unique, special loves that rival Romeo and Juliet. Skip the justifications. I'm investigating murder, not adultery. Now, Mr. Hearst, are you sure she couldn't have left during the night?"

"Positive. I'm a very light sleeper."

Denise added, "I so much as move the wrong way, and he wakes up."

Hearst smirked at me. "See? She's got the perfect alibi."

Only if you've had a lot of mistresses. "How does she sleep?"

"Once she's out, it'd take an earthquake to wake her before morning."

I grinned and cleared my throat. "That doesn't leave you with much of an alibi, Hearst."

"No worse than I had before."

True. I sighed. "Okay, I guess that's all. Thanks."

Hearst folded his arms. "Are you going to tell the cops and Hernandez?"

"Probably. The police need to know where everyone was."

"How could it be relevant to them that she was really in the next room when the crime was still committed thirty miles away?"

"Good point, but I do have to tell Hernandez. Your little game of hanky panky is putting his campaign at risk."

Denise tilted her head back. "We're very cautious."

I chortled. *You're so cautious, you try and bed a guy on the first date.* "Oh yeah, political people are never, ever caught in sex scandals. Plus you guys had us waste time tailing Gordon Thomas, lest we stumble onto your little peccadillo. You put the campaign at risk to protect yourself."

Hearst shook his head. "People were upset."

I glanced at Denise.

"They were," she said while looking at me with cherub-like innocence.

Hearst said, "Ustick, I've been winning elections since before you were born. Hernandez needs me, but he believes if a man's wife can't trust him, no else can. If you tell him about us, he'll get rid of me. That will kill his campaign and my career." He took a breath. "And then there's my wife and my family."

Laughing, I slapped my hands on the conference table and stood. "After two years of you having an affair, you want me to think about your family? And you mention them after your career and after the campaign." I shook my head. *Poor kids, poor wife, poor Hernandez, poor everyone, if this comes out.* "Somebody's got to put your family first, but that's up to Newton. I'll do my best to persuade him to not report it on two conditions. First, no more liaisons during the campaign. If you do, and I find out, I'll go straight to Hernandez. Second, I want complete cooperation with the investigation from here on out."

Hearst shook his head. "We don't have much choice. Very well."

Denise nodded. "Sounds reasonable."

"All right, I'll go and talk to the boss." *After a couple of stops I need to make first. I think I'll start with a trip home for a shower.*

I stood ringing the doorbell of a third floor apartment of a periwinkle building in West Boise.

On the fourth ring, a female voice shouted, "Go away!"

My face warmed. What had I been thinking, visiting newlyweds without calling first?

Jared Bach voice sputtered. "Who is it?"

"Cole Ustick." My voice came out half an octave softer. I swallowed. "I can come back."

Bach called, "I'll be out in a minute."

I waited for closer to five minutes before the door opened.

Jenny Bach stood at the door. She wore a pair of jeans and her husband's Broncos t-shirt which was two sizes too big for her. She was five foot two, had long, fine black hair, and a clear beige complexion. "Come on in."

She led me into the studio apartment. I sat on the couch. Beside it was a small Broncos t-shirt. Bach came from the closet while he was pulling on a red polo shirt. He and his wife flopped across from me on the love seat.

Bach put his arm around Jenny. "What did you need, Mr. Ustick?"

"I wanted to check with you again about the night of the murder. Did you go anywhere at all where the keys could have been stolen or in anyway compromised?"

Jenny tugged at her shirt. "The police questioned us twice, and this is the third time either you or your boss have been by. Does Mr. Hernandez suspect us of foul play?"

"He doesn't suspect anything. It's our job to do his suspecting."

"But it wouldn't make any sense. What motive could we have?"

It would be something if the people in Idaho best known for premarital chastity had committed murder. I chuckled. "If you'd like, I could refer you to the records from the California Secretary of State's office." I glanced to her husband. "Mr. Bach, did you know that her parents are both Democrats and that she voted in the 2012 Democratic primary?"

Jared Bach raised his right eyebrow. "So?"

"Some think, if Hernandez wins this election, he will become a national Republican figure."

Jenny cracked up, grinning. "You've been talking to Tara. She's mixed up the word 'Democrat' with the word 'vampire.' Sure, my parents are registered Democrats, but they vote for whoever they want in November. They were out to see us and met Mr. Hernandez. They liked him on a personal level so much, they gave his campaign a $500 donation. I voted in the Democratic Primary because a cousin was running for State Assembly. I'm strictly a Jesus freak. I hate that I have to become a Republican to vote for Mr. Hernandez." Her smile faded. "You didn't give that information to Tara, did you?"

"No."

Jenny wiped her brow. "Thanks. Sometimes, it is hard to avoid getting offended when she goes off on one of her tirades about Democrats."

Bach smiled. "She doesn't mean all Democrats, dear. She's usually talking about party leaders and activists."

"It sounds like she means everybody who has ever voted Democrat. That stinks." Jenny added to me, "We know some nice folks who are Democrats."

Bach nodded. "Once, I was up at U of I for a Young Republican meeting, and someone was trying to talk to Tara about that. He began by telling her not to be so intense and finished with, 'I even voted for a Democrat once.'"

I asked, "What did Tara say?"

Jared's grin widened and he touched his wife's arm. "She patted his arm and said, 'That's okay. Everyone makes mistakes.'"

Jenny said, "Oh gosh, that is Tara."

The two burst out laughing. I started laughing, too.

So the two biggest paragons of virtue in the state were human after all. They had insecurities and could feel like they were being judged. They laughed. They made love and grabbed the wrong shirts afterwards.

I cleared my throat. "It's good that she believes in things very strongly. Too many people are wishy-washy."

The two glanced at me and each other before laughing even harder.

"What did I say?"

Jenny smirked. "Don't you know? You're supposed to be the detective."

"If it's got something to do with the case—"

That brought on more laughter.

Bach said, "Let's give the guy a break."

Jenny stopped laughing. "I'm sorry. I get the giggles some times."

I asked, "Where were we?"

"Oh, you accused me of sabotaging the campaign for the glory of the Democratic Party of the Socialist States of America." Her tone was sarcastic.

I leaned back on their couch. "Sorry, I meant to illustrate that, in theory, everyone is under suspicion. I don't consider you a likely suspect, but someone took Mr. Hernandez's car and used it to murder Katrina Robles. We'd hate to think that anyone who he trusted with the keys betrayed him. But, somehow, the car was used, and it was not hotwired. If someone he trusted didn't do it, someone must have inadvertently given a murderer access to the keys."

"No." Jared ran his hand over his face. "I've thought about it. I've never lost these keys. Well, except around the house, and I've always found them before I left."

I nodded. Another sign of humanity.

Jenny said, "I thought you were here about the vacuum?"

I raised my left eyebrow. "Vacuum?"

"Yes, the police came with a warrant and impounded our Kirby."

"They took your Kirby? That's kind of a big vacuum for this little space."

Bach nodded. "It was a gift from my uncle Wally for our wedding. I told him it was too big for our apartment."

"It could come in handy when you upgrade."

"That's what he said."

Jenny said, "Only we're heading to India after the campaign, and it isn't coming with us."

"What's in India?"

"A lot of people who need help."

"You're going to be missionaries?" I asked.

Bach bit his lip. "It's going to be a challenge finding all the money."

So he'd given up an NFL contract to move to the third world? Why would he do that? That wasn't really a question I needed answered–or wanted answered for that matter. I stood. "I'll be going now. You have things to get to. I'll check on that vacuum for you."

Newton and I sat in the conference room back at Newton Investigations.

I swallowed bile. "After I left Hearst and his lover, I indulged an urge to take a shower and took one last stab at Jared Bach and his wife."

"They're not likely suspects."

"I did find out one thing. The police took their vacuum cleaner."

The boss raised his right eyebrow. "Interesting. What brand is it?"

"It's a Kirby. It's one of the newer models."

"Probably a model that also functions as a shampooer. The police asked everybody if they owned a Kirby vacuum and took it if they did. The shampoo was from likely from a Kirby, so they're checking out any Kirby machines to see if they can link it to them. I doubt it says anything about the Bachs."

"Agreed. They're leaving to become missionaries to India. That doesn't add up to people who'd commit murder for political or monetary reasons."

"Unfortunately, that leaves us with a huge problem. There were four keys to that car. Mr. Hernandez had one in his room at the motel, Mr. Hearst had another in his motel room, Jared Bach had his thirty miles away from the car, and Mrs. Hernandez had hers in Twin Falls. We haven't found any additional duplicates were made. So if Mr. Hernandez didn't do it, who did?"

I nodded. "Speaking of quandaries, what are we going to do about our illicit lovebirds?"

Newton scrunched his nose. "Tough call. Hernandez would want told. However, this revelation would ruin the campaign." He tapped his fingers on the conference room table. "Even if this by some miracle didn't leak out, if he fired his top two campaign officials without explanation, that'd look bad. Plus, I think they're still suspects, and I like to keep my suspects handy. They stay—for now. When you write up the report, simply summarize the conversation with the maid by saying no information of apparent relevance to the murder investigation was discovered."

"Unless Hearst is the murderer and he is trying to sabotage the campaign from the top."

Newton shook his head. "If Hernandez loses this campaign, the only thing it does for Hearst is tarnish his legend. Plus he'd only been to the house once. I doubt he'd know his way around there well enough to steal the murder weapon. There still may have been collusion between him and Ms. Waters, but we don't have proof."

I sighed. "So we still have what we had this morning: a big fat nothing."

Chapter 12

The score remained the same for the rest of the week.

After brunch on Saturday, I wore an olive green suit with a black tie as I strolled in the conference room of Jake Donaldsen, Attorney at Law. The walls were beige and the carpet was dark blue. Eight black rolling chairs surrounded the oak table. The boss sat on the right side of it and was dressed up in a gray suit with a red tie. I plopped in the chair beside the boss. "Can we hold our conferences here?"

Newton nodded. "Sure, if we start taking sleazy divorce jobs."

I clicked my heels together. "There's no place like home." I leaned back in my chair. "Something's occurred to me. We've let the question of the sexual assault claims drop."

"Doesn't seem important when we're talking about a murder."

I shook my head. "It goes back to why I found Robles. Whoever killed her wanted us to drop that investigation. If we find who started this rumor, we'll find the murderer."

"You may be right. Depending on how things go here, I may have you go over that ground, but the lawyers are going to be driving our investigation."

I grunted.

At ten till one, Denise entered wearing a dark green blouse and matching slacks. She carried a large purple purse over her shoulder. She placed it in front of her as she settled at the table, seated diagonally from the boss.

Tara entered followed by Jared Bach. He carried a file folder and placed it on the table as he plopped at it across from the boss.

She ambled over to Denise and pointed at her bag. "Oh, I haven't seen that since your birthday."

Denise nodded. "It's come in handy. Thanks for getting it."

Tara took her seat across from me.

I smiled. *At least the view will be nice during the meeting.*

Mr. and Mrs. Hernandez entered and took seats at the head of the table.

At three minutes after the hour, Hearst made his entrance dressed in a blue sports jacket and khakis. Trailing in his wake was a distinguished-looking, square-jawed man and a man a few years older than me with brown hair and a pointy chin. Their blue suits and gold ties were identical twins. The younger man sat by my boss and the older one sat by the younger man.

The older twin spoke. "Gentlemen, I'm Mr. Hernandez's attorney, Jake Donaldson." He pointed to the younger man. "And this Conrad Metcalf, my associate. We're here to coordinate the legal, political, and communications strategy of Mr. Hernandez, so we will cooperate rather than hinder each other. We'll go around the table with quick introductions before we get started."

That took about one minute. I noted the arrangements. Political people on were one side of the table, lawyers and investigators on the other.

Donaldson pointed at my boss. "Mr. Newton, you have conducted a pre-discovery investigation. Would you mind reporting your findings?"

Newton spoke. "To my knowledge, my associate and I have found all the evidence the police have. We're positive Hernandez's car and one of his guns were involved. However, there is no proof Mr. Hernandez himself was. They have a legitimate question as to how anyone else could have obtained the gun and ammo used, as well as the car. We haven't found an answer yet."

Donaldson said, "It's the prosecution's job to establish Mr. Hernandez's guilt, not our job to establish his innocence. How sure are you that you grasp the whole case?"

Newton looked Donaldson in the eye. "One of the investigators is my former partner. I know his methods. I know where their case stands, unless they have a secret eye witness. We've been to all of Mr. Hernandez's neighbors and to all of Ms. Robles' neighbors, and we got nothing you could build a case on. A neighbor who lived across the street from Hernandez saw his car and a silhouetted figure approaching his house sometime between 10:30 and 11:00. Three different people in Ms. Robles' apartment building saw a Lincoln Town car out front. However, no one saw the driver. One person saw the car in back of the house about two. Again, no driver."

The lawyer nodded. "Then the county prosecutor is going after my client for political reasons. We need to call them on it. Overall, our best strategy is to force a preliminary hearing before the primary. Based on the evidence, I doubt the judge will allow this to go to trial. Getting the hearing scheduled for only two months out is going to be a challenge, but I should be able to pull it off."

Hearst glared. "Leave the political strategy to me. We can win this even if the case hasn't been resolved by primary night. Bach, could you share that poll you emailed me?"

Bach pulled a piece of paper out of his file folder. "We had our pollster do a survey of likely Idaho Primary Voters. It found us trailing the governor by only eight points. By a 54-39% margin, primary voters didn't believe he was involved in the murder. Only 49% believed he wasn't involved in the sexual assault claims with 44% believing the charges."

Hearst rubbed his hands together. "With work, we can win by moving past the issue publicly. If we have the candidate brought before a preliminary hearing right before the primary, that will dominate the news completely."

Donaldson shook his head. "Yes, but exoneration would be positive, if they're not able to produce a believable case."

"But who says this will end in exoneration? We're not talking about a jury trial. They don't need to prove guilt beyond a reasonable doubt. They just need to prove probable cause."

Denise wrinkled her forehead at Hearst and glanced at Donaldson. "Sir, probable cause means it's more likely than not, right?"

Donaldson gulped. "Well, yes."

"Would it really would look improbable to a judge? Mr. Newton, you were a detective. Do you think they have enough for probable cause?"

Newton leaned back. "I've never been part of a murder case with this sort of evidence, but I have seen burglary cases go to trial on less."

Hearst grunted.

Newton added "But the hearing would be two months away. Evidence could yet be uncovered that might exonerate Mr. Hernandez."

Donaldson said, "Mr. Newton, I believe you were the arresting officer for a couple of my clients, the Irving and Blackwell case? Didn't I stop the case at the preliminary hearing?"

Newton bit his lip. "You did."

"You thought there was probable cause, which shows the limits of the police's imagination. I've never lost a criminal case. That's why Mr. Hernandez hired me. I have a sixty percent success rate at preliminary hearings, and I feel this case is ripe to be thrown out."

Hearst glowered and leaned toward the lawyer. "Donaldson, I've won a hundred percent of my campaigns. I don't need the help of a sleazy criminal defense attorney. More than likely, you'll end up torpedoing the campaign."

Great, it's the ego roller derby. I sighed.

The drama kings went at each other for over fifteen minutes.

Hernandez finally extended his hands. "Gentlemen, you are both the best at what you do. I appreciate your expert opinions and give them equal weight. Mr. Donaldson, please proceed with this case in the way that will best serve my legal rights without any regard to political consequences. Marc, you will handle those. I have every confidence in your ability to keep the campaign rolling with whatever legal strategy is indicated."

The two men glanced across the table at their opposite like they wanted to stick out their tongues at each other. Both grunted and nodded.

Hernandez continued. "Now, we're going to talk about communications and media strategy and how we can coordinate that, Jared."

I glanced at Newton. *Is there any reason why we have to stay here? We don't have anything to do with media.* I pulled out my notebook, ducked low, and doodled.

The voices around me went on at some length.

I looked up at the boss. He was scribbling notes, but he did that all the time. It didn't matter if everything said was a mass of irrelevancies. I returned to doodling. This stank. We were increasingly invisible and unnecessary but couldn't leave without being rude.

Finally, I checked the time on my iPhone. It was three in the afternoon. *There goes two hours of my weekend. There ought to be a law against dragging people to irrelevant meetings.*

Tara spoke up. "We've been going on a while. If you'd like, I could go and get us some coffee from the espresso stand downstairs."

"I'll go with you!" I shouted.

She waved me off. "I can get it myself, but thank you."

Hernandez grinned. "That sounds like an excellent idea. I could go for a chocolate mocha."

Mrs. Hernandez cleared her throat.

Hernandez sighed. "Make that a latte with sugar-free chocolate syrup and skim milk."

About half the room chuckled including the boss.

I raised my hand. "I'll have a peppermint latte with a double shot."

Everyone gave their order to Tara with the lawyers abstaining.

She wrote down the last order and looked around. "Mr. Hernandez, may I please borrow some cash? I just realized I left my purse at the office when I rode over with Jared."

"No problem. The campaign will cover it." Hernandez pulled a secretary wallet out of his inside suit jacket pocket and handed her two twenties. "Let's all stretch our legs for ten minutes. That will give Tara time to get the coffee."

I trotted into the men's room.

After I'd finished in there, I took the elevator downstairs. I passed by the espresso stand. A chubby, middle-aged male barista was filling each order and writing the contents on them. Tara stood waiting.

I glanced at Tara. "Are you sure you don't need any help?"

Tara raised her left eyebrow. "I'll be fine, thanks."

I walked outside and inhaled some cool March air. *What is it with her? She's sending more mixed signals than a confused third base coach.*

I checked my cell phone. I had a text message: *I love you, Dad.*

He was something.

I beamed. How many four-year-olds could text and even come close to being right? I texted back, *Love you too, son.*

I climbed up the stairs and resumed my place.

Tara entered carrying the trays of coffee stacked on one another. She handed me mine first. "You had the peppermint, I believe."

I nodded. "Thanks."

She handed everyone their coffee and left a pile of white, yellow, and blue sweetener packets on the conference table. The boss grabbed one white packet. Denise and Tara each added three yellow packets to their coffees. Only Mrs. Hernandez and I abstained from using any of the additives on the table.

Mrs. Hernandez placed her purse on the table and pulled out a medicine bottle. It looked like it'd once held five hundred Tylenol, but she'd recycled it. She opened it, held it over her cup, and shook out a white powder. She closed the bottle, put it back in her purse, and stirred her coffee.

The meeting got back underway, and I got back to my doodling. *At least they're paying me $40 an hour to bore me to tears.*

At two minutes to four, Hernandez spoke. "If there's nothing else, we'll be adjourned. Thank you for your time."

Tara and Jared Bach headed for the restrooms. I walked out into the hall and stood at the door as I waited for the boss. Inside, Mrs. Hernandez spoke softly with the attorney and Hearst while Mr. Hernandez stood behind her.

The boss started collecting empty, disposable coffee cups and putting them in the trash can at the end of the table. He picked up Mrs. Hernandez's cup. "You want this? It's still got about a third left."

Mrs. Hernandez shook her head. "It wasn't very good, but thank you."

The boss tossed it out and joined me. The Hernandezes also exited the conference room along with Hearst and Denise.

Once downstairs, we headed out the front door and toward our cars.

A dozen and a half journalists descended on us with lights, microphones, and cameras. A loud female reporter said, "Mrs. Hernandez, do you stand by your husband?"

She responded, "Yes, of course."

Mr. Hernandez thrust out his right hand. "This is my wife. She is not a candidate."

A tubby male reporter shouted at her, "Is it true you've told friends you expect your husband to go to prison?"

"No!" She glared, shaking her head.

Her husband grabbed her arm and moved to lead her away, but it was like a zombie movie where they herded around us, ready to close in for the kill.

Hernandez shouted. "Jared!"

Newton and I glanced at each other, ran out in front of the Hernandezes, and pushed our way forward.

Gordon Thomas said, "Is it true you were here to discuss divorce with the attorneys?"

"Absolutely not!" Mrs. Hernandez rasped, turned white, then collapsed.

Mr. Hernandez shouted, "Liu!"

The boss and Mr. Hernandez rushed to her side. The boss felt for a pulse and began to perform CPR.

Hernandez stood clear and stared at her. The lines on his face seemed to multiply. His lips moved like he was speaking too softly for me to hear and he bowed his head.

I pulled out my cell phone and dialed emergency services. I glanced back at the reporters. They'd stopped shouting questions. Most were slack-jawed.

"My God!" A pretty young reporter cupped her mouth and fingered her messy braid.

The operator answered the phone. "Nine, one, one, emergency."

"Yeah, we have a woman down. I believe she's suffered a heart attack." I provided the attorney's Front Street address.

Except for the woman with the braid, the reporters all began to scribble in notebooks or type on iPads. The photographers were setting up shots.

I sneered. No time for human compassion. This was news and the news had to be covered.

Jared Bach ran up with Tara a few steps behind him. The burly, former running back looked around and pushed the media back. "Give them room."

The operator said to me over the phone, "We'll have an ambulance there as soon as possible. Is someone performing CPR?"

"Yes, my boss is."

Newton pumped Liu's chest with both hands and shouted at me, "Tell them to have a defibrillator ready."

I relayed the message.

The operator said, "We'll have someone there right away. Should be within three minutes. I'll wait with you until they arrive."

Three minutes later, the paramedics arrived in an ambulance. A short-haired blonde took over performing CPR on Liu Hernandez.

The boss shouted, "Jared, Ustick, Tara, form a barrier between them and the press!" He glared at the reporters. "Ladies and gentlemen, stand back."

Most of the press backed off. One lady with an eyebrow ring dashed to the left to get past the boss's perimeter with a camera.

The boss and I ran after her. He snatched the camera out of her hand.

She crossed her arms. "Hey, freedom of the press!"

The boss scowled. "File a civil rights suit if you like. I'm not going to let you get pictures of Mrs. Hernandez like this. I'll give your camera back to you once they leave."

The male EMT shouted, "Stand clear!"

We took a step back as they used the paddles.

They checked her pulse and continued to work on her.

The city police showed in three squad cars.

The boss briefed a sergeant, handed him the camera and police officers took our positions on the perimeter. The boss ran inside the building.

Hernandez stood frozen, gaping.

Gordon Thomas was texting like a teenage girl.

I imagined breaking each one of those dancing fingers. *Slime Incorporated's poster boy.*

The EMTs gave Mrs. Hernandez another shock.

"She's got a pulse," the EMT said. She and her partner loaded the patient into the ambulance. She glanced to Hernandez. "Sir, you want to ride along?"

He nodded, and she let him into the back of the ambulance with her. It tore out of the parking lot, headed towards St. Luke's, sirens screaming.

A black Ford Explorer pulled up outside. Detective Weston climbed out wearing a BYU sweat shirt and a pair of jeans. He scurried in the building. A couple minutes later, Weston came out carrying Mrs. Hernandez's coffee cup.

The boss was at his heels. "Get that checked."

Weston nodded. "You told the medical people?"

The boss nodded. "Of course."

Weston got in his SUV and drove off.

"What was that about?" I asked the boss.

The boss grimaced. "Hopefully nothing. Let's get down to St. Luke's."

Chapter 13

The boss was already there when I walked into the ER's waiting room. Denise and Hearst were seated beside Newton. I flopped in a blue chair across from him, removed my hat, and eyed the boss. "Where are the others?"

The boss took a bite out of a Heath bar. "Jared's talking to the press."

"So how are the jackals?"

Hearst grimaced. "Happy. They've been fed today."

I swallowed. "What about Tara and Mr. Hernandez?"

Newton said, "They're in the chapel."

Jared plodded in from the parking lot and headed toward the chapel.

The boss got up and fed two dollar bills to the vending machine in the corner. "Anyone want anything?"

"I'm not hungry," Denise said.

Hearst and I shook our heads.

The boss got a Three Musketeers bar and a bag of pretzels and paced as he ate them.

After Newton had finished, Jared Bach returned from the chapel stone-faced. "Mr. Hearst, Mr. Newton, come here."

They got up and followed Jared. He spoke to them for a minute and then walked back towards the chapel. Tara came out of it as Jared strolled to Denise and I. Jared bowed his head. "She didn't make it. I'm sorry."

Just one week ago, I'd played for her. Now she's gone.

Denise wept softly. "I can't believe it."

Tara stumbled over, her eyes and cheeks red, and embraced Denise. The two women stood sobbing and hugging.

My cell phone buzzed. I read the text.

It was from Newton. *I failed. Go home.*

Good. I didn't belong here.

Tara quivered as she bawled on Denise's shoulder.

Denise led her to a chair, and the two women sat beside each other. Tara held her head in her hands and heaved tears. A couple ladies in the waiting room were staring at her.

Poor kid. I touched Tara's shoulder. "I'm sorry."

Shoulders slumped, I headed out the exit and headed across the street to the underground parking garage. What had the boss meant by him failing?

"Hey now, you're an all-star, get your game on, go play," my phone sang as if all were right in the world.

Yawning, I ripped my black sleep mask off and grabbed the phone from my nightstand. "What?"

The boss said over the line, "Ustick, come down to the office."

I glanced at the time on my phone. "It's six fifty a.m. on a Sunday."

"You called me once about that time."

"So this is revenge?"

"No, it's important."

I sighed. "Give me twenty minutes."

Twenty-four minutes later, I was wearing a navy blue suit as I entered the office. The boss slumped at his desk. He wore the same suit he wore yesterday, his face was covered with a day's growth of beard and his eyes were bloodshot.

I blinked. "So what cat drug you in?"

The boss rubbed his hand across his unshaven face. "I apologize. I know my appearance isn't up to our dress code. Let's call this Casual Sunday."

"If you say so." I took my place at my desk.

"What did you do after you left?"

"I cancelled my date for the night, went down to Wahooz Family Fun Center, bought an unlimited pass, and played laser tag until the place closed."

The boss grunted. "You have an odd way of responding to a tragedy."

"I needed to work out my aggression so I didn't track down Gordon Thomas and punch him in the nose. What did you do?"

The boss grimaced. "Tracked down Gordon Thomas and punched him in the nose."

I half-smiled. "If we were at a bar, I'd offer to buy you a drink. So when do you surrender to the authorities?"

"Never. He didn't even have me thrown out of the pub he was at."

"That was decent of him."

"The video of Liu collapsing is all over the news. Thomas is even getting flack in the national media. CNN's doing a segment on it this afternoon. He didn't want to risk getting any more negative attention himself. I made clear I wasn't speaking to him as an employee of Hernandez but as a family friend."

"And that's when you belted him?"

"No, I asked him if he knew Mr. Hernandez had told them to lay off her because of her heart. He said they had."

"And that's when you smacked him?"

"No, he explained the media had thought Hernandez was being overly protective, exaggerating, or lying. That's when I smacked him."

"You should've done one for me."

"He got up and pointed out Mrs. Hernandez had given an interview on a radio show before Hernandez even thought of running. She'd explained how she managed to live an almost normal life with medication, diet, and exercise."

"So the media decided to play doctor."

Newton nodded. "They weren't without a point. She lived a remarkably active life. She ran in the half-marathon, Race to Robie Creek. She shouldn't have collapsed due to some stupid questions. I think she was murdered."

Murder? Committed right in front of both of us? "How?"

"I think the coffee was poisoned. I've never known her not to finish a latte. I was such a fool. If I'd realized sooner, I might have saved her."

"Boss, her death was beyond your ability to control. The poison theory may appeal to you so much because it allows you to regain control over life by blaming yourself."

The boss blinked hard. "Ustick, at times, I regret paying for that psych course." He rubbed his eyes. "I'm fairly sure it's not an invention of my guilty mind, or I wouldn't have called Weston to have the coffee analyzed. If it is just my imagination, be assured you're being paid."

"By what client? Does Hernandez know about this?"

"No. For now, I'm the client."

I sighed. "I guess you're the boss twice over. I hate to be crass, but how long do I have to keep at this? You may be able to go 24/7 but I haven't had a full day off since last Sunday, and I'm not supposed to get another one until next Saturday."

"The attorney provided us two surveillance videos. One shows a good overview of the lobby. We can use it to determine when everyone arrived and if anyone left the building during the break. Watch that one. I've got another one that shows the espresso stand. I can get an idea of whether the barista put something toxic in her drink, if we can compare when Tara came to when he was serving others. Shouldn't be more than an hour or two."

I raised my left eyebrow. "Wait. This is Sunday morning. Shouldn't you be in church like a good Protestant?"

Newton groaned. "I'm in no condition to go to church."

Then you're in no condition to work. "I drove by your church a couple days ago. The sign said, 'Come as you are.' Go home and get a couple hours sleep. You'll be fine."

"Ustick, thank you for your concern for my spiritual welfare, but my faith doesn't depend on me being in that building every Sunday. I'll listen to the podcast later."

I shrugged. How could I press the point when I'd planned to sleep until noon? Newton's church attendance may be spotty, but I wasn't in a position to needle him. "I'll admit watching surveillance footage beats going to Mass."

"Good." Newton handed me a DVD.

I popped a piece of Juicy Fruit into my mouth. The DVD loaded on my PC, I fast forwarded to eleven o'clock when the first people began to show up.

After an hour, I carried my notes over to Newton and dropped them on his desk. "This was almost as boring as tailing Gordon Thomas, but here's a complete list of everyone's arrival and departure times to the minute."

He scratched his head. "What about during our recess?"

"I came downstairs. So did Mr. Hernandez. He walked around the lobby for exercise. I got fresh air. Tara came and got the coffee. No one else came into the building at that time or entered or exited the stairwell or the elevator."

"You seem to be a little ahead of me."

"It happens, particularly when I practice that ancient Oriental discipline known as sleep. You might want to try it sometime."

"Later." The boss grunted. "The espresso guy didn't kill Liu. He seemed pretty cool and collected. But he could have been a professional."

"Yeah, a professional killer who has obviously been working food service for years and has an arthritic knee, judging by the way he was hobbling on the video."

"You don't need to be swift for poisoning."

I sighed. *You're firing on half a cylinder, maybe.* "Boss, take it easy. You could be right, but I wouldn't bet on the police lab telling us anything until Monday. I'd like you to be conscious tomorrow. You know, instead of tracking down every long shot we can think of."

"I can't sleep."

"Have you tried some herbal tea?"

"That doesn't work."

I grinned. "It does when I make it. I'll go down to the break room and get you some. Now don't run off and get yourself in an accident."

"Well, if that doesn't work, I'm going to need coffee."

"I'll drive you. I know this fabulous little place. It's run by a professional assassin."

The boss growled.

I dashed to the common break area for our floor, and put a cup of hot water in the microwave, and heated it for two minutes. The microwave dinged. I put a chamomile-peppermint tea bag in the cup of water and mixed in sugar and two herbal sleeping pills.

The next evening, I wore a black suit with red pinstripes to Dugan's Bar and Grill. It was dimly lit with the NCAA Basketball tournament on all the plasma TVs. The interior was baby blue and chipped badly. BSU pennants and sports pictures adorned the walls. I strolled to the blue and orange bar. A male bartender with half-bleached hair stood mixing a drink.

I slid in front of him. "Get me a strawberry margarita."

"Yes, sir." He put the drink in front of me. "They're all over at the table in the corner."

"And you swear they're all regular customers of Katrina's."

The bartended frowned. "Look, man. Those guys have built a shrine to her memory." He pointed to the edge of the bar. "It's been more than a week, and the management doesn't dare remove it."

"Where are they sitting?"

"Back of the bar, four at a table."

"Just four guys?"

"Oh, more than four guys contributed to that shrine, but most wouldn't even talk with you."

I reached into my wallet and handed him a twenty dollar bill

"You promised me ninety."

"Yeah, twenty when I hired you, twenty now, and fifty once I'm done talking to them."

The bartended grimaced. "You're not a trusting sort."

"I'm not paid to be." I grabbed my drink and ambled to the end of the bar. A large poster board had Katrina Robles' picture on it. Brief messages were written on the cardboard. Three flameless candles blazed out front.

I strode to the back of the room.

Four gentlemen in their 50s and 60s sat in the far corner. Three of them were dressed in blue jeans. One wore a BSU Sweat Shirt, another wore a red flannel shirt, and the fattest man wore a denim shirt. The oldest man wore khakis, a white dress shirt, and a light blue sports coat.

I offered the latter man my hand. "My name is Cole Ustick. I'm a private investigator looking into the death of Katrina Robles."

"Johnny told us." The guy in the sports coat had spoke with a thick New England accent. "Have a seat."

I pulled up a chair and eased into the chair.

"We're speaking to you in the interest of justice. My friends and I here know that sometimes the police get it wrong and we want whoever murdered our friend to be punished. If we think you're going to pursue a strategy of besmirching Katrina's character, we will wish you a good day, sir. We would rather go to jail than support such an abuse of the system."

Denim shirt clapped. "Well said, Senator."

"Senator?" I asked. "Where's that nickname come from?"

Sports Coat smiled. "I was a State Senator in the Vermont for six years. That was twenty-six years ago."

I smiled. "About my lifetime."

BSU Sweatshirt cackled as he clutched his empty beer mug. "Senator got voted out of office. Has been doing honest work ever since."

"Quite right." Senator grinned.

I leaned forward. "Gentlemen, I'm not in the besmirching business. I'm in the fact-finding business. I simply want to ensure justice is done."

"Then we are in agreement, sir."

"Let me get you a round of drinks." I took their orders, went to the bar, and returned with the drinks. "A sherry, two Coors Lights, and a Budweiser." I gave the senator his sherry and distributed the beers. "Now, that that's out of the way, can I get your names?"

The senator said, "My name is Ulysses Lee."

"Albert Hastings," Denim Shirt said.

Flannel shirt said, "Nick Leiber."

"Fred Kenner," BSU Sweatshirt said.

I jogged them down in my notebook. "All right, so tell me about her."

Hastings said, "Katrina was such a sweet young woman. She'd been here about two years."

Kenner slurred, "She was a little quiet at first, but she got over that. She was a great listener. I was always so glad to see her bringing my drink."

The senator nodded. "She cared quite a bit. Even in the way she handled the customer who was having too much. She'd engage you in conversation, find out if something was wrong."

Kenner pouted. "But she was too quick on the car keys. She'd go to any length to keep you from driving out of here if she thought you were too drunk to drive good. I always wished she'd stop pestering great drivers like me and focus on the crazy slouches who really need that."

"Anyone make trouble over it?" I asked.

The senator waved. "Oh, she could handle rowdies. It was always surreal. She'd be laughing and joking with us one minute. Someone would get out of hand." The senator made a fist. "She'd take care of it and then two minutes later be back to laughing and smiling."

Leiber said, "Didn't she rescue you once outside the bar?"

"Someone tried to attack me outside the bar, and she flattened him." The Senator sipped his sherry. "I hate that memory. I've gone from being a young man who is a protector to an old one who needs protected by a woman."

"She was no ordinary girl." Kenner grinned and whistled. "What a strong young woman."

Hastings sat up a little straighter. "I beat her at arm wrestling once."

"She let you win." The Senator guffawed.

Hastings guzzled his beer, his face crest-fallen. "She was nice anyways."

I asked, "Did she have any recurring problems with anyone round here?"

Everyone shook their head.

I made a note. "Did she talk about family at all?"

Senator said, "I gathered that she and her sisters journeyed from place to place, and her mom went from man to man all her time growing up. I don't think she had anyone to come home to as an adult."

Hastings nodded. "Poor kid had been through a lot. It was a miracle she'd turned out as well as she did."

Kenner raised his glass. "I'll drink to that."

I joined them in a drink and raised my hand.

The waitress scurried over. "Yes?"

I said, "Another round for everyone but me."

"Yes, sir." The waitress hurried toward the bar.

Senator said, "You're not much of a drinker, are you?"

"Two is my usual limit. When I'm working it was one."

"Good for you, sir. A sober man." Senator slapped my shoulder. "I once asked Katrina about how she managed to be such a wonderful person with the background she came from. She credited her faith. It made me think of Sunday School and things I'd given up long ago. It seemed to work for her."

Last thing I wanted to talk about in a bar was religion. "Do you know where she went to church?"

Kenner rubbed his chin. "She used to go to some funny church, Azusa something."

Senator frowned. "Isn't that place out in California?"

I nodded. "I believe so, but I know which local church she was talking about. I saw the name over on Orchard. Did she have any friends there?"

"She mentioned a cop who she hung around with."

"Sally Montoya?" I asked.

"Yeah."

"She's on my list of people to talk to, but she's out of town this week. Anyone else?"

"No, and she stopped mentioning the cop like six or seven months ago. And then she started going over to a Vineyard church. I think it was the big one in Boise."

"Did she mention anyone there?"

They all shook their heads.

I turned a page. "Did she ever mention any romantic relationships?" Again they all shook their heads.

Senator said, "One night, after I had a couple beers in me, I asked when she was going to get married. She said she didn't plan to. I don't believe she ever met anyone special enough to change her mind."

Hastings nodded. "She was warmer to guys our age than she was to guys her age." He took another sip. "I always thought it was a shame with a nice girl like that."

I noted it. "Were any of you here the last night she worked?"

Senator said, "I was. She seemed distracted. On her breaks, she grabbed her cell phone and went into the backroom. Whatever happened, she wasn't happy about it."

Hastings said, "She did her best to bear up under whatever strain she was under. She even gave me advice." Hastings patted his beer belly. "I says to her, 'Katie, I've found a new way to lose weight. Hypnosis.' Then she looks at me real serious, almost like she'd stepped into the Twilight Zone, and says, 'Albert, don't do that. They'll mess you up.' She says, 'What you need is some physical training. I'd like to start that as a side business, but I wouldn't charge you for it, since I'd be experimenting with you. Come in tomorrow, and we'll talk.' I told her I would and was looking forward to it." Tears welled up in Hastings' eyes. "You know how that turned out."

A woman shouted from behind me, "Cole Ustick!"

I whirled in my chair and eyed a short-haired blonde about five seven with a slightly stocky build. She was wearing a pair of tan pants and a blazer.

Was this a girlfriend I'd forgotten I had? I said coolly, "Yes?"

She put her hands on her hips. "Where the hell have you been? I've been trying to find you for two hours."

"Sorry, I'm booked solid. I couldn't possibly consider a date until May."

"I'm not your type." She pulled a badge out of her blazer pocket. "I'm Detective Maggie French, Boise Police. I need to ask you a few questions."

"In a minute. I'm about finished here." I spun back to the guys I'd been questioning.

Detective French said, "No. Come now."

"Am I under arrest?"

"Not yet."

"Then let me wrap this up, and I'll be right with you." I glanced around the table. "Gentlemen, is there anything else you can tell me?"

Senator said too loudly, "Sir, you're a good man. I wish you good hunting as you investigate this heinous crime. Ms. Robles was a special woman. I am a miserable old man paying for a lifetime of vices. I've lived too long."

"You're not even seventy," I said.

"Just the same, I've outlived the love of two ex-wives and the respect of my children. The only thing I haven't outlived is my money. In Ms. Robles, I found a good friend who was kind simply for the sake of being kind. Having spent years in politics, I can't tell you how refreshing that is. I disagree with Mr. Hernandez's politics, but my experience tells me he is not the murderer. That being the case, you must find the real murderer and punish him. If you need additional funds in this endeavor, I'm at your disposal, sir. But you must find him, you must see that Katrina's murderer does not go unpunished."

"I'll do everything I can, Senator." I pulled out four business cards and put them on the table. "Here, call me if you remember anything else."

The men took the cards.

I walked over to the bar and gave Johnny the cash for the bar tab.

Johnny said, "How was your conversation?"

"Enlightening." I handed him a fifty dollar bill.

Detective French glared at me. "What's the fifty for?"

I smiled. "I'm a generous tipper. Is that a crime, Detective?"

She snorted. "We need to go down to City Hall. Can you drive?"

"I only had one, and I took a girl for dinner and dessert before I came."

"You're dating a teenager?"

"No."

"Then you took a woman to dinner."

Was she the political correctness police, too? "Yes, Detective. I took a woman out and forgot my cell phone. I know it's a shocker I managed to survive without it."

"Don't get cute with me." Detective French waved me out. "I'll follow you downtown."

Detective French escorted me into the Boise Police Department and led me to back to her desk. Several other workstations were in the area. She leaned against hers and folded her arms. "Have a seat."

I settled in an office chair.

She took a seat opposite me. "We're looking into Mrs. Hernandez's death. I don't have too many questions. Could you tell me in your own words what happened?"

I went on for ten minutes.

Detective French finished taking notes. "Ms. Burke declined your offer to help with the drinks. How do you two get along?"

"Fine, I guess."

"How'd you meet her?"

"I met Tara in my professional capacity."

"Have you spoken to her outside of that?"

"Four times. First day I met her, I asked her to dinner. She declined."

French chuckled. "And after that?"

"Two weeks ago, I went to the campaign office and I volunteered to help with the mailing and we talked."

"About what?"

I sighed. *I hate being on the other end of these questions.* "I'll just say I made a pass at her. I wasn't intending to be disrespectful, but she took it that way."

"So pass intercepted. Then what?"

"Ten days ago, I was eating dinner at the Fish Shack, and she joined me. She asked me about investigating an aspect of her libel case against the paper. Then I ran into her at the Hernandez's place. Ms. Waters and Mr. Newton were also there. We played music together and we ate lunch at the same table."

"Anything else outside of work?"

"Tara and I are Facebook friends."

"So would you describe your relationship as cordial?"

When it's not stiff, formal, and cold. "That's a good word."

"So you can't explain why she refused your offer of assistance."

"It could be that she was using the trays for weightlifting."

Detective French rolled her eyes. "Any serious explanation?"

"Aside from the fact she can't seem to make up her mind whether she hates me? No."

French rocked in her chair a moment. She pointed to the computer at another desk. "Turn this into a statement. We'll have you out of here soon."

After I'd printed out my statement, I brought it back over to her.

She scanned it. "You forgot to include that you're not aware of why she refused your offer."

"Why do you need that? As I recall it, I said maybe she doesn't like me."

"Unless you know that for certain, say you don't know."

"Why does it matter?"

"The day I start giving you information on my case is the day I check myself into the state hospital in Blackfoot. Can you think of any reason you shouldn't include it?"

"No."

"Then add it to the statement, so we can get out of here."

"Are you going to hold me if I don't?"

Growling, Detective French folded her hands together into the shape of a gun. "Fine, if you insist, sign what you have and go home."

I pulled out my pen, signed it, and slid it at Burke to her. "Here you go."

She scooped it up. "Thank you."

I left the police station.

Once I was back at the office, I typed up my report on my interview with Katrina's four friends.

As I finished that up, Newton stormed in our door and stood over me, glaring. "Where have you been? Why haven't you answered your phone?"

"Sorry. I'd left it at home."

"You should never leave home without it."

"True, Boss. I was so naked without it. I'm surprised I wasn't arrested for public indecency."

"Cut the clowning. I got news for you. That case I thought was a murder is now officially a murder. The police have even made an arrest."

"Who?"

"You won't believe this." The boss took a deep breath. "Tara Burke."

Chapter 14

I stared at Newton. "Tara Burke, a murderer? What, did she have a nun for an accomplice?"

The boss sighed. "I understand where you're coming from. I'd have bet against her being the culprit. That was why I was so interested in the guy who ran the espresso stand. With him out of the picture, that leaves Tara as the only one to touch the coffee before Mrs. Hernandez got it."

"Didn't Mrs. Hernandez put her own sweetener in the coffee? Anyone could have poisoned the sweetener."

"Yeah, the police also had the sugar bottle analyzed. No poison at all, but there was poison in the coffee. That's highly suggestive. Logically, I can't see how anyone else could have done it."

I leaned back. "It's not in her character. And what's her motive?"

"She helped discredit Gordon Thomas with that planted story."

"That isn't true, and it'd be irrelevant if it were."

Newton waved. "It bolsters the theory that she's in love with Hernandez, would do anything for him, and wanted to get his wife out of the way."

Great job, Ustick. No one can know it was you, or it'll blow your credibility and the campaign's to pieces. I swallowed. "Who came up with that theory?"

"Detective French."

"Apparently her schedule allows her to TIVO *The Young and the Restless.*"

"I don't like the theory much myself. They jumped the gun on this arrest, but I thought you should know. Tara is spending the night in lock up and will be arraigned in the morning."

"Thanks for letting me know. Let me email you my report. It's time I headed home." I did so and left, frowning. Now what I was going to do?

119

I stood outside the Ada County Courthouse as I pulled my ponytail tie out for the fifth time that morning and retied my hair. Hopefully, I got it neat enough this time. *I could have used some sleep last night.*

A ravenous herd of journalists gathered before me.

My cell phone rang.

I picked it up. "Ustick."

Newton said over the phone, "Where are you? You were supposed to be here at nine."

"I'm waiting for Tara Burke to come out of the courthouse and give her statement."

"Are you working for me or *Boise Weekly*?"

"Boss, I'm following the case."

"I didn't assign you to watch Tara."

The reporters stirred like a pool of sharks. A bald, bulky man in a black suit and a light green shirt strode out with Tara Burke behind him. She was wearing the same wrinkled gray suede skirt suit she'd worn in court.

"Hold on a minute, Boss," I whispered.

The bald man extended his hands to the press. "I'm Kenneth McKenzie, attorney for Ms. Burke. She has prepared a brief statement."

Tara stepped forward and unfolded a piece of paper. "Members of the press, in court this morning, I pled not guilty to the charge of murder." She stared around. "This charge is absolutely false. On the advice of counsel, in the interest of justice, and to ensure a fair trial, I'll have no further comment on this case. Thank you for your time."

McKenzie led her to the car.

The reporters shouted questions. "Were you involved in the murder?"

"Are you in love with Ignacio Hernandez?"

Mackenzie used his ample frame to part the pack of reporters like Moses at the Red Sea. Tara headed towards a waiting SUV.

I glared at the reporters before stomping back to my Jaguar.

Once back at the office, I stomped to my desk. The boss grunted at me. I glared. "Don't grunt. You had me here early on a Sunday morning." I flopped into my chair. "And there was nothing scheduled on the calendar."

The boss sighed. "Fair enough."

I tapped my fingers. "So what is on the agenda today?"

"Two murders and a sexual assault allegation."

"Let's talk murder number two."

"All we can do with that mess is interview Tara and find out her side."

"I can do that."

The boss laughed. "No you can't. You're not even remotely open to the possibility she did it."

"She didn't."

"I've met plenty of murderers who were nice people. You have to go by the evidence."

"All you have is circumstantial evidence."

The boss grimaced. "People have been executed on that basis."

I folded my hands. "Let me interview her. Afterwards, if you don't feel I did a professional job, you can do it yourself."

The boss sighed. "We need to know exactly what happened when she got the drinks. Did she put something in Mrs. Hernandez's drink that should have been harmless? Second, how much did she know about her bogus news story? I want to find out who was behind it and why. Check the surveillance archives. The tails we had on Thomas may have some clues."

It's rare someone is asked to investigate himself. I swallowed. "Sure."

"Do you have any other ideas?"

"We need to think about the crime. We can imagine there's no chance she did it, and then figure out how it could have happened otherwise."

The boss raised his left eyebrow. "You want to bill the client for merely thinking about the case?"

"It's only a thought experiment."

"I'll save it for when I'm desperate. Now on to the first murder."

After two hours of tedium, the boss's cell phone rang. "Jerry Newton speaking." He cocked his head for a minute before he nodded. "We'll be there, sir." He hung up and glanced over at me. "There's a meeting about Tara Burke at noon at campaign headquarters. Mr. Hernandez wants us there."

Rather than get stuck in traffic, we ran the three quarters of a mile to the campaign office. Panting hard, we stumbled into the conference room. Sitting inside were Hernandez and Hearst. We sat across from them. Newton buckled over like he had a cramp and might pass out.

Hearst snarled at us. "I have no idea why you brought them here."

"I want someone who isn't in politics to be in the meeting." Hernandez spun to us. "This meeting is about Tara Burke's status with the campaign."

Hearst waved. "There's nothing to discuss. We have to distance ourselves from her and make it clear you had no idea she was stalking you, let alone that she'd sink to murder."

Hernandez glared and clenched his fists. "She's innocent."

"Only the naïve think the courts get to determine that." Hearst waved it away. "The media are already prosecuting her. The public will convict her long before this comes to trial. After her rubbing it in Thomas's face over the false report, he's having a good time crucifying her. He and his cronies will use her to destroy you. We have to get away from this."

"But Tara is my most loyal supporter! I'd have quit long ago, if it weren't for her."

"Yesterday she was a valuable asset. Today she is a class one liability. Let her go. Remember, Idaho's economic future is on the line as well as a quality education for our kids. We can't sacrifice that for our personal feelings for one person. Victory or defeat, that is our choice. For the future of our state, we must tie all the campaign's negative baggage to her, with a little whisper here, a little whisper there, and give her a swift kick to send her on her way."

I grimaced and pointed at Hearst. "You'll ruin the rest of her life."

"It'll hardly matter, where she's going."

My jaw dropped. "You were serious! You've got her convicted already."

The boss sat up and leaned forward. "This case is premature at best. The police have yet to find how she supposedly got hold of this poison or provide a believable motive."

Hearst leaned back in his chair. "Let's say you found out how she got the poison, and you found a motive you could buy. Would you arrest her?"

The boss cupped his hands over his mouth and took a breath. "Yes."

"I rest my case. The police have got their woman. Once they find the source of poison, she's done for—and they will find it. She was the only one who could have done it."

I clinched my fist.

The door swung open. Standing there, red faced, was Tara Burke.

She made eye contact with each of us in turn. "Gentlemen, no need to fight about this. I'm leaving the campaign. However, I want you know." Her lip quivered. "She was—I'd never—I love her! How could any of you think I'd do something like that?" She ran out of the room.

Hernandez scowled at Hearst and got up.

I followed him out. *Somehow, I don't think a collection of political books will square this with Tara.*

She sat at her desk, loading her belongings into a cardboard box. She'd cleared off her desk and was emptying the first drawer.

Hernandez was seated in Denise's chair and looking in Tara's eyes like a father at his daughter. "Tara, he was wrong."

"He was wrong about my guilt, but I am a liability to the campaign. You can't have an alleged murderer sitting at the front desk."

"They're alleging I committed murder, too."

"Their evidence is far weaker in your case." Tara held her chin high. "I resign."

"I don't accept. You've done too much for me to throw you overboard."

She wiped her eyes. "My dear Mr. Hernandez, no one is throwing me over. I'm jumping to save the ship, like Jonah did. I'm no good to you now."

Hernandez bit his lip. "How about a paid leave of absence?"

She sat back in her desk chair. "That's very kind of you but no."

"Please reconsider that and let me be kind, for Liu." Hernandez's mouth wobbled. "She wouldn't forgive me if I let you go unemployed."

Tara smiled. "That's generous."

Hernandez opened his arms and then drew them back and extended his hand. She shook it and returned to packing.

Hernandez groaned, strolled back to the conference room, and closed the door behind him.

I stood and tapped my foot. What was I supposed to do? I was kind of worthless here, as well as being the source of her problem.

She buried her face and sobbed.

I grabbed an office chair and sat across from her. "What's the matter?"

"Mr. Hernandez used to make an exception to his usual restraint and hug Denise and I."

"Why?"

"He and Liu loved us like the daughters they lost." She wiped her face off. "Now, with all the lies, he can't do that without it being taken wrong by the press. They're dirty people, and they have to make everything else as dirty as they are." She resumed packing. "Sometimes, a hug could be nice." She glanced at me and wiped her eyes. "That wasn't an invitation."

"I didn't take it as one." I bit my lip and reached for my notepad. "I did have a few questions I needed to ask. Is this a bad time?"

"No, go ahead. My life's falling apart, but you have questions just like the police. I doubt I'll feel more like it later. Let's see, it starts by you asking me if I did it."

"No, you've answered that."

"Then you'll ask what I know about poisons. The answer is not a thing. I've read some murder mysteries where poisons are used, but that's it. I was lucky to get a 'C' in Chemistry." She slammed the top drawer and opened the second. "I suppose you will want to know why I didn't accept your offer to help with the coffee."

"I was wondering a little. Do you usually go and get coffee?"

She scooped a few things into her box from the second drawer. "Yes, I offer quite often. On rare occasions, I get an offer of help. Usually, I say yes. This time, I told you no. I don't know why. The police spent twenty minutes on that, and I still don't know why."

"Would you mind discussing your feelings for Mr. Hernandez and your overall relationship with him?"

"My father left when I was eight. God has blessed me by sending men into my life to fill that role. Mr. Hernandez is among them. I interned for his Moscow corporate office in college and came to work for the campaign."

I smiled. "So you have no designs on being the next Mrs. Hernandez?"

She made a face like she'd bitten a lemon. "He's old! It's gross. A woman my age would need to have her head examined to chase a man his age."

Denise strolled in the front door. She wore a pink blouse, jeans, and pink sneakers. "Tara! My God, I just heard that you're leaving the campaign. This whole thing stinks."

Tara stood. "Thanks, Denise. I'm packing up. I have one more drawer."

Denise wrapped her arms around Tara. The women wept together.

"I'll leave you two alone." I fled.

I came into the office at six the next night, chewing a stick of Juicy Fruit.

The boss sat at his desk reading a well-worn hardback copy of *The Casebook of Sherlock Holmes.*

I frowned. *Here I'm out doing his job, and he's catching up on his leisure reading.* I cleared my throat.

The boss put the book down. "Is that Densmore case wrapped up?"

"With a bow on it."

"I want to apologize. You shouldn't have to handle these administrative and supervisory things all alone. I've been spending too much time helping on the Hernandez case."

"That kinda does make your help counterproductive, but I don't mind." I glanced down at the book. "Provided you're doing work."

The boss followed the line of my gaze. "Oh that. I finished my report to the client about twenty minutes ago and picked this up, but it wasn't for fun. It was something about this case. I didn't know what but then I found it. 'The Problem at Thor Bridge.' That's what this is like."

"Huh?"

"Don't tell me you haven't read Holmes."

I shrugged. "I read three Holmes novels and a short story collection the summer before I discovered girls. After that, I didn't do much reading."

"You missed another novel and four short story collections. In the last collection is a story called 'The Problem at Thor Bridge.' Eerily reminiscent of our current case. A beautiful young woman not at all disposed to committing murder is nonetheless accused of murdering her employer's wife."

"What's the solution?"

The boss frowned. "The solution isn't applicable, but the case was solved because of something Sherlock Holmes missed the first time. Just like Holmes, we're missing something."

I scratched my head. "You needed a book to tell you that?"

"No, I knew that. Reading the book simply re-enforced the point. Now, I can take action."

Apparently Newton's Bachelor's degree had come with a minor in over-analysis. "This makes me glad I had less than two years of college."

"Tonight, I'm going to spend quite some time mentally going back over the case step by step. I'd ask you to stay, but I couldn't afford to pay you."

Apparently the idea that was bad when I'd suggested it this morning was good after we'd spent all day on tedium and drama. "Thinking is easier before a long day of work, so I'll pass, but maybe I'll come by later."

Someone knocked on the door. I opened it. Standing there was a Pizza Hut delivery man.

The boss walked over and handed him two twenties. "Keep the change."

The delivery man handed the boss three medium pizzas. "You want any packets of red peppers and cheese?"

"Yes."

"You have a good night, sir." The delivery man handed the boss several packets and left.

I glanced at the pizzas. "Three pizzas?"

The boss nodded. "This is a three pie problem."

I rolled my eyes. "Night, Newton."

On my way home, I stopped by the Albertson's on Vista. I grabbed a stray cart that had been left in the adjacent parking space and took it inside. I fetched out my credit card as I passed a "ten items for ten dollars" display on my way to the deli counter. The server's badge said his name was Chuck.

He grinned at me. "What can I get you? No charge."

"I'll take one of your roast chicken dinners for four dollars." I held out my credit card.

Chuck waved it away. "This one's on me."

I shook my head. "No, Chuck. I put up with people buying me stuff for the first month or so after I shot Durant, but it's got to stop."

"But what you did was heroic. I wish I could shoot a child molester."

"I was protecting my boss. That's all there was to it. Now, let me pay for my own stuff, or I'll start buying my meals at the Albertson's on Orchard."

"You win." Chuck's shoulders fell as he handed me the hot roast chicken dinner with a price tag on it.

I headed up the aisle closest to the produce. I grabbed a jar of peanut butter there before heading to the shelves on the back wall near the bakery. I fetched a loaf of whole wheat bread and made a dash past the sweets into the lunch meat, sausages, and cheese section.

"Get away from me!" A woman's voice.

I left my cart in front of a cream cheese display and ran toward the sound of the scream. By the sea food display cases, Tara Burke wore an Anaheim Angels sweat shirt and knee length skirt and black hose. She was facing a short man in his late thirties with stringy brown hair.

He leered at her. "You killed a woman so you could kiss Hernandez. So give me a kiss."

My hand automatically grasped my gun in its holster as I ran faster. The slime was at the same time latching onto Tara's sides.

She stomped on his foot.

He let go of her. She slammed her knee into his stomach. He stumbled backwards a few inches from me.

I pried my hand away from my gun. "If I were you, I'd get out of here while fathering kids is still a possibility."

The man hobbled away.

Tara spun toward the selections of lobster and stared hard at them.

I panted. "What are you doing here?"

"Even murder suspects need groceries."

"Why aren't you at your mom's house?"

"I'm a fighter, Mr. Ustick. I will not be driven from my home by these slimeballs in the press, nor am I intimidated by the comical antics of Detective French and the county prosecutor."

"So how far did you drive?"

"My apartment is on Broxton."

That street was right across from one of the exits from the store parking lot. I laughed. "Was your commute to the store one minute or two minutes?"

"Nine minutes. I walked."

"Are you suicidal, Tara?" I clenched my fists and my teeth. "You're on the front page for the biggest murder the state's seen since someone blew up the governor a hundred years ago."

She pressed her hands into her hips. "What would you suggest? Hiding to protect myself from every crackpot unfortunate enough to read the paper?"

"Tara, someone broke into Katrina Robles' apartment and killed her. She was a lot bigger and stronger than you."

She glanced in my eyes and smiled. "You're sweet. But I'll be fine."

"Can I at least drive you home?"

Backing away from me, Tara frowned. "I'd rather walk."

"If you're nervous about getting in my car, then let me walk you home."

"That's very kind. Thank you. So how goes the case?"

"It's growing more complex."

"Well, you're not the only private investigators on the case. I've hired the Fortieth Street Detectives to find out who set up Gordon Thomas."

Uh-oh. Busted. I swallowed. *Maybe not.* "They're a whimsical bunch of rank amateurs. What are they charging you?"

"A hundred dollar donation to the Idaho Food Bank." I laughed. "That's whimsical, all right."

"Whoever planted that story's not going to be laughing."

She led us into the dairy section as she spoke. "The Fortieth Street guys have a network of contacts all over the city. They'll find out where Thomas was. Once we find the person behind this foolish idea, and get him or her to admit I wasn't involved, the police's claim I had motive to kill Mrs. Hernandez will be shown for the fiction it is."

At least there was that. I grabbed a half gallon of 1% milk. Tara chose a bowl of Blue Bonnet margarine and slipped it into her cart

After Tara and I had left the store, we stopped by my Jaguar. I unlocked it with my key fob, tossed my groceries onto the back seat, and relocked the car. I gestured for her to lead the way.

I said over the wind, "You handled yourself well back there. Where'd you pick that up?"

"When I was a teenager, I worked on my uncle Mike's fishing boat. On a few occasions, I'd run into men who either didn't have manners or drowned them in beer."

"You worked on a fishing boat?"

"For six summers, starting when I was fourteen. By the time I quit at nineteen, I could pretty much do anything on the boat."

"Sounds like you liked it."

"Have you ever been to Alaska?"

I shook my head. "No."

"That's where my uncle's boat was. Its summers are heavenly. The sun shines nearly all day. When you're on the sea, staring out over the vastness and breathing that salt air, it grips you."

I said, "You sound like my dad. He was in the Navy, and he used to tell stories about the sea."

We reached the end of the Albertson's parking lot, stepped on to the sidewalk, and headed South on Vista.

"The sea off the Alaska Coast at Summer Time." Tara sniffed as if she could smell Alaska from here. "There's nothing like it."

"You go back often?"

"Haven't been there in years. I picked up bad habits there that really were not consistent with where the Holy Spirit was directing my life."

"What do you mean? You don't seem the type to have bad habits."

She smiled. "Let's just call it unladylike habits."

I couldn't imagine her having any of those. *Watch it, Ustick. This could get flirty real quick.* "Some pretty unladylike behavior came in handy back there."

"Being a lady doesn't mean being defenseless. It means being gentle whenever possible. Sadly, it wasn't, though at least I didn't have to use the pepper spray."

We turned down Targee, a curved road that led to a residential area.

She said, "My place is toward the middle of the block, near the shrubs."

"I'll walk you to the door."

Tara grinned. "How about that! You truly are acting like a gentleman."

I smiled. "Maybe I just don't want to get pepper sprayed."

"Don't be a silly, I wouldn't."

An explosion ripped through the air.

Tara collapsed to the ground, bleeding from her chest.

My body temperature and pulse soared as I whirled in the direction the shot had come from, the fitness club across the street.

A middle-age woman with a .22 pistol stood thirty feet way in the parking lot. She fired again.

Pain ripped through my left shoulder. I reached for it instinctively, but I stopped myself. Instead I reached into my shoulder holster and whipped out my nine millimeter Glock. Wincing, I fired at the woman.

The slug ripped through her torso. She dropped the gun, clutched her stomach, and collapsed to the ground with blood seeping through her fingers. The gunwoman retrieved her gun and clambered onto her knees.

Tara lay out on the ground, blood flowing out of her chest.

I held my Glock as steady as I could one-handed. "Drop it!"

The gunwoman put the pistol in her mouth.

"No, don't!" I shouted.

She pulled the trigger.

Chapter 15

I should've known better than to trust Newton. I sat sipping a cup of coffee in a baby blue waiting room at St. Al's. The shooting had ruined my last suit, and Newton had brought me the navy blue suit I normally wore to funerals.

The boss glanced at me from the next chair. "They didn't give you a cast. That's a good sign."

I shrugged. "I'll live. It's Tara I'm worried about."

"If it was going to happen, there couldn't have been a better spot for her to get shot in. Charlie Weston said an emergency room doctor was just getting off shift and came by as he was heading home. He took care of you and got you here all right. I guess Tara's guardian angel was watching out for her."

I frowned. "I never thought it was guardian angels' job to let us get shot conveniently. I intend to file a complaint with the union."

Newton laughed. "This is a right-to-work state."

I rolled my eyes. That was what passed for humor from him.

Detective Weston strode in carrying a woman's handbag.

The boss stood. "Charlie, what can you tell me?"

Weston eyed me. "Do you have your statement ready?"

I handed in a statement form. "Sorry, I waited until I stopped bleeding to fill out the report. Hope you don't mind. Add this to the Cole Ustick papers when you send 'em to BSU."

"In my nightmares, Ustick." Weston pocketed my statement and turned to my boss. "The shooter was Patty Lorraine."

The boss grimaced and glanced to me. "In one of my early cases, Patty Lorraine found her husband in bed with another woman and shot them with the gun she kept by the nightstand. She pled to voluntary manslaughter. She should have gotten second degree."

I glowered. "Why didn't she?"

"The county prosecutor didn't want to spend the money on a trial. She was out in a couple years and was in therapy, I thought."

Weston nodded. "Her parole officer said she'd been doing fine, but she switched therapists. Check out who the new one is." He flipped out a business card. It read, "Diana King, Hypnotherapist."

I gaped. "A hypnotist? What? Did she do juggle therapy, too?"

Weston shrugged. "Hypnotherapy is legitimate in my opinion, but it's completely unregulated in the state of Idaho, kind of like private detectives. So, yeah, the parole officer made a bad call."

I fumed. "A beautiful lady's hanging between life and death, and you say it's a bad call? Oh, and I don't think she would be in there if the newspaper hadn't printed your department's trashy theories. Was one of you cops singing to Gordon Thomas like Miley Cyrus at an awards show another bad call?"

"Sir, I know you're upset, but this isn't helping."

Newton asked Weston, "Did you get my text?"

"Yeah, we're running the tests. I'll let you know." Weston sauntered out.

I asked the boss, "What was that about?"

Newton leaned back, eyes closed. "My pizza party was cut short, but I had one idea. It may turn up something useful. What about you? How are you holding up?"

"Fine."

"No, really. How are you?"

I shook my head. "When something bad happens, I find something to do. Go play laser tag, or listen to whatever music strikes me, or work out till I drop." Or find a woman. "Now, I don't know what to do."

"Is her family here?"

"They've taken over the chapel."

"You could go there and pray. That's something to do."

I grunted. "God and I aren't on speaking terms."

The boss sighed. "We're off work, so you can tell me to shut up any time you want."

"It'd be my pleasure."

"God doesn't hold grudges. My mom always says God is always only a prayer away."

Does your mother subscribe to the cliché of the month club? Nah, Newton was the type of guy you didn't say anything to about his mother. "That's trite."

The boss glared. "Hey, my mom said it! Why is it not true?"

I leaned back. Did I really want to talk about this? No. Did I need to talk about this? Maybe. "God started it with what happened with Sis. She didn't deserve to be molested. She didn't deserve to die of a drug overdose before she graduated high school. He could have stopped it, but He didn't. God and I have carried this feud on for five years. There's no going back."

The boss said, "So that explains it."

I blinked. "Explains what?"

"You have this regretful tone of voice when you talk about Jared Bach and his wife or Tara, like what you see in them is something you don't see ever getting for yourself."

I leaned back in my chair. "When I went over to their apartment in the early afternoon and knocked the door, it was hilarious. And she comes to the door in his t-shirt and he's stumbling around looking for some shirt he can put on." I sighed. "If I ever get married, it'll just be a ceremonial recognition of the fact I'd already settled down. We'll no doubt have been living together for however many years I can stand my mother's nagging. Then there's Tara." I shook my head. "She's got it all: beauty, integrity, and brains. I know she's got brains. She slapped me down cold. The dumb ones think I'm cute."

Newton patted my shoulder.

I snorted. "The crazy thing is, at my worst, I was trying to get even with God. Boy did he get even with me. He gave me a son but never lets me see him. Maybe I deserve that. I knew what I was doing, and it's my road to walk."

"Come with me." The boss led me to the deserted, far end of the waiting room. "I'm gonna tell you something, but I don't want it repeated."

"Being confidential is in the job description. I can handle it."

"My mom had an abortion when she was seventeen. It haunted her. She believed it was wrong and punished herself for years. At a funeral, she heard something that changed everything." Newton bit his lip. "It was something by the prophet Jeremiah. He was mourning for Jerusalem and, out of the ashes he says, 'Your mercies are new each morning.' She later told me she'd squandered mercies with the choices she'd made, but God had new mercies for that day and each day after." The boss wiped his face. "She told me God would always have new mercies available for me, no matter what mistakes I made."

A chill ran down my spine. "I don't know."

"You'd better decide, Ustick. This is your war, my friend. You've fought it for five years. You want to fight it for another fifty?"

Moisture flowed from my eyes. "I still don't understand how he could let her slip away."

Newton half smiled. "You don't know how many times I've wished God would turn off criminals' free will. I know he did everything He could to reach her, and I know you did everything you could."

I needed to think. "I've got to go. You'll text me if you hear anything?"

The boss nodded.

I strolled out to the parking lot.

Hernandez trotted toward me carrying a Bible. "How's Tara?"

"She's going into surgery. Newton thinks she'll make it."

"Thank God. I've got to see her as soon as she's awake." He strolled past me and into the hospital, clinging to the Bible.

Once behind the wheel of my car, I stayed in park in the dark garage. I swallowed hard, stared at my shoes, and rubbed my hands together. Would God want to talk to me? Did I have anything to say to him? I inhaled deeply.

"Lord have mercy, Christ have mercy." The words had come out of my mouth like helium escaping from a popped balloon. Tears flowed down my cheeks. Even being able to bring myself to pray at all was a new mercy.

At St. Joan of Arc Church in Eagle, I strode through their parking lot, whispering prayers for Tara's safety and recovery. I got in the Jaguar.

Buzzing came from the glove box. I opened the glove box and grabbed my ringing phone.

It was Newton. "I've been trying to get a hold of you for an hour."

"Sorry, boss. I was in confession and then in the chapel."

"It's been three hours."

"I had trouble finding a priest." And confession had taken longer than I cared to admit.

"Well, the good news is Tara Burke's pulled through. She wants to talk to you. She's most grateful for you saving her life."

"Er, thanks."

"You can't see her tonight, but late tomorrow morning should be good."

"Sure. Could I take an unpaid personal day tomorrow?"

"Not a problem. I hope you have a good visit with her."

"Yeah, see you later." I hung up.

Not on Tara Burke's life was I going to talk to her until the truth of what I'd done was public knowledge. After that, she wouldn't be so grateful.

Late the next afternoon, I was typing on my home computer.

My landline rang. The caller ID said, "Fontaine Ford." I picked it up.

"It's me," she said.

That was useless. I snorted and rolled my eyes. "Thanks to caller ID, I know that, Fontaine."

Fontaine's voice frowned. "Ustick, I have to come clean. When I think of that poor girl charged with murder, and the police assigning her a motive based on a stunt we pulled, it makes me sick."

"I'm ahead of you. I'm typing up a statement now."

"How is she?"

"My boss says she wants to thank me for saving her life. I'm the one who put her life in jeopardy by not admitting you and I were the ones who made a fool of Gordon Thomas."

"Do you name me?"

"You want me to?"

"You'll need corroboration. Besides, any publicity is good publicity for me. My God, did I say that? A woman has been shot, and I'm . . . . " Fontaine sputtered. "Either this whole thing has got to me, or I'm the most shallow and selfish person in the world."

I smiled. "If you were the second, you wouldn't have said it out loud, and you wouldn't feel bad about it. You're a good person at heart."

"What'll happen to you when this breaks?"

I grimaced. "Career change and probably a move."

"You could come to LA. We could split the rent."

"If I'm going anywhere out of state, it's to Seattle. I got a kid there."

Her voice fell. "Oh."

I added her name to my statement and hit the print icon. "I've got to get going, Fontaine."

Once I'd hung up and printed my document, I strolled down Ladera out on to Canal and walked about a block to tan and brown townhouses arranged as four quadplexes. I stopped at the fourth unit and walked up to the second door and knocked.

Blogger Doug Witherley opened the door. Give him a beard, whiskers, and fur-lined red suit, and he could have a part-time job during Christmas. It was still only March, but he wore jean shorts and a Palin Power T-shirt.

Witherley grinned at me. "This is an unexpected pleasure. Come on in."

The house was adorned with pictures of Reagan, both Bushes, Palin, and various other politicians. The couch had an anti-IRS couch cover.

I smiled. *To his credit, Doug wears his political biases on his sleeve and on his house.*

"Have a seat." Witherley pointed at the couch. He sat in an office chair at his imitation wood desk. It had a flat panel monitor and a green custom built bright orange computer. He turned towards me. "So, what I can do for you?"

"It's what I can do for you," I said.

He grimaced. "You have gone in to selling insurance?"

"No." I handed him my statement.

He read it and put it by the computer. "So you brought this actress here to imitate Tara Burke with no involvement from Hernandez or your boss."

I nodded. "Yeah."

"People aren't going to buy this."

"Do you?"

"You could be telling the whole truth, or it could be that they did hire you, but you got squeamish when the Burke woman was shot."

"I got squeamish, all right, but I wasn't acting for a client or an employer. You can check with Fontaine Ford. She'll confirm it."

"I'll do that. Can I have her number?"

I scrawled it down on the statement. "How long until this comes out?"

"First I've got to check sources. I have Jared Bach on speed dial, and I'll call your boss. It'll probably be about an hour, if I get all the confirmations and comments I need."

I nodded. "Thanks."

"Why'd you bring this to me rather than the paper?"

I laughed. "You kidding? Go down to the newspaper, hand them a rope, and ask them to hang me? At least this way, when the local media types get a hold of the story, they'll have a friendly original source."

"A totally unbiased and fair source, I assure you."

One that was all in for Hernandez. Right. I eyed the book shelf over his desk with big political books. "I had one question for you."

"Sure."

"How would someone under forty get elected to the US Senate?"

Witherley leaned back, his hands behind his head, exposing a small hole under the armpit of the Palin Power shirt. "Legally, you only have to be thirty, but in Idaho? If you're not rich or the offspring of a powerful political family? It's not probable. Unlike other states, Idaho conservatives don't run insurgent campaigns nor do moderates. Only middle-aged business people and lawyers get elected. That and elderly ranchers."

"Is there any way someone under forty could run a strong campaign for the Senate in Idaho?"

He bit his lip. "The people began to eye State Senator John McGee as a potential candidate for Congress or even Governor, and he was under forty. Then he had a few problems that ended his career."

"So if you could get elected to the State Senate or State Assembly, you could potentially end up going to the US Senate."

He nodded. "Provided you impressed the right people, but Idaho's lower house is the House of Representatives. I'm not certain a younger person could get past a primary, after the McGee thing. Voters are wary if people don't have much life experience. There is one way. If a legislator resigns, their local party submits three names to the governor, who will name the replacement."

I said, "So, if a young person could get appointed to the legislature, they could then run as the incumbent."

The blogger smiled. "Exactly. Why do you ask? If you're thinking about it, this wouldn't be a great springboard to a political career."

I raised my hands. "Oh no. I talked to someone who had boasted they would become a US Senator from Idaho before they were forty."

Doug let out a hearty laugh. "They were being fanciful."

"Probably, but thank you for your time." I headed out the door and back to my place.

Denise wasn't the fanciful sort of girl. She was a high stakes gambler out to get herself appointed to the legislature, make a name for herself, and get to the US Senate. To her, it'd all happen if she got that first break.

Could it be a motive for murder?

I frowned. I'd never find out. I'd officially be off the case by the end of the night. I kicked at loose pieces of gravel on the sidewalk. That was what I'd liked about the job. Uncovering secrets. What would I do now? Did a blogger ever need a leg man? Nah, that probably wasn't in his budget. I glanced at the exterior of the eight hundred square foot townhouse.

Forty-five minutes later, I was sipping green tea at a sushi place on Vista. I took out my smartphone and pulled up the Witherley Wire. Doug's article was already posted.

After finishing it, I grunted. *About what I expected. Time to face the lions.*

Down at the police station, I strode to the front desk. The short-haired, skinny guy at the front desk glanced up at me. "What can we do for you?"

"I'm Cole Ustick. I'm here to see either Detective French or Detective Weston regarding the investigation of the Hernandez murder."

"Just a second." The skinny guy picked up the phone. "Detective French will come get you."

Two minutes later, she blustered out. She furrowed her brow. "What do you want, Ustick?"

"You read the Witherley Wire?"

"That right wing nut?"

"You better take a look." I followed her back to her desk.

She settled at her computer, pulled up the Witherley Wire, and gasped at the headline. As she scrolled down, her eyes popped out like Jackie Gleason's in a *Honeymooner's* rerun. She glared at me, placed one hand on her hip, and pointed at a conference room. "You. There. Now."

I shook my head. "Sorry, I haven't been to obedience school."

She put her thumb and index finger a centimeter apart. "You're this close to getting booked for concealing evidence. Now go."

"Fine." I marched over to the conference room. It was brightly lit despite the drawn blinds. I flopped on one of six chairs.

She returned twenty minutes later with a captain I'd met the night I killed a child molester.

French scowled at me and folded her arms. "What the hell did you think you were doing? Why did you keep this secret?"

"I've explained that to the blogger, and he's reported it. I knew Newton wouldn't approve of that tactic and figured I'd get Tara out of this some other way. That incident yesterday persuaded me otherwise."

The captain grimaced. "You still concealed evidence."

"Don't try and scare me. What I hid was not relevant to the question of who committed the murder. It only had to do with motive."

French snorted. "Yeah, and that motive part isn't minor."

The door banged opened. Weston and Newton entered.

The captain said, "Burke's still the only one who could've done it."

Weston cleared his throat. "Tara Burke didn't do it."

The captain said, "What are you talking about?"

Weston pointed at Newton. "At Jerry's suggestion, we did another once-over on Mrs. Hernandez's purse. We found some grains at the bottom that we missed the first time. The lab tested them and reported they were a mix of her sweetener and the poison."

French said, "But the bottle didn't have any poison in it."

Newton sneered. "The one you tested didn't, but she put her sweetener in her cup while holding it over the purse. It's evident the murderer replaced the poisoned bottle with Mrs. Hernandez's normal bottle while we were all distracted with the emergency."

French cursed.

The captain frowned.

Weston flinched.

French paced. "That was a big bottle. Who could've had it on them?"

The boss shrugged. "Everyone had briefcases, purses, or overcoats."

I spoke up. "Not Tara Burke. She came in there in a knee-length skirt and a sweater. She forgot her purse at the office."

French scowled.

My mind flashed to the moment Denise had entered the room with that big purple bag. "I know who did it. It was Denise Waters."

French's scowl deepened. "Clue us in, Sherlock."

I sighed. "Her bag didn't match her outfit."

"Oh, yeah, let me go haul her in on that. Who do you think we are? The Fashion Police? I only own two purses. A black one and a bright pink tote. My tote doesn't go with anything. So how many people have I killed, genius?"

I shrugged. *You can find this out your own way.*

The captain cleared his throat. "I will get in touch with the Ada County Prosecutor. He won't be happy."

"He shouldn't be." Newton glanced at Detective French. "Detective, this was your case. You botched it. Look for the truth, not an easy scapegoat."

The captain said, "Come off it, Jerry. She brought it to me first."

"I'm sure it's only a coincidence your wife gave $250 to the governor's re-election campaign and got appointed last year to the Arts Commission."

The captain turned beat red. "Are you accusing me of pressing the case against Burke to help the governor?"

My boss crossed his arms. "Just saying what it looks like to outsiders."

"I've been in this department for twenty-five years. No one's questioned my integrity. My wife's the one into politics. I only vote in general elections."

The boss nodded. "Uh-huh."

French said, "I blew it. I'll go by and apologize to her."

The captain put out his hand. "You'll do no such thing, French. You'll open us up to a lawsuit."

Newton glanced at me. "Unless you need my associate, we'll be going."

"You know the way." The captain jerked his thumb at the door.

I followed Newton out to the parking lot and asked, "Do you really think the captain arrested the wrong woman for the sake of politics?"

Newton shrugged. "I hope not, but who knows? In politics, you can't trust anyone. I sent that detail to your blogger friend."

"How long have you known the captain?"

"Five years, but I don't know him well. Let's go back to the office."

Yeah, it was Newton's turn to chew me out.

I reached the office first, opened up, and turned on the lights.

The boss plodded in and paced a full minute before speaking. "Ustick, I don't know what to do about this."

"Yeah, you do. We both do. You should fire me. You're a stickler for operating by the book. It'll simply be hard after all of our heart-to-heart talks."

"Ustick."

I pulled a document from my inner pocket. "Here is my resignation. I'm taking the heat off you."

Sighing, he took my resignation. "I'll write you a severance check."

"You're not severing me. I'm quitting."

"Shut up." Newton glared, wrote out the check, and handed it to me.

I glanced at it. He'd given me $4,267.20. Four week's pay at forty hours per week.

The boss said, "Don't cash it until Friday."

I stuffed in my wallet. "That's generous of you."

"You've been good for the agency. We'll miss you."

"One thing before I go. About Denise's purse."

Newton extended his hands. "I appreciate your intuition, but a purse that doesn't match isn't evidence. It is odd, though. Unlike most women in Idaho, Denise does match her purse. Trouble is, it could have been an accident or a coincidence."

I'd lost my credibility with Newton, too. "Okay, well, I need to give you my keys." I dropped on his desk the office's key as well as the company car's key. "I also need to delete that GPS tracking app you put on from my phone. You'll want to remove my user profile from the network."

Newton nodded. "Yeah, I'll do that."

"I'll be off." I swallowed, plodded to the door, and took one glance back at the boss.

He reached into a drawer and grabbed a bag of potato chips.

Chapter 16

I jogged toward my townhouse with the newspaper pinned under my arm. Gordon Thomas was waiting for me on my front lawn.

He pointed his index finger in my direction. "You made a fool of me."

"I had good material to start with." I smirked and kept going.

He followed me all the way to my door. "Do you have any comment for my column? I'll be fair if you give me an interview."

"No comment. Off the record, I have a gun, so don't enter my house without permission." I went inside, slammed my door in Thomas's face, and unfurled the fish wrap he wrote for. Doug Witherly's scoops had made the front page, but the lead item was about the potential conflict of interest with the captain who'd authorized Tara's arrest.

I poured a glass of Florida orange juice, sipped it, and leaned against the counter. My vintage 1950s red replica house phone rang.

I picked it up.

A weary woman's voice said, "Oh, son!"

"Mom, is that you? What's wrong with your voice?"

"I've been worried sick, trying to get a hold of you."

"Oh. Sorry. I turned my cell phone off last night to dodge the reporters."

"What were you thinking?"

"About what?"

Her voice went up an octave. "About what? I don't know. Maybe I'm talking about you hiring an actress to impersonate my best friend's daughter and getting poor Tara charged with murder!"

I leaned against the fridge. "Sorry, Mom. I was trying to break the case. I knew Tara was a good Catholic girl, and it'd be a perfect set up for Thomas. You don't know how much I wish I'd come up with something else."

"So what are you going to do now?"

"Check the want ads."

"Good call, but check them in Seattle. You need to be near your son."

Sure, like letting Jensen's mother take him hundreds of miles away was my bright idea rather than Mom's. "You sure I wouldn't be a bad influence? You can't have it both ways, Mom."

Silence buzzed on the line. "Son, I didn't mean—he misses you."

"I miss him, but I'm so far underwater on my house, the bank must think I'm trying to find Nemo."

"Then I'll take a loan out on my 401(k) and help you get out from under it and get to Seattle. I'm sure you could work for Catherine."

Me work for Jensen's maternal grandmother? I winced and wrinkled my nose. "That'd be pleasant."

"Sometimes you have to make sacrifices for the good of family."

I bit my lip. "Again, you can't have it both ways. Do I have to give my son up for 'the good of the family' or not? It's cruel of you to change your mind on me now that I can't un-sign the papers that gave his mom the right to take him away from me with only one week visit per year."

Even if that move did grow stupider as each day passed.

"Prove me wrong now and stop abandoning your son."

Clenching my fist, I growled. "We have good, long talks three or four times every week. We video chat on Skype and play games together online. He looks up to me. That wouldn't be the case if I were a deadbeat."

My stomach churned. Would I still be his hero if I went to Seattle with my tail between my legs and worked as a low-level stooge for his grandma?

"Cole?"

Had she said something I'd missed? "Ma, I'll think about it."

"He's your son. It's an easy choice."

"Sure, the death of someone else's dream is always an easy choice. I need to go." I hung up, popped a stick of gum in my mouth, dialed voice mail, and entered my PIN.

The machine's female voice intoned, "You have thirty-two messages."

Then again, this chore could wait. I slammed down the phone's receiver, and glanced out through the peephole. Only my car was out there. I slipped out, scanned my deserted street, and dashed into my car. Made it.

An hour later, I was inside a warehouse converted into an aquarium. It managed to be both well-lit and shadowy. The tank before me held dozens of seahorses. I made my third trip to the shark's petting pool. It was waist-high, stone, and stocked with little guys uninterested in dining on humans.

I reached in as a stingray swam by and stroked its back.

"Mr. Ustick," a familiar male intoned from behind me.

I spun and faced my former boss' client. "Hello, Mr. Hernandez."

"What brings you here?" He brushed lint from his suit.

I shrugged as I stared into the petting pool. "Nothing to remind me of politics. No elephants or donkeys."

A shark about the size of a salmon whizzed by.

Hernandez frowned. "If only all sharks were that small."

I nodded. "So what brings you here?"

"Jerry sent me here after he checked your cell phone's location tracker."

"Oh." I glanced at my pocket. "I got to get around to deleting that."

"Tara would like to see you."

I sucked in my gut. "Best get it over with. She still at Saint Al's?"

"Yes. I'll meet you there." Hernandez plodded out.

At St. Al's medical complex, I panted as I neared Tara's hospital room in a tan hallway with pink handrails.

Tara's door swung open. Detective French exited dressed in jeans and a San Diego Chargers long-sleeved t-shirt. She grunted. "Ustick."

I gaped. "You actually came to apologize?"

"What makes you think that?"

"Police detectives don't dress like that unless they're either off duty or undercover."

"Sherlock, stay out of my affairs." She stomped away.

I glared at her backside, sucked in a deep breath, and tiptoed into Tara's hospital room.

Tara was sitting up in bed and holding an iPad. She laid it in her lap and smiled. "Hello, Mr. Ustick."

I waved. "Hi."

She looked me in the eye. "Thank you for saving my life."

"Don't." I bowed my head. "I got you into this."

She sighed. "I don't appreciate the position you put me in, but I know the bad consequences were unintended. You're forgiven. I respect the guts it took to come forward."

"The boss, uh, Newton would've cleared you anyway."

"Do you wish you'd hid the truth?"

"Coming forward was the right thing to do."

"Then I want to hire you to investigate the murder of Mrs. Hernandez."

I crisscrossed my hands. "I'm not a private investigator any more."

"Start your own agency. Only you can solve her murder."

"How about you save your money and let the police handle it?"

She gripped her sheets and blew out a loud breath. "You know what's wrong with politics?"

I chuckled. "You want the long answer or the short one?"

She waved her arms. "Too many campaigns are uncreative and cumbersome. Everything is scripted. It's the same way for police investigations. That works with most murder cases, but this one is different. Solving the case will require a creative investigator who can think outside of the usual patterns. You're that man, Ustick. I believe you can do it."

My shoulders slumped. "Okay, to pay the debt I owe you, I'll temporarily go to work for myself and take you on as a client."

"At what rate?"

What would be the steepest discount I could give without being as nutty as her friends on Fortieth Street? "Um, a hundred a day plus expenses."

"Deal." She sat up and extended her dainty hand, which had tape and an IV plug on it.

I shook her cool hand, lingering longer than necessary. I smiled.

She grinned. "What are you standing here for? Get your business set up and get to work."

"Yes, ma'am." I left and closed the door behind me.

Hernandez stood outside. "What did she hire you for?"

Did I look like a guy with a job or a guy with a conscience? I grunted and shoved my hands in my pockets. "A hundred a day plus expenses."

"Take your orders from her, but send the bill to me."

"Okay."

"I'd like to hire you at the same rate. Jerry has dropped the investigation into the sexual assault allegations, saying he no longer has the staff needed to cover both them and two homicides. I want you to get to the bottom of them. I'll pay my bills when I pay Tara's bills."

I laughed. "Okay, so whose idea was it to set me up in business?"

Hernandez spread his hands like a politician. "Tara spent an hour this morning talking to Mr. Newton and me about the case and your unique skills. She's quite persuasive."

"What about the press? I just admitted to deceiving them."

"The campaign isn't hiring you, I am. As far as the staff will know, you're working for Tara with an order from me to provide full cooperation."

Good. If he let everyone on staff know, my secret work for Hernandez wouldn't be secret for long. "Are you staying in the governor's race?"

Hernandez nodded. "I wish I'd never gotten in it, but Liu wouldn't want me to let her killer win by dropping out. So I won't, for her sake."

"All right then. I'll do what I can."

A completed, business license application sat on the dash of my car.

I was parked at a street side meter two blocks away from the Hernandez campaign's headquarters. I tossed the last bite of my beef gyro in my mouth, chewed, and swallowed.

Time to ask a huge favor.

I reached into my lilac suit's inner pocket and fetched out Senator's card. I dialed his number on my cell. "This is Cole Ustick. We met over at the bar a few nights ago. I was investigating the murder of Katrina Robles."

He groaned. "I remember."

"Are you following what's happened with me on the news?"

"Sorry, son, no. I had a long, hard night."

"Oh, well, my good news is I've had an opportunity to go into business for myself. The downside is I can no longer investigate Ms. Robles' murder until a client hires me to do so."

"That I can assist you with, but one question. What if one of your other clients is responsible?"

I bit my lip. I'd bet anything that neither Tara nor Hernandez were guilty, but that wouldn't convince Senator. "Should I get a client arrested, I won't bill them. I'm after the truth."

"How much do you want?"

"A token amount will be fine. I only need enough to prove I'm working for a client."

"In that case, how about twenty-five dollars a day plus expenses? The wage of the great Philip Marlowe. May his luck go with you."

"Much obliged, Senator. I'll send you a contract tonight."

"I'll look forward to receiving it. Now, if you'll excuse me, I have a round of golf."

"Score low." I hung up and leaned back in my seat. If I guessed wrong, I could blow up the whole investigation.

I got out, locked my Jaguar, and jogged the two blocks to the Hernandez campaign office.

Denise was out front in a white blouse and a gray skirt. She smiled at me like a crocodile. "Mr. Ustick, I knew Tara had hired you, but I didn't expect to see you so soon."

Given you're my prime suspect? Good. "Is Mr. Hearst in?"

"Let me check if I can get you in to see him." Denise scurried toward the back office.

I settled into a guest seat and played Angry Birds.

She returned. "He's got a lull in his schedule."

"Thank you, kindly." I glanced her over. Did she know I was onto her?

Hearst strode out, frowned at me like I was an unexpected parking ticket, and sneered. "If it isn't Idaho's best dressed detective. I thought you were looking for a new line of work?"

This was getting off to a great start. "Nah, I'd decided to retire, but that lasted about five minutes. Could I talk to you alone?"

He waved at me, snapped back around, and stomped to his office.

By the time I caught up, he'd already settled in at his desk.

Pictures decked the room from wall to wall. Most were of strangers, but one photo showed a younger Hearst with Ronald Reagan and another showed Hearst with both of the presidents named Bush.

Hearst leaned forward in his executive chair. "Well?"

"I'd like to know how the affair started."

Hearst chortled. "I thought you didn't want to hear about it."

"What I didn't want to hear were attempts to morally justify it."

"Really, I expect someone of your generation to be more open-minded."

"Hey, I'm Catholic. If you've got a problem with adultery being wrong, take it up with God, not with me." I swallowed. Enough defensiveness. "Truth is, I owe you an apology."

Hearst's jaw dropped. He blinked. "You do?"

I nodded. "Hating you for your sin made it easier for me to live with my own. That said, I got to ask some questions. Everyone I talk to says you're a political genius. Even leaving morality aside, I don't understand why you'd do something that could end your career in disgrace."

"Son, have a seat," he said quietly.

I lowered myself down.

He leaned back. "You're young. You don't know what it's like. To bring more freedom to Idaho, I sacrificed time with my family. I barely know my wife. My kids regard me as a human ATM machine." He laughed. "I spent three decades building the governor's political career. Twice, I've uprooted my family for him, when he went to the Senate and when he returned to Idaho. I poured my life into that man, and what's become of it?" Hearst shook his head. "The governor has become part of the problem. He lives for one more election, one more term."

"So you had an affair to get back at the governor?"

"Shut up, boy. I'm not finished." Hearst cleared his throat. "With my reputation and all I'd accomplished, what prize did I get? Not freedom but being a good little vassal in Flanagan's Fiefdom. Then Denise showed up, young, full of energy and full of faith in me."

He smiled. "That woman saved me. She thought I could still accomplish those long-forgotten dreams. She inspired me to seek a candidate concerned about Idaho's real problems. I found Hernandez." He laughed. "The governor called me when he learned who I was supporting. Do you know what he said?"

Who cared? I sighed. I wasn't about to close his floodgates. "Tell me."

"How could you betray me like this, Marc?" Hearst emitted a mirthless chuckle. "The governor had that much nerve. The sellout's betrayed us all."

I clasped my hands together in front. "Did Denise tell you about her goal of becoming one of Idaho's US Senators before she's forty?"

Hearst raised an eyebrow. "She's still bent on that? I've told her it isn't possible."

"She thinks she has a trump card. I need you to help me figure out what such might be, in your game. Would Hernandez give her a big state job if he were elected governor?"

"At best, a staff position." Hearst shook his head. "Ignacio is convinced that businessmen should run government agencies, not political operatives."

"What about the theory my blogger friend has proposed? What if she got herself appointed to the legislature and impressed people as the up and coming woman of Idaho politics?"

He shook his head. "You can't predict that."

"Who is her legislator?"

"She lives in the North End. That is the state's most solidly Democratic district. She couldn't get elected there." Hearst looked past me. "Though, after the primary, she is marrying a doctor who lives in another district, and she'll move there ahead of the wedding."

"Does the doctor know about you two?"

"Not specifically, but he's said he'll let what is in the past rest. You've ended the physical part of our relationship, but we knew it wouldn't last. She told me she wanted to be discreet as not to create scandal for me."

Or for her? I wrinkled my brow. "Who are the doctor's legislators?"

"Let's see. Senator Madden and Representatives Birch and Harley."

"What are the odds of one of those guys getting an appointment by the governor that would leave their seat vacant?"

Hearst bit his lip. "Harley's been rumored to be interested in becoming chair of the Tax Commission, and the governor likes her."

"Could Denise get appointed to replace Harley?"

"Maybe. She's taken time away from the campaign to recruit candidates for the legislative district central committee up there. That's the committee that'll pick the appointments." He glowered at me. "What are you suggesting?"

"I've been looking for a motive. Someone on the staff had to be in on the plot against Hernandez. Gordon Thomas quoted a campaign source over and over again. Plus think back to that Saturday when Mrs. Hernandez died. How did the reporters know we were at a confidential meeting? This is Idaho. Hernandez hadn't reached the point where the media would normally be in scary stalker mode. Someone on the staff had to tell them. I've studied the staff for the past few weeks and only one person had a motive. Denise."

Hearst shook his head. "I don't buy it."

I leaned forward. "Then why has she been organizing the precincts in the legislative district she's moving into?"

He shrugged. "To get a good reputation with the locals. Nothing sinister about it."

"Face it, Hearst. Of the people on staff, only Denise and Tara knew the Hernandez house well enough to find the gun the murderer stole. Aside from yourself, only Denise could have taken the car to Katrina Robles' apartment. And she's the only one I can find a remotely plausible motive for."

"What do you want me to do?"

"Let me investigate her." I stood and spread my hands. "I need to look around her place. I assume you're paying part of her rent."

His cheeks reddened. "How'd you know?"

"Somebody is. She couldn't afford an apartment in that building on what Hernandez is paying her. You got a key?"

"I can't let you go in there." Hearst hid his hands under his desk. "She trusted me."

"And you trusted her. She's selling you out by selling out the campaign."

"You're asking me to betray a woman I loved. She saved my career."

I peered into Hearst's eyes. "If it turns out she didn't do anything wrong, you'll have done what was necessary to regain your peace of mind. If she did this, then she betrayed you first and has been manipulating you all along."

He stared up at me.

I stood and leaned over his desk. "You told me once that we couldn't let personal feelings interfere with doing what's right for the campaign. Well, how about it?"

He ripped a key off a key ring. "Be careful."

"She won't know I was there. Be sure she doesn't leave the office for the next hour or so." I shoved the key in my pocket and headed for the door.

Chapter 17

I had my gloved hands in my pockets as I stepped out of the stairwell on the seventh floor of Denise's apartment building. I glanced up and down the empty hall. The green carpet looked almost new, as did the paint on the peach colored walls. There was no trash can, so I couldn't remove the formerly kiwi strawberry gum I was chewing. I walked up to her door, 704, and glanced over both shoulders. The coast was clear. I put Hearst's key in the door, swung it open, and walked in.

The living room had a brown leather couch and two matching recliners. A sixty-inch, flat-panel television set was in the living room along with a newer looking sound system. I pulled up my phone and checked the price on the Internet. The system ran a little over $800 and had about a four and a half star rating. I whistled, pocketed my phone, and strolled over to the kitchen.

The furniture was perfectly matched to the interior. I opened every oak cupboard's doors. Barren shelves greeted me in the three closest to the wall and the one over the sink. Inside the next cupboard were a box of Special K cereal and several pill bottles: a multi-vitamin, an expensive brand of Vitamin C, Gingko biloba, ginseng, and birth control pills. I opened the cupboard next to that. It contained four champagne glasses, two plastic drinking glasses, and a couple dozen mugs bearing various candidates' names. Most were unknowns, but two were the last two Republican presidential candidates.

I shut the door and checked in the drawer of the stove. It held one pan. All that was under the sink was cleaning supplies. In the cupboard nearest the one under the sink, I found two bottles of wine, one of them champagne.

Inside the stainless steel fridge was a half-gallon of milk that was almost empty, a half-dozen bottles of PowerAde Zero, and an unopened wine bottle. In the freezer compartment were six Healthy Choice TV dinners.

So she's a political nerd who doesn't cook and likes champagne.

I entered the master bedroom. The room had oak paneling. The bed had a sturdy, steel frame. The headboard boasted a carving of the Greek goddess Aphrodite. At the foot of the bed was a black dresser with five drawers. On top of it sat a CD player with a $300 sound system, as well as a stack of CDs, mostly pop music, 1990s stuff, and folk music.

A perfectly good sound system wasted.

I walked up her large dresser and began to open drawers. The first three drawers contained underwear as well as t-shirts. I opened the fourth drawer. Inside were several, neatly folded outfits. One pink dress was labeled, "Aunt Bernice." A checkered blue skirt was labeled, "Mom." A purple mini-skirt was labeled "Dad." Designer jeans with holes in them were labeled, "Barbara." A pink over the shoulder bag was labeled, "Susan."

The pattern continued in the fifth drawer. Each item was not her style and was labeled with a name.

Probably the name of the person who gave it to her.

On top of the nightstand was a digital alarm clock. I opened the nightstand's drawer. It held a contact lenses case, an orange prescription bottle, a copy of *Sun Tzu's* book on war, and a perfume bottle.

I glanced at the prescription. It was dated two months ago and the label's instructions read, "Take at bedtime as needed."

Most likely it was a sedative. I clucked my tongue. Best I double-check. I opened my phone and did a Google search. Yep, sedative.

I made my way to the closet. At the far left hand side were seven hangers. Two had nothing on them and five had complete outfits.

Since its Tuesday, this must be what she'll wear Wednesday through Sunday.

Wednesday would be a light green sweater with black slacks. I checked behind the hanger. Behind it hung a pair of light green pumps in a light green handbag. Thursday's outfit was a navy skirt and white top with a pair of blue heels and a navy blue handbag. Friday's outfit was a dark green shirt, brown slacks, a pair of gray flats, and a zebra-striped handbag. Saturday featured a red sweater, black jeans, red pumps, and a red purse. Sunday would be a Broncos sweatshirt, jeans, a blue and orange handbag, and gray sneakers.

I grinned. That confirmed my suspicions about the purple purse.

On the back of the closet door, seven outfits without shoes and purses hung on hangers from a dry cleaner. At the end of the closet were two pairs of gray overalls and a tool box. Over head on the closet shelf were car magazines and car owner's manuals to three different cars, including an '85 Jaguar and a Ford Thunderbird.

I sauntered out over to the next bedroom. It had a filing cabinet and a large desk with an HP laptop on it. One wall sported a minor league version of Hearst's photo collection. One showed Denise with the governor. In a few more, she was posed with people I didn't recognize. Last, a beaming preteen Denise shook hands with President Bush Junior. I touched the picture and stared at the smiling eleven-year-old.

How'd you grow up to be a murderer?

The book shelf was mostly political titles but it also had a few chemistry ones, including *Poisons in Humans*. It was on the shelf at an angle, as if it wasn't put back correctly. Looked like it hadn't been read recently. I snapped a picture with my cell phone.

Her fiddle case was in the corner. A humidifier was on a table beside it.

On the desk was a black plastic file folder. I opened it. Inside were bills neatly filed going back six months. I pulled her latest credit card bill and cell phone bill. I read through the credit card statement. Two days before Katrina's murder, Denise had purchased a pay-as-you-go cell phone.

Strange. She already has a cell phone.

I put the page of the credit card statement on the desk, took a picture of it, and replaced it in the folder. I scanned through the cell phone bill. Three weeks before the murder, calls and texts had been going to a number in the 206 area. They stopped after she purchased the new phone.

Wow, 206 is a Seattle area code. Newton's old high school pal comes from there.

I took pictures of Denise's current cell phone's bill, pulled out the last two months, and snapped pictures as well for each page with a call or text to the 206 number. I checked November's statement.

The 206 number wasn't on there.

I put the bills back in the folder and made sure everything looked as it had when I'd come in. I double-checked the bedroom and looked both ways before fully stepping out of the apartment.

A woman emerged two doors down, glanced at me, and smiled. "Hi."

Sweating, I smiled back. "Hi."

I strode down the hall and took the elevator downstairs.

Out in my car in a parking lot downtown, I emailed my photos to myself, pulled out my iPad, and did a reverse directory search for the 206 number. I grinned. *Bingo!*

I drove to Hernandez's campaign office and marched in his door.

Denise was sitting up front. "Back again?"

"Yes, is Mr. Hearst available?"

She nodded. "He's reviewing some reports from the field director."

"Then I'd better go right in. He's expecting me." I strode into the office, shut the door behind me, and cleared my throat.

Hearst looked up from his computer. "Didn't find anything, did you?"

I pulled up the photo of the first cell phone statement. "In February, she started making calls to a Seattle number. The number belongs to Bart Bradley. He's a labor union politico who hired a local private investigator to investigate Hernandez."

Hearst buried his head in his hands and stood up scowling and grabbed a pen knife. He paced, muttering, "I should've known better." He thrust the pen knife in the air as if he were stabbing someone. "That witch is gonna be fired so fast, it'll break the sound barrier. By the time I get through with her, she'll never work in politics anywhere in the Western hemisphere ever again!"

Once a drama king always a drama king. I snorted. "I'm glad you're taking this so well, but we'd need to explain to Hernandez how we got the evidence. I doubt you'd want him to hear the reason you had a key to her apartment. Secondly, she and Bradley are probably in on both the murders and the sexual assault rumors, but I've got to prove it. If you fire her, she'll know I'm on to her, and I'll never get her. For now, we have to keep this a secret."

"Ustick, you must believe me. The physical relationship is over." Hearst made a face like eating raw onions. "You have to keep that from leaking out."

I raised my eyebrows. That was Hearst attempting to ask nicely. "I'll do the best I can on that count, but I can't make any promises. It also won't do any good if you try to recapture your youth again."

He ran his hands through his thinning hair. "You don't need to worry about that."

I arrived at Leah's enclosed porch. The new cuckoo clock above her front door clicked and whirred. An action figure of the seventh incarnation of Doctor Who came out wearing a white suit and a panama hat.

The clock said, "Who, who, who, who, who, who, who."

Wow, seven o'clock already? And Leah was a hacker, a local alternative rock singer, a painter, and a carpenter? No doubt she was talented at all four, but she had way too much time on her hands. I guess she was having a baby to remedy that.

A male voice shouted through the door, "What about my rights?"

I knocked on the door. "Ustick."

Leah's shouted, "Come in."

I entered.

A man in a checkered shirt and khakis stood red-faced, facing Leah.

She grabbed a windbreaker off the couch and tossed it at the man. "Ah, Ustick, Patrick was just leaving, weren't you?"

He jabbed his index finger at her and grabbed the jacket. "If you think you'll get a penny from me, you're more neurotic than I gave you credit for."

She slapped him. "I have more money in savings than you owe in student loans. If you come back again, you're getting a taste of pepper spray."

Cursing, he stormed out past me.

I raised an eyebrow. "What just happened?"

Leah stomped her foot and glared at me. "Ustick, it's all your fault!"

I put up a hand. "Could you sit down? You're not making any sense."

She plopped into her favorite chair. "That was the father of my child. I'd listened to what you said, read all the research online, and thought maybe kids do need fathers. So I met him here and I told him about her." She grabbed her stomach. "He blew up, demanded I get an abortion or else he'd . . ." She made quotation marks with her fingers. "Take care of it himself."

"Sorry," I said, frowning.

"I was about ready to Tae Kwon Do him in the head when you came in."

Six months pregnant and using Tae Kwon Do? That'd be a sight. I looked around. "You got a gun around here?"

"No way! I hate guns."

"Then please stay somewhere else, or I can stay in the spare bedroom."

"Ustick, you're overreacting. I don't need a big, strong man to take care of me. Tae Kwon Do and pepper spray will be enough to take care of that wimp. He might have done something in the heat of the moment, but he's not dumb enough to come back here."

"Look, I'm not sexist. I simply don't want you taking chances." I glanced down at her belly. "It's not just about you."

Leah sighed. "Fine, Ustick. Stay in the guest room but only tonight." She tightened her shoulders. "I remember last time you stayed the night was two years ago. It was in my room."

I coughed. "Well, there won't be a repeat of that incident. I've decided to live a life of chastity."

She cracked up. "You? You'll become a monk, shave your head, sing chants all day, and copy down the Bible on scrolls? You?"

"No, I said chastity, not celibacy. Big difference."

"Actually, no difference. Those words are synonyms."

Was she a master grammarian, too? I rolled my eyes. "Teach, I meant I'm not having sex again until I'm married."

She roared, slapping her thigh. "Thanks, I needed a good laugh."

I leaned forward. "I'm serious. I'm making changes in my life. One of them is chastity."

She raised her eyebrows. "Really?" She looked at me as if she'd found out I didn't like *Doctor Who*. She sighed. "If it makes you happy."

"At least you're being more supportive than others. I've lost three girl-friends over this, so I'm down to two, unless I go back to counting you. Would that be okay?"

151

Leah laughed and slapped her thighs. "No, by all means, use me to inflate your girlfriend census." Leah blinked and narrowed her eyes at me. "Wait, you only had four girlfriends. You should have been down to one."

Curse her being good at math. "Okay, only one girlfriend on my active list stuck with me, but I met this cool senorita named Marcella at the motel, and she'd ended up on my reserve list."

Leah gaped. "You have a reserve pool of girlfriends?"

"Had. Marcella was the only reserve who stayed. She's Catholic, too."

"How is 'I'm living in chastity' and 'I have three girlfriends' compatible?"

"So long as she's okay with nothing physical, I'm handy for a date."

Leah winked at me. "I'd rather hear you play the piano."

"Are you complimenting my piano playing or ins—"

"—yes. When you play the piano, it's meaningful and it's beautiful." She rubbed her stomach. "Creating life is meaningful, too, but I didn't realize how much so until tonight."

At this rate, she'd be in church by Easter. I nodded. "You want to hear some meaningful piano playing?"

"Sure."

I got her a glass of fake wine from her refrigerator, sat at her piano, and played, "As Time Goes By."

She sung along in a way her death metal fans wouldn't recognize.

I played "Mr. Belvedere," but she only sat there, feet up and sipping her fake wine. She did the same while I played Mozart.

I got up, poured myself a glass of fake wine, and joined Leah on the couch. *Now to get to what I came for.* "Would you mind if we talked business?"

"No, but I don't need an assistant."

"I need your help on a case."

"But you're out of the private detective thing. The paper said you quit."

"I'm in business for myself now. I'm on the same case." I unloaded all the details, including my conversation with Hearst, and finished, "So, I called a Seattle Private Investigator and hired him to find out about the whereabouts of Bradley on the night of the Robles murder."

"And what do you need me for?"

"Cell phone records. I've got Denise Waters' records, but I need more."

Leah pulled a piece of paper off the coffee table. "Write 'em down."

I wrote down Gordon Thomas's and Bart Bradley's numbers. Newton had gotten Katrina Robles' numbers from the police and had sent them over.

"It will be a hundred dollars," Leah said.

"I'll pay it out of pocket." I bit my lip. "Maybe I shouldn't have you do it. You could get caught, and you got a baby."

She waved it away. "Only boy hackers get caught. They act like animals, marking their territory by spreading viruses. I just get what I need and get out.

Contrary to what you've heard, pregnancy doesn't inhibit my work. I might not be up to a hardcore concert now, but come on, I can hack in my sleep."

"Sorry."

"One thing I don't get. What was with the looking at all her clothes?"

I smiled. "I found a couple of things that were highly suggestive."

Leah grimaced. "That's sick."

I rolled my eyes. "Suggestive about the crime. All of her brightly colored outfits were in a drawer with the name of the giver on it, including all of her purple stuff."

She blinked. "And that has what to do with murder?"

Everything probably. "I'll tell you once I have all the pieces together."

She leaned back and pointed at me. "I see why you're being mysterious. It's so when you catch the killer, I'll say . . . " She did her best imitation of a British old man. 'Egad, Ustick, how the devil did you know it was her?' And you'll say, 'Elementary, my dear Leah, it was when I saw she kept her purple outfit in a drawer.' And then I'll say, 'Astounding Ustick!'"

"It's not that."

She raised her left eyebrow.

Cheeks warming, I put up my right hand. "Okay, it's not entirely that. The thing is, I have a sound hypothesis, but I'd rather not accuse people of murder and get myself sued for slander until I have solid proof. Speaking of which, do you mind if I check my email to see what the Seattle PIs found?"

"Yes, I mind, but it's the twenty-first century world we live in. I've got to check my PayPal to see if I got a payment I'm expecting."

"Thanks." I pulled out my cell phone. Leah grabbed hers.

I opened the email.

From: Douglas Wiggins, Confidential Investigations
To: Cole Ustick, Private Investigator
Mr. Ustick,
Our office has completed an investigation of the whereabouts of Mr. Bart Bradley on the day in question. Mr. Bradley spent the day meeting with the political leadership of the Washington State Brotherhood of Labor at their annual conference. According to hotel staff, he left the Hilton at seven thirty in the evening. He later made an appearance at a ten o'clock roundtable at the Brotherhood of Labor conference. See the attached photo from Flickr, taken by an attendee. It suggests an injury had occurred.

At the bottom of the message, the photo showed Bradley's face covered in bruises. A deep gash was held together by some slipshod bandage and all too visible stitching.

That could be explained by a close encounter with Katrina Robles. I smiled.
I read down. The message continued:

There is a stretch of time of over fifteen hours where Mr. Bradley's actions couldn't be accounted for. We can look into this further, but this would not be a good use of your resources, since Mr. Bradley was found to be still in Seattle as late as 11 P.M. MT. Since the murder occurred by one in the morning, the only way he could have arrived in time was to take a flight to Boise. However, he caught no flight and no charter flew between Seattle and Boise International Airport that night.

Well, there goes that. I cursed.
Leah looked up from her phone. "What's the matter?"
"The guy I thought did the Robles killing couldn't have done it. Bradley would have to fly in, but he didn't go commercial and there were no charter flights into the Boise airport."
Leah crossed her arms. "Ustick, there are other airports around here."
"Yeah, the municipals. I'll email back on that." I did so and pocketed my phone. "By the way, what's the last name of that professor?"
"Jessup, Patrick Jessup."
I noted the name, mentally breaking his nose.

Chapter 18

I sat on my couch, sipping a cup of gold tea, while Sonny Bono sang, "I Got You, Babe" through my sound system. The phone rang. I turned Sonny Bono off and answered the call.

Leah asked, "What are you doing?"

"Taking a tea break. It must come from my British ancestor."

"I got a call from the professor this morning. He said a wild-eyed private eye who thought he was the Godfather had been by."

"Did I leave an impression? I did say I was the baby's godfather."

She said, "He said you threatened to kill him."

I smiled. "Not at all. I only made it clear I didn't appreciate his attempts to intimidate you and told him about some of my accomplishments. If he took any of that as a threat, that's his problem. So did he say anything else?"

"He was very apologetic." Leah laughed. "He said he was pro-choice and that he would respect my decision."

"Thoughtful of him."

She giggled. "You scared the jerk half to death."

I shrugged. "Any creep who goes around threatening pregnant women deserves it."

"Gender shouldn't make any difference."

"Fair enough. I'll do the same favor for any pregnant men I know who get threatened."

She laughed. "So anything new on the investigation?"

"You were right. There was a chartered flight from Seattle over to the Caldwell Industrial Airport. According to the agency in Seattle, the pilot's a known associate of Bart Bradley. The flight plan indicates no passengers, but that doesn't fly."

"Not funny, but what do you mean?"

"The guy landed at about ten thirty at night and took off at two thirty in the morning. No passenger, no cargo, and four hours in Caldwell on a week night? Please."

"He could just be a drug smuggler."

"I doubt it, but it's now up to me to place Bradley in the Treasure Valley at the time of the murder. And that's going to be a challenge."

"If it helps any, I've got his cell phone records at the office." She flipped a paper. "He didn't make any calls on the night of the murder."

"I'll swing by and pick them up. The other thing is I contacted the Idaho Brotherhood of Labor and got no comment from their office flack on whether they hired Bradley. And I've been working on Denise Waters' background."

"Is there anything else I can do to be of service?"

"Not unless you can get me the Kirby that was used to clean the Robles murder or the purse that Denise brought with her on the day Mrs. Hernandez was killed."

"For that, you ought to see the Fortieth Street Detectives."

I rolled my eyes. "Newton says they're a bunch of amateurs."

She chuckled. "You're not exactly an expert at solving murders. I had to use them for something once, and I found them pretty good at what they do. I bet they know someone who can find your missing items."

I nodded. "Maybe it is worth checking with them. Besides, Tara's already paid the Idaho Food Bank for those jokers' services, and they didn't end up being needed. Thanks for the tip." I looked at my watch. "I got to get back to work. See you in about an hour."

"Talk to you later." She hung up.

After another sip, I put the tea cup down. Back to work. On my iPhone was a list of my compiled list of as many known out of state associates of Denise Waters as could be found on the Internet. There were three names left and so far nothing but praise or generic references.

Next up on the list was Erica Fuhrman.

The phone rang. A businesslike voice answered. "Hello."

"Is this Ms. Fuhrman?"

"Not anymore. I've been Mrs. Rodriguez for the past year."

"Right. Mrs. Rodriguez, I'm Cole Ustick. I'm conducting a background check for Denise Waters. She's under consideration for an important job in the Idaho Republican Party."

"So important you're investigating?"

"Yes, ma'am."

A baby cooed in the background.

I asked, "Mrs. Rodriguez, are you still there?"

"Yes, I was just thinking. I won't be quoted on this?"

"No, ma'am."

She took a deep breath. "I'd rather not say this, but—Let me be clear, Denise is a very talented person, great fundraiser, very outgoing. However, she has a nasty streak. She ran against me for Vice-President of College Republicans her freshman year and played dirty."

"How dirty?"

"Thanks to her, I didn't make it to the vote. Three days before the election, she invited me to chat over coffee. I got gravely ill afterward and went to a doctor." She paused. "He found out I'd been poisoned. At the time, I was naively mystified at how that had happened and dismissed it and the loss of the vice-presidency. That changed when I got to truly know Denise."

"When was that? What happened?"

"After I became treasurer, in my last few months of school, I noticed that people who got in Denise's away ended up having accidents. The first President Bush was coming to town. The President of College Republicans was going to introduce him, but his car broke down and his cell phone battery was dead, so he wasn't able to call anyone. Denise ended up doing the honors. Another time, one of her rivals for a boy got gravely ill exactly as I had. I can't help but suspect that both of us had been poisoned by the same person and that Denise engineered the car accident. Of course, I can't prove it."

I gripped the phone. "Did anything else make you suspect her?"

"Her bad attitude. Plus Denise worked in her mom's pharmacy during summers and was very good in chemistry. She actually had a minor in that."

"Interesting. I'll have to take note of it."

"You don't believe me, do you?"

"The opposite. I agree that isn't enough to prove it, but what you have is suggestive and worth looking into. You have a good day, Mrs. Rodriguez." I hung up and pulled up Denise's Facebook timeline. On it was a picture of her behind a pharmacy counter with her mother. "Gotcha."

I drove through the part of Garden City that made the residents from its respectable precincts tell friends that they lived in Boise.

This street was lined with title loan places, car dealerships, auto shops of variable reputations, run-down hotels, and an adult book store. Its residential areas were littered with trailer parks.

The trailer park on 40th street featured single-wide manufactured homes that were about thirty years old, the lawns were well-maintained, and there was no graffiti. I parked and got out of the car.

A red-haired, fat man wearing an American flag baseball hat and a Boise Hawks windbreaker sat on the front porch of a black and white trailer. He was reading a paperback book.

What sort of redneck operation was I hiring? Maybe this guy wasn't part of the group and was just someone who lived in the neighborhood. I called to him, "Do you know where the office of the Fortieth Street Detectives is?"

"You're looking at it."

So much for that. "My name's Cole Ustick. I'm a Private Investigator."

"Is that a fact?" The man squinted at my orange suit, green tie, and black shirt. "You sure you're not the Great Pumpkin?"

I crossed my arms. "You don't scream Philip Marlowe, Bubba."

Bubba chuckled. "I guess not. Well, what can I do for you?"

"My client, Tara Burke, hired you to find out some information."

"Yeah, but you took care of that by coming clean." Bubba smirked. "The beauty of our system is, no one ever goes to the Idaho Food Bank and asks them for a refund."

"No, but we can ask you to do another job without another donation. I'm looking for an item that may have been thrown away that's relevant to a murder investigation she's having me investigate. It's a large purple purse."

"Whereabouts would it have been tossed?"

"North end. I doubt they'd have driven all over town to get rid of it."

"I know some folks who look for items like that at the landfill. Was it in good shape?"

"Yep, looked brand new. Was a gift last Christmas."

"I'll have them get on it."

"I also need to know if you find an aluminum softball bat. I found a twin to it at a sporting goods store, and it's a 34 inch Demarini Bat. It's silver and teal. I'll give a $100 to anyone who finds it."

"Anything else?"

"Also, I'm looking for a Kirby vacuum."

"Paul, he lives in 16, sells them part time."

"I'm looking for one that was thrown away but in good working order."

The redneck frowned. "Do you realize how much those things run for? Nearly two thousand bucks new. It'd be crazy to throw it away."

"Murderers often are mentally unbalanced. The one we're looking for was used to destroy evidence at a crime scene and it may have trace evidence. You'll find it at solid waste."

"We'll check."

"There's a $200 bounty for the vacuum if anyone finds it."

"We'll do our best. Let me get you one of my cards." The redneck fished into the pockets of his jeans, pulled out a card, and handed it to me.

It said, "Ray Davis, Fortieth Street Detectives, You Don't Have to be Smart to be a Detective."

Awe inspiring. I slipped it in my pocket. "Much obliged."

"We'll be in touch." He picked up his book and resumed reading.

A guy like him was likely reading something by the *Duck Dynasty* guys. I glanced at the title. *Henry VI, Parts 1, 2, and 3* by William Shakespeare.

I climbed up the stairs to a second floor apartment in Garden City. Each unit opened to the building's exterior and their doors could use a fresh coat of blue paint. I knocked. By the side of the door was a name plate for Sally Montoya, the police officer friend of Katrina Robles.

"She's not there," an old lady said as she shuffled toward me. She had hair cropped like a man's and wore a black sweater and black slacks. "She's at church tonight."

"Do you know where she goes?"

"Some place on Orchard. Spanish service. She's always talking about it."

"Thank you, ma'am."

"Whatever." She continued on toward the next apartment.

Ten minutes later, I was driving up Orchard. Where was that church?

I got to the Albertson's near Overland. *I must have missed it.* I turned around and drove back down Orchard.

About half way between Franklin and Fairview, I spotted a sign. "Azusa Pentecostal Church." I pulled into the parking lot, closed the door, and walked to the church's glass door.

A woman was standing up speaking at the pulpit. She wore brown slacks and a brown jacket with a white shirt. She had a pixie cut, a dark complexion, and two small diamond studs in her ears.

I opened the door. It squeaked.

What a way to make an entrance. I removed my hat and crept to the back row. The church was packed with around two dozen tan and olive skinned worshippers. I claimed the last folding chair on the back row.

A woman in her early twenties traipsed over to me and whispered, "Do you understand Spanish?"

They must have some people who speak English wander in and want someone to translate. I said in Spanish, "Yes, I understand very well, thank you."

She handed me a worship bulletin and returned to her own seat.

I glanced at the bulletin. Sally Montoya would be easy to find.

Montoya was the preacher.

The service lasted fifty minutes, including a half-hour, discordant session of the regulars all praying over each other. Afterwards, she visited with people.

I fidgeted in my folding chair. *I should've waited for her at her apartment.*

She came up to me and gave me a hug. "Welcome. And who are you?"

I said in Spanish, "My name is Cole Ustick."

She stiffened and released me as if I'd said I was a Satan worshiper. She glared as she said in English, "What do you want?"

I replied in Spanish, "May we please discuss together what happened to Ms. Robles?"

"Meet me at the Fish Shack on Fairview."

I nodded, put my hat on, and left.

My bowl of clam chowder was almost empty by the time she slapped a basket of hush puppies on my booth's table.

She settled across from me. "Forgive me. I was a little abrupt."

I waved. "I wouldn't have come to the church, if I'd known you were preaching."

She nodded. "I'm a part-time assistant. Even if I hadn't been, I wouldn't be gung ho about talking to you. I can't help but think, if you hadn't talked to her, she'd still be alive."

"Of course. That's the police's theory, and you're a cop. I suspect myself that someone got scared of the truth coming out."

Montoya put up her hand. "Katrina had her faults, but she was no liar."

"Someone hurt her, but it wasn't Ignacio Hernandez." I related the story she told me.

After I finished explaining why for the millionth time, Montoya shook her head. "She was definitely confused. The perp in her case was a tall, blond guy with long hair."

"Was that how you met her?"

"Yeah." Montoya cut off half a hush puppy with her fork, popped it in her mouth, chewed, and swallowed. "I could tell she'd been through a terrible ordeal. She was kind of awkward, very skinny, all arms and legs, and that gave her a lot of issues, so I had invited her to my women's self defense class. We became friends, and she came to the Lord."

"She definitely wasn't awkward when I met her."

Montoya smiled. "No, she became fanatical about building muscle. She'd even considered going out for the Miss Fitness Idaho contest." A tear slipped down her right cheek. She wiped it away. "I'm sorry, Mr. Ustick. It's so tragic. I mean, Katrina worked so hard to build herself up, and one guy with a gun destroyed it in a few seconds."

I nodded. "From what I heard, it seems like you two had a falling out."

"Who told you that?"

"Her customers indicated she'd stopped talking about you. Why?"

Montoya lowered her head. "She was one of the first women I discipled, and I dealt with her rebellious streak poorly."

Stiffening, I asked, "What do you consider rebellious?"

"Oh, she insisted, 'I can be a witness' justified her for refusing to be like Mathew and quit her worldly job in that dive. I left that to the Holy Spirit, but then she started going to this hypnotist for therapy. That I couldn't let go, for her safety. She was making herself vulnerable to having her mind negatively influenced, but she insisted a true friend would support whatever she wanted to do and be happy the hypnotist was helping her work through her personal issues. I pushed too hard, and she said she didn't want to see me any more."

I leaned back and scratched my head. That was the third time hypnotism had come up in this case. "Who was the hypnotherapist?"

"Dr. Diana King. I was on a mission trip when Katrina died. When I got back, she'd left me a sweet message saying she was sorry how things had ended and asked me to call her. It was three hours before she died." Montoya wiped the tears from her eye. "Sorry."

It all made sense now. I touched her arm. "For what it's worth, it appears the hypnotist she saw truly was up to no good. She might even be still alive, if she'd listened to you. The hypnotist is the key to the whole case."

Officer Sally Montoya straightened up in her chair and stared at me. "Tell Detective Weston about your conclusion."

I shook my head. "I only have to share evidence with the police. You can tell Weston what you know about Katrina. Once you do, he'll have all the evidence I have and may reach the same conclusion. What I need is evidence."

"If you need any help on that count, let me know. I want this guy and I want him bad."

"You and me both." I cracked my knuckles.

Chapter 19

I stood in the bathroom combing my hair.

The doorbell rang.

I tied my ponytail quickly, slipped on my baby blue suit jacket, and went to the door.

Tara Burke stood in a navy blue skirt suit with black stockings. "Ustick, I came by to get a status update on the case."

She might try calling. I grunted. "Come on in."

She glanced over her shoulder. "I don't know if I should."

I put up my right hand. "Look, my home is my office, and I would really hate to discuss this standing in the doorway."

"Okay." She sighed.

I led her to the dining room, which included a glass table with a purple table cloth and purple vinyl chairs. She sat and smiled as she glanced around.

I settled across from her and cleared my throat. "Right now, I'm working on the original assault complaints. If I crack them open, the murders won't be far behind. My theory involves a hypnotist named Diana King. The Robles girl went to her. So did the woman who shot you. My working theory is that the conspirators hired King to plant in the minds of real sexual assault victims the suggestion that Hernandez was the perp. When they reported it to Thomas, he believed them because they thought they were telling the truth."

Tara's eyes widened. "That's quite a fantastic theory. How are you going to prove it?"

"I checked with Newton and got a copy of the reports from everyone who'd been following Thomas. After he left Robles' apartment, he drove to a diner and asked for Karla. Turned out she was off that day, so Thomas left. I found out from a confidential source where Karla lives, and I think she's one of the women who accused Hernandez. She should be home, and I'll have a talk with her. She lives between Meridian and Kuna."

Tara stood. "I'm coming with you."

"Thanks for the offer, but—"

"But don't be absurd. You're driving out in the middle of nowhere to talk to a woman who's been a victim of sexual assault. If she doesn't shoot you on sight, what are the odds she's going to believe you that her memory of her assailant is the result of a bad hypnotist? I mean we still might fail, but you'll have better odds if you have a woman along."

I regarded her a moment. "I concede the point, counselor."

"What's her last name?"

"Dearing."

Tara nodded. "Very well, Mr. Ustick. We'll see Miss Dearing." She eyed my hair. "You didn't quite get that ponytail right. Let me help you with that."

Yeah, she'd run her cool, soft hand across my scalp simply to get my hair just right. I shook my head. "That's okay, I can fix it before we go."

"You sure?"

I bit my lip. Most of my girlfriends would be consciously making a pass at me, but virgins were often being manipulated by their own bodies. "No. You'd better not."

She smiled. "Be sure to wear an overcoat. It's muddy out that way. I'll follow you in my car."

I nodded. Why wasn't it annoying to be told that when it was forty-five degrees outside? Guess it was nice she cared.

Once in my Jaguar, I pulled out of the garage and drove onto the street. She followed behind me in a late model dark blue Volkswagen Beetle.

The GPS led me down I-84 West to the Eagle road exit. I took a couple back roads outside of Meridian. The trees were close together and the houses far apart. I smiled. This was one advantage of living in Boise. I'd been a mile from the airport and about five miles from the State Capitol when I'd started. Now, I was out here in God's country.

"You have reached your destination," the GPS said.

I stopped and got out of the Jaguar. Tara parked right behind me.

She walked past the Jaguar. "Nice car."

I walked ahead. "Yeah, I got it three years back at a police auction. Some idiots messed it up running from the cops, but I got an engine overhaul, new breaks, and a new paint job. It's perfect."

She laughed. "Some men are more proud of their cars than their kids."

"Cars are easier to get right." Unlike my kid, I could see my car any time. We arrived at the front door and I knocked.

It opened. A woman scowled out at me. She was dressed in a blue tank top and green shorts. Her long, gray hair was all tangled. "What do you want?"

"We're here to see Karla," I said.

The woman raised an eyebrow. "You two Jehovah's witnesses?"

I said, "No, we're Catholics."

"Catholics go door to door?"

Tara laughed. "We're not on a religious mission, at least not directly. The work of truth and justice is a God-given call."

The woman wrinkled her nose and glanced over her shoulder. "Karla! Some folks are here to see you." She added to us, "Those Jehovah's witnesses are persistent. We live half a mile from anyone and somehow they miss the no soliciting sign. If I wanted to be bothered, I'd live in the city. God knows it's coming out here quick enough."

I nodded.

A woman in her mid-twenties jogged over. She had chin-length black hair and wore an Idaho Steelheads sweatshirt and black jeans.

The old woman said, "Karla, these folks are here to talk about truth and justice." She pointed at me and laughed. "This one is really Powerhouse."

Okay, that was a new one. I coughed. "She was kidding."

"Sure I am, Powerhouse." The old woman retreated.

Karla eyed us. "What do you want?"

I said softly, "Ma'am, we're hear to discuss your assault case."

Karla folded her arms. "What assault case?"

"The one you told Gordon Thomas about."

Her eyes bugged out. She cursed. "He said he'd keep my name out of it!" She reached for the door.

Tara said, "Please don't, Ms. Dearing. I know you're very scared, but we need to talk. You could be in danger."

Karla tapped her fingers "I'm listening."

Tara glanced over her shoulder. "Could we come in? This discussion would probably go better inside."

"Sure." Karla shrugged and led us to the living room. The furniture was well-worn, with an easy chair on three legs, and a couch that looked twenty years old. In the center of the living room was a playpen with a baby in a pink onesie. Ricki Lake was on the TV. Karla grabbed the remote and muted it. "All right, you got twenty minutes until Judge Judy."

I said, "You ever hear of a hypnotherapist named Diana King?"

She blinked and pressed her lips together.

"A woman who had apparently been on the road to recovery went postal and took a couple pot shots at us. She also went to Dr. King."

"So what's that have to do with anything?"

"Likely, she shot us under Dr. King's post-hypnotic suggestion. Further, another of Mr. Hernandez's accusers also went to Dr. King. The story she told was impossible. Her assailant towered over her. Hernandez couldn't have."

Karla's eye grew wide. "Who do you work for?"

I pointed at Tara. "She's my client. I'm the detective."

Tara stiffened. "In this matter, he's employed by Ignacio Hernandez."

Karla shouted, "You get the hell out of here!"

How had Tara convinced me to bring her along, again?

Tara put her hand on Karla's shoulder.

Karla shoved Tara away. "Get your hands off me, lady."

Tara tightened her firsts on her hips. "Miss Dearing! We're here to help."

"Yeah, help your boss get rid of me. He's the guy who went to see the other accuser before she died. He's Hernandez's freakin' angel of death."

"We are not here to hurt you, and we won't even tell Mr. Hernandez we found you, if you don't want us too."

We wouldn't? I coughed.

Karla growled. "I mean it. I want you two out."

I said, "Your life is in danger, but not from us. Let us explain."

The mother came in carrying a shotgun. "You two head for the door, nice and slow."

I cupped my hands together. "Please hear us out."

Karla sighed. "It's okay, Mom, but keep the shotgun handy."

The mother pointed the shotgun at me. "I want your heater."

"Huh?"

The old woman sneered. "Your gat, your rod, your piece."

Karla reddened. "Not everyone watches those old gangster movies." She rolled her eyes. "Mom wants your gun. Do you have one?"

"Don't ever leave home without it, I say." I glanced up the barrel of the shotgun. "You'll give it back after we're done?"

"If you're in any condition to use it."

I slowly pulled my nine millimeter out from my shoulder holster and handed it to her handle first. "Here."

She tucked my gun into her shorts and plodded away, calling, "Mind your manners!"

I said, "How long ago did the assault happen?"

She leaned back. "It was four years ago."

"Did you have any idea who did it? Height, weight, hair color."

"No, it was dark. I didn't remember until—" She bit her lip.

"One of your hypnosis sessions?" I asked.

She glared. "That doesn't mean it wasn't him!"

I blinked. "Why did you go to Gordon Thomas with this?"

"Duh. It allowed me to safeguard my privacy while helping protect other women from becoming the next victims."

"What are the odds of you, Robles, and the woman who shot us having the same hypnotherapist? I believe King gave you and Robles the suggestion that Hernandez was the perpetrator, and planted a suggestion with that woman that led her to come after Tara. And then take a listen to this." I pulled out my cell phone and pulled up the audio of my interview with Katrina Robles and fast forwarded.

I played the part where she said, "It allowed me to safeguard my privacy while helping protect other women from becoming the next victims."

Karla gasped. "It's a coincidence. Diana wouldn't, she couldn't—"

"We have a way to find out. I've got Dr. Jonathan Ravenhill downtown and ready to meet with you. He's an independent expert on hypnotism with no ax to grind in Idaho. He'll be able to give us an opinion we can trust, whether my theory is true or not. I'll help you."

"Like you helped Katrina Robles?"

I sighed. "I don't want you to end up like her. We're going to take every precaution."

Karla stood and paced. "I don't find that reassuring."

Tara smiled. "You could always run."

Boy was she a ton of help.

"What?" Karla put her hands on her hips.

Tara continued. "Run. All you'll lose is your self-respect. If we don't talk to this Dr. Ravenhill, you won't know if you're justified in running. If you hang around here with your eyes closed, you'll be risking your life."

"No, I'll just go on like you two never came here."

I laughed. "Sorry, this isn't the Matrix. You can't take the blue pill. If I'm right, these people are desperate. If your memory is false, you're a big liability to them, if they find out about our visit."

"Think about it." Tara stared at Karla. "Are you still seeing King? Do you really want to go now that you're not sure you can trust her? If you cancel suddenly, that could also set off red flags."

I nodded. "It's possible King called the killers. Robles made a bunch of calls to King's cell right after our conversation."

Karla glanced at her child and glared at me. "So you put us in danger?"

"We're dealing with killers. You might have been in danger already, and they'll stop at nothing. They don't care who they hurt."

Tara said, "Miss Dearing, if Mr. Ustick's right, these people victimized you a second time with a therapist who promised to help you, but sold you out for money and used you as a pawn. Will you let them get away with it?"

Karla sighed. "I'm not going to run around afraid of my shadow. I'll find out the truth."

I said, "All right, I'll take you downtown to see Dr. Ravenhill."

Karla grimaced. "No, you won't. First, I'll Google this Dr. Ravenhill. Second, I'll call a friend to take me. My friend has a CCW permit."

A Concealed Carry Weapon permit. "Good for him."

Tara glared at me. "That's sensible. I think you'd be a fool to come with us just because we claim to want to help."

I cleared my throat. "Whatever you do, don't call Dr. King."

Karla rolled her eyes. "I'm not an idiot."

"Sorry, miss. If I'd known to give Ms. Robles that bit of helpful advice, she might be alive." I handed Karla a card. "Give me a call if you guys run into trouble and need another friend with a CCW permit."

Karla nodded. "Will do."

Tara and I walked back to our vehicles. I stopped us by them. "What was with telling her that I work for Hernandez?"

"You do. I only hired you to investigate the murder of Mrs. Hernandez."

"What if she hadn't gone along with us?"

She glared. "Sorry, unlike you, I don't lie. Besides, she did agree while we did things my way. Your lie was actually quite silly. She would ask why I cared, and then I'd have to improvise a lie."

I shrugged. "Or I could do it."

"Another thing. Avoid your whole hard boiled private eye shtick when talking to a victim of abuse. It can be endearing, but not in that context."

"I stopped myself from saying I'd compare permit expiration dates with her friend."

"Good for you."

I glanced at her. "I'm curious. Do you find my shtick endearing?"

She glanced at me. "I'd better get back."

"Come on, you called me on honesty. Dodging a question doesn't strike me as being honest."

She frowned. "At times, you can be endearing."

"Thank you." I smiled.

I got in my car and began the drive back to Boise, frowning. Was I a jerk or what? I'd started a big argument with my client because she hadn't done things my way. I probably should've thanked her instead. And why had I done that whole thing about her finding me endearing? That was stupid, particularly if it was meant to be flirty.

Oh yeah, Ustick, nothing says romance like manipulating a woman into expressing minor fondness for you.

I shouldn't even be thinking about romance with her. Tara was out of my league. I needed to become a better person before I dragged a woman like her into my life. This would be more material to talk about at my next confession.

My cell phone rang while I was half way to the freeway.

I turned on my hands-free device. "Ustick here."

A voice came over my earpiece. "Hello, this is Paul Veneau, with the Brotherhood of Labor. You've been trying to get a hold of me. I'd like to have a 'clear the air' meeting."

"I'd be happy to oblige. You ready to answer some questions?"

"Absolutely. I'll tell you everything you need to know."

"When you want to meet?"

"Now."

Eager beaver. "I'll grab some lunch."

"We'll order in. Sandwich okay?"

"Can you get pastrami on whole wheat with Swiss?"

"It'll be there to greet you."

After depositing the Jaguar at a downtown parking garage and walking three blocks, I arrived at the Brotherhood's office. It was a two-room suite on the second floor of a building on Ninth.

I sat in the outer office waiting for ten minutes.

A teenage intern came in with some white lunch bags. She handed me one. Inside was a small bag of Lays potato chips and a wrapped sandwich. It proved to be ham, but, hey, it was free.

I bit into my sandwich. A little dry and too much salt. The meat tasted like it'd come from Walmart, three days ago. I ambled to the water fountain, grabbed a Dixie cup, and filled it up four times.

After I'd gotten half-way through with the chips, a bald man in a gray sweater came out of the inner office. He shook my hand. "Pleasure to meet you, Mr. Ustick. My name's Steven Danner. I am the president of the Idaho Brotherhood of Labor. Come on in. Sorry to keep you waiting."

"It's okay." I tossed the sandwich in the trash, stuffed the potato chips bag in my pocket, wiped my hands with the napkin, and walked into his office.

Danner crossed to a desk. He gestured to a gray upholstered chair in front of it. "Have a seat."

I did. "I've been looking forward to this conservation."

"Excellent, Mr. Ustick. You know, there's a road named after you."

If I had twenty dollars for every time a Boisean made a crack about that. I gritted my teeth. "I discovered that regrettable coincidence my first month in town."

"Oh. I guess it's an old joke for you. I could tell you're not from around here. Brooklyn?"

"Philly."

"So you must have quite a different perspective on unions than the less enlightened. Was your father in one?"

"No, he was in the Navy when he died. All the men in my family going back to the Revolution were Navy men or worked on private boats."

"How'd you end up working as a private detective in Idaho?"

"I was visiting my aunt and got seasick on the Staten Island ferry. Took it as an omen." In truth, I'd suffered from motion sickness ever since my dad died at sea. "Why do I feel like I'm being stalled?"

Danner frowned. "Do you know anyone who was fortunate enough to be in a union back in Pennsylvania?"

"Actually, at one time, my mother was the vice-president of her local hotel workers' union." Though she hadn't had much nice to say about unions since they'd move to Idaho. Would Honest Tara have admitted that? Probably.

"So you understand how important it is that unions represent the rights of workers. And you appreciate what a horrendous situation Idaho workers are in due to the right to work laws."

Wait a second. I put up my hand. "I know right to work is what people complain about whenever their boss acts up or their work situation's not what they'd like. I don't know anything about it myself. I've told conservatives, I've told liberals, and I'll tell you, I'm here to solve a crime and clear my client."

"So you're not concerned with his political fortunes?"

"Hernandez is a really nice guy, but I don't know whether he should be Governor. I don't vote, okay?"

The union president leaned back in his chair. "I have some information that I can share. But I need you to promise to keep it away from your boss's political people and from the press unless it's absolutely necessary."

"Given the build up you're giving it, my guess is it's necessary, but if it's not, sure."

He slid a piece of paper across the desk to me.

It was a fax from the office of Bart Bradley. It read:

> I was hired by the Idaho Brotherhood of Labor to consult for them on the upcoming gubernatorial election. During this employment, I and my agents conducted standard investigations into the background of Ignacio Hernandez. I had no involvement in the allegations regarding Mr. Hernandez's past misconduct, nor was I involved in the murder of his wife or Katrina Robles. Such statements are patently false and may be grounds for a slander and/or a libel suit.

It was signed at the bottom. I asked, "May I keep this?"

Danner nodded. "Certainly."

I shoved it in my inside pocket. "So a couple questions. You paid the private detectives?"

"No, he did the opposition research. We reimbursed his expenses plus a five thousand dollar fee."

I smirked. "Union dues payers' hard at work. So did he do anything other than hire private detectives? Any other recommendations?"

He frowned. "If there were, it'd be privileged."

"Did you know about the allegations against Hernandez before they hit the paper?"

"Of course not."

Based on the thirty thousand the union had paid to Cheryl Thompson, and assuming a thousand in expenses, they'd spent a chunk of change. "What did you get that was worth thirty-six thousand dollars?"

Danner gaped. "How did you know how much we spent?"

I smiled. "Just an estimate. I assume I'm in the neighborhood."

"You're not only in the neighborhood, you're on the front step. I don't know how'd you guess something like that."

The less he dwelled on how I knew that, the better. "I'm really good at estimating. So did you get your money's worth?"

"No comment."

Let's try another tact. "How important is it to you that Governor Flanagan get re-elected?"

Danner sighed. "Off the record?"

"I'm not a reporter. I'm not recording, and I know you can deny it."

"If you'd told me twenty years ago that I'd try to get Flanagan re-elected, I'd have said that you were crazy. He's been an enemy of labor throughout his entire career. However, that Hernandez is a terrorist. He wants to have public dollars pay for private schools, and he wants to decimate the state workforce. It's all about cheaper with him. He's a typical right-winger who knows the cost of everything but the value of nothing."

"What value do you place upon keeping Hernandez out of the governor's mansion, then?"

"We don't have a governor's mansion, at least not one anyone lives in. So you're really asking about keeping him out of the governor's office."

I groaned. There was nothing worse than a smart aleck politico. "Okay, I stand corrected."

"It'd be too bad, if Hernandez won, but we'd manage just like we have before. He has got a big agenda, but he can't steamroll his agenda through like he would in a corporate boardroom."

"What about the changes Flanagan made to state policy that favored the unions?"

Danner chuckled. "It'll give unionized shops a chance to pick up maybe two to three hundred jobs. It's not much, but we'll take what we can get."

I leaned back. The policy differences between Hernandez and Flanagan weren't big enough for the labor union to engage in this complicated game of murder and blackmail. Bart Bradley seemed like a good candidate as Denise Waters' co-conspirator in bribing Diana King to plant false suggestions.

None of that worked unless Bradley had a motive.

What motive might Bradley have? King wouldn't risk her practice for peanuts, and Bradley wouldn't pay her big money and commit murder unless he expected to get something significant out of the deal.

"Sir, are you okay?" Danner asked.

I shook my head. "Sorry, I was just thinking. Can you give me an official total on what you paid Bradley?"

"Sure, lemme print this up." Danner clicked on the computer. "Total was $37,325.58." He pressed a button and the nearby wireless printer produced the document. He handed it to me. "There you go."

"Thanks, you've been helpful." Almost too helpful. If the guy had been green, it'd been understandable, but that model had plenty of miles on him and shouldn't be so forthcoming. I shook the guy's hand. "Have a good day and thanks for the sandwich."

I headed for the door. My phone buzzed. It was a text.

Karla had arrived to meet Dr. Ravenhill.

The digital clock in the rented doctor's office read 3:52. Dr. Ravenhill sat behind the desk. He wore a white sweater and khakis. He had his hair pulled back in a blond ponytail and had a small hoop earring in his right ear. Karla was there along with a guy a few years younger than me, with a crew cut, medium complexion, and wearing a green hoodie.

Dr. Ravenhill said, "Karla and I have talked through what she's been through, Mr. Ustick. Based on a careful examination, my opinion is that her memory of the sexual assault is real, but her memory of the perpetrator had been altered through suggestion."

I glanced at Karla. "How are you doing?"

She grimaced, and voice choking. "Your friend was right. It's like being violated all over again." She sniffled. "Diana betrayed me. I don't know if I can ever trust anyone again."

I nodded. "I'm sorry. I'll do everything I can to see her held to account. I know this hurts, but you're brave to face it."

"I'm scared to death."

Dr. Ravenhill smiled. "That's what makes you brave."

I said, "Karla, can I count on your help to get these people?"

She raised her eyebrows and shook her head. "Mister, I have a daughter. I can't put myself at risk."

"We'll take steps to protect you. First, we'll have you sign an affidavit. The existence of written proof lessens any incentive to harm you. Second, we'll get you out of town for the next few days."

She frowned. "What about my job?"

"Explain you had a family emergency come up. I'll arrange some place in Oregon for you to stay until this blows over."

She sighed. "Promise me you'll get them and that you'll try to keep my face out of the paper."

I nodded. "I'll do my best."

Outside the offices of Jake Donaldson, I strolled to my car, pulled up Gordon Thomas' cell phone number from my iPad, and called it. "This is Cole Ustick. I'd like to talk to you."

Thomas growled. "I'm busy. You should have taken the chance to talk a few days ago. Now you're old news."

"Oh, too bad. Then I guess I'll visit Doug Witherley with a story that'll knock your journalistic career out of the water."

"What are you talking about?"

"Another Hernandez accuser has recanted. Seems you've been taken in by a hoax twice. I wasn't behind this one, either, but I uncovered it, so I'll be suspect. Do you want to discuss this?"

Thomas sighed. "I'll be at the office for an hour. I'll be waiting for you."

I hung up and started the car, and put it in reverse.

The cell phone rang. I pressed the hands free button. "Ustick here."

"It's Ray Davis, Mr. Ustick. I've found the purple bag, and I may have found the Kirby."

Fortieth street wasn't the place to go in a nice car and it'd be tempting fate to take it there again. "Can you meet me at the newspaper office in about half an hour to forty-five minutes? I have a meeting with Gordon Thomas, and then I can talk to you."

"I'll look forward it."

"Thanks." I drove to the newspaper office in West Boise and turned into the parking lot.

It was nearly empty, so I targeted a space right in front of the concrete barrier near the building. I turned into my chosen space and hit the break.

My car sped up like it was possessed. It lurched forward, hopped over the curb, and raced toward the concrete wall.

Chapter 20

I whispered a prayer.

The car scrunched into the barrier, jerked, and came to a stop.

I took the car out of gear, turned off the ignition, and walked around to the front. A thick muddy patch of dirt was between the car and the wall. My tires had dug in there pretty good, and the mud had slowed the momentum. However, my beautiful pink Jaguar's front bumper was crushed in, the hood was off its hinges, and the lights were smashed.

For a full two minutes, I stood, staring open-mouthed at the wreckage.

My car, my beautiful car! Blinking back tears, I dialed the number of my auto club and had them tow it to the body shop I used in the North End. It'd be twenty minutes until they arrived.

Might as well go see Thomas. I strolled into the office.

Behind a fiberglass desk sat a plump woman with shoulder-length black hair. "Can I help you?"

"Cole Ustick here to see Gordon Thomas."

She nodded. "Head on back."

I walked back to an area full of open cubicles. I glanced around the gray areas. With all the unoccupied cubes, it looked like a ghost town. Guess there had been a lot of layoffs or everyone had gotten off early.

Thomas stomped over, scowl. "You took your sweet time."

I swallowed. "Had a mishap in the parking lot. I'll have my insurance company call your business office."

Thomas waved. "Not my problem. I'm fed up with your Gestapo tactics. You tried to intimidate me by having people follow me, your buddy Newton used my chin as a punching bag, and then you threaten me over the phone. Your girlfriend regards me as a threat to democracy. Well, contrary to what the NRA tells you, an AK-47 in every house is the sign of a fearful people, not a free people. This is a free country because we have a free press!"

I put up my hand. "Enough with the speech, Patrick Henry. As I've had to say way too many times already. When it comes to politics, I'm as neutral as the Swiss. I've not once tried to intimidate you—until now."

I whipped out the affidavit.

Thomas grabbed it and sat at a vacant cubicle's desk. "Undue influence due to hypnosis? You expect me to buy it."

"Karla's hypnotherapist saw Katrina Robles and the woman who shot at Tara and I. The public will buy it, and you'll look like the ultimate dupe."

He stared past me. "This statement could've been obtained under duress, or Hernandez could've pealed back a few thousand to pay these guys off."

"If you'd been this skeptical in the first place, neither of us would be in this position. You'll be able to talk to the victim on Monday. I'm keeping her out of harm's way while we wrap up the investigation."

"So why did you bring this to me rather than your blogger friend?"

"I need you to get in touch with the other three women."

"Why should I?" Thomas asked.

I put my hand inches from his head and made a knocking motion. "Anybody home? Our murderers could kill them so they can't come forward. I need you to find out for me whether Diana King was their hypnotherapist, too, and get them to safety."

Thomas folded his arms and narrowed his eyes. "I meant, since when am I working for you?"

"Since whenever you want to have something to do with this correction coming out rather than having it ramrodded down your throat."

"Your employer wouldn't approve of this."

"If you mean my clients, Mr. Hernandez isn't the type to want women to die so he can score political points against you. Even if he was that sort, I have to look at myself in the mirror in the morning."

Thomas smiled. "You guys are nuts, thinking I'm persecuting him."

"No, I'm willing to give you the benefit of the doubt. However, that does require you generally write shoddily sourced stories about everyone. If that's true, I wonder why you last in this business."

"The real shoddy practice is the courts re-victimizing ninety-nine women who've been sexually assaulted on a hunt for the one unbalanced woman who fingers an innocent man. When a victim bravely comes forward, she deserves to be taken at her word and given justice."

My cell phone rang. I glanced at the caller ID. "My tow truck is here, sir. I expect to hear from you tomorrow."

I turned on my heels and headed out into the lobby.

The tow truck driver stood by his vehicle, which was parked across the driveway from my Jaguar. "Cole Ustick?"

"Yeah."

"Towing by Dan. I see where your car is."

I snorted. "It'd be hard to miss."

"There's someone under it."

Oh not another one. I frowned. "Is he dead?"

The driver raised his greasy eyebrows. "What do you think I mean? The guy appears to be a mechanic playing the good Samaritan."

"Oh. Sorry, it's been quite a few weeks." I got outside, just as Roy Davis was coming out from under my Jaguar.

How had he found out? Oh yeah, I'd asked him to meet me here. Still. I frowned. "Do you go under everybody's wrecked car?"

"Only ones I'm suspicious about." Davis reached into his back pocket, pulled out a red rag, and wiped his forehead. "A bolt under there was broken. Usually, when that happens, the engine overheats and burns out. In this case, it caused you to accelerate rather than brake. Personally, I'd bet on sabotage."

I bit my lip. If he was right, the car could have failed at any time. What if that trick had happened downtown or on the Connector? Rather than having to deal with the headaches of insurance companies and body men, I'd have killed myself or someone else.

"You want to call the cops?"

I shrugged. "I don't want to spend all night here. I'll have the shop check for damage that could be deliberate. If someone's trying to kill me, then I'm sure I know why, who, and how. They already have enough to answer for."

"Suit yourself." Davis shrugged. "I can give you a ride once I'm done."

I nodded. "Let me tell the tow truck driver where to take my Jaguar, and I'll be right with you."

A few minutes later, I hopped into the passenger seat of Davis's mint-condition, 1981 F-150 truck.

A paper bag sat between the seats. Davis pointed to it. "I think we found your purse."

I opened the bag. Inside, wrapped in plastic, was a purple purse in almost new condition. If it wasn't Denise's, it was a perfect twin. "Nicely done. What about the softball bat and the Kirby Vacuum?"

Davis started the car and headed toward Garden City. "Neither has been recently dumped."

"Oh. So where are we going?"

"To get the vacuum cleaner."

I raised an eyebrow. "I thought you said you didn't find it."

"Didn't say that. It wouldn't go out with the trash. You'd have to take it to the dump yourself. Too many people would see it, perhaps even a cop. The easiest way to dispose of it is to sell it or give it away."

We pulled up in front of a ramshackle single wide trailer on West Thirty-sixth street with a beat-up, rusting, red 1993 Ford van.

Davis added, "Easiest way to get rid of something is to list it as a free item on Craig's List. The likely guy to get anything on Craig's List is in this trailer, Bargain Bill we call him. I checked with him, and he has it."

I whistled. "You're not bad, Davis."

He smirked. "Flatterer. Come on, let's go see Bargain Bill."

We climbed out of the truck. Davis glanced around at the broken-down trailers and eyed a graffiti-laden wall. "Man, this is run down."

I smirked. "Yeah, it's totally unlike the Biltmore where you live."

"Yeah, I'm blessed." He shook his head. We walked up the creaky steps to the door of the single wide trailer. Davis knocked. "Bargain Bill, it's Roy."

"Roy who?"

Davis sighed. "Davis!"

"Just a second." Bill opened the door and glanced over my lime green suit. "I got another suit just like that. I think it's in your size. Oh, come in." He led us into a living room chock full of junk. "Have a seat."

In what? I glanced around. There were two bean bag chairs: one pink and one orange, along with two lawn chairs: one dark blue and one golden brown.

Bargain Bill flopped on the orange bean bag that was leaking stuffing.

I removed from a brown lawn chair a bread maker and the board games Operation and Landslide. I shoved them underneath lawn chair. They almost fit. I lowered myself down. Even if the chair broke, all the stuff under the chair would hold me up.

Davis cleaned off the other lawn chair and crashed in it. "Bill, you got the vacuum?"

Bill flashed us a toothy grin. "In the kitchen. You'll have to move a few things to get to it."

Davis and I waded to the kitchen. We grabbed a couple Coleman camp stoves, a doll house, and three bags of dog food. We shifted them around until I found a Kirby vacuum. I slipped on latex gloves, pulled out the vacuum, and glanced back toward the living room. "Other than storing it here, have you done anything with it?"

Bill shook his head. "No."

"How'd you get it?"

"I saw an ad for a free Kirby vacuum. Strangely, I received an email back that said I could come and get it at three o'clock in a parking garage and it'd be on the third level. Went downtown and there it be in a vacant parking spot."

"What day was that?"

"Last Thursday at three in the afternoon."

"Did you see anyone?"

"Nope."

I bit my lip. "This may be it."

"Do I get my money?"

"Not yet." I put up my right hand. "We have to ensure this is the right vacuum, but if it is, the two hundred will be yours."

"How are you going to find out?"

"We'll take it to the police, and they'll test it. They'll need to come by and take your fingerprints for identification."

"They already have 'em. Had a couple run-ins with the law when I was younger, and I haven't changed my prints since then." Bill eyed the vacuum cleaner. "Whoever bought this paid nearly two thousand dollars, and here I got the vacuum free. You'll pay me $200 if you use it for evidence, and I can probably get it back after the trial. There's a lesson for you, boy."

I blinked. "Uh, yes, sir."

"Hold on now. I've got a few things for you boys." He waded through the junk in the hallway to the bedrooms.

Davis leaned in and whispered to me, "Whatever he gives you, take it. He'll be insulted if you don't. He gives stuff away to make room for more."

In addition to the vacuum, I left with three dress shirts and four suits. Only two of them would fit me, and one of those I could only wear after I got it dry cleaned. Davis left with three baseball bats, a cribbage set, and a copy of *Plato's Republic*. We piled into the cabin of the truck.

Davis smiled. "Got anything you could use?"

"The maroon suit and the pink dress shirt. I might have bought them myself, if I'd been looking. I get most of my clothes through eBay."

"I wondered about that."

"What's that guy's deal?"

"Oh, he grabs up free stuff. He says it keeps his bills low and makes sure not to feed the corporate machine, but he gets a lot of junk in the process. He sells some stuff, but some things won't sell. He unloads it on likely passersby to make room for more. If it's a vice, it's got to be one of the more harmless ones in Garden City." Davis started the car. "So, police headquarters?"

I nodded.

Once there, I stuffed the wrapped purse into my overcoat. Davis helped by carrying the accessories for the vacuum while I lugged the vacuum cleaner inside. Davis dropped the items on the front desk and headed back out.

The lady at the front desk eyed the items. "What's this?"

"Gifts for either Detective Weston or Detective French."

The clerk bit her lip. "I think Detective French is in. Let me call her."

I sat in an uncomfortable brown plastic chair in the lobby. I popped a stick of gum in my mouth and checked Facebook on my phone.

Detective Maggie French emerged frowning. "What do you want?"

"I have some evidence for you." I pointed to the Kirby.

"Come on back." She led me back.

I lugged the vacuum clear to her desk, released it, and wiped the sweat from my brow. *Never realized how much these things weigh.*

She pointed to a chair. "Sit."

I lowered myself down. "You're so polite."

"Where'd you get the vacuum and what makes you think its evidence?"

I told her the whole story.

She arched her eyebrows. "Trying to dispose of evidence on Craig's List? That's a new one on me."

Big whoop. Newton said she'd only been a detective six months

French frowned. "I'll get you a receipt for this. "

"There was one more thing."

"Out with everything, Columbo."

"This is all." I pulled the purse out.

She smirked. "Lovely. Doesn't quite go with your ensemble though."

If anything was worse than a smart aleck politico, it was a smart aleck cop. "It's Denise Waters purse. It was found at the landfill."

French sniffed it. "Yeah, I'll buy that. Your point?"

"She threw away a purse in like-new condition. Why? Perhaps she used it to transport poisoned artificial sweetener to the meeting and threw it out for fear that there was trace evidence."

"Couldn't it be that she used the purse for completely non-sinister reasons, decided she didn't like it, and tossed it?"

Why toss it now? You should have that tested."

She stared at the purse. "I think you're crazy, but okay."

After she wrote me out the receipts, she led me to the lobby. I headed out the front door and got in Davis's truck.

Davis sat there, thumbing from through *The Republic.* "So how'd it go?"

"Good." I patted his shoulder. "You've come through pretty well. Sorry. I kind of misjudged your whole group."

Davis nodded. "We're not super-geniuses, but we do have specialized knowledge. Though no one specializes in homicides. This is our first murder investigation."

"We're even on that. Do you know how to get in touch with security at the Caldwell Airport?"

"I do, actually." Davis pulled out a cell phone and dialed a number. "You mind if I sit here a few minutes?"

I shook my head. "Be my guest."

While Davis made his phone call, I played with my iPhone. I pulled up Tara's Facebook page. She had a couple pictures she'd taken of the office. One was a visit of a group of Young Republicans who took a picture with Denise Waters and Jared Bach.

Another picture was of a Canyon County Commissioner that'd come by and endorsed the campaign. The picture included Hernandez, Hearst, with Denise smiling on the side of him.

What was that on her hand? I zoomed in on Denise's hand. It had a light coating of black that looked like grease. She could've gotten that while she'd slipped away from the office to tamper with my car.

I glanced at the time stamp on the Facebook post. This had been taken soon after I'd left the union headquarters, so she could've gone there and had no time to give her hands a thorough washing before the photo op.

Davis hung up. "On the night of the murder, my contact at the Caldwell airport saw a black Lincoln Town car drive in and an attractive woman with long, blonde hair get out. An hour or so later, a man drove the same Lincoln Town car out. He got off at three that night and hadn't seen it return."

"Anything else?"

"Yep, the police asked him about it and showed him some pictures. He picked out the woman. The female cop told him a private detective named Ustick might come asking about it, but to say nothing."

I grimaced. "Somebody in there doesn't like me, and her name is Maggie French. Thanks for the help. What do I owe you extra?"

Davis nodded. "If you could give another fifty dollars to the food bank, that'd be nice."

I smiled. Newton had misjudged the Fortieth Street Detectives. They were good guys, even if they were whimsical.

I ran upstairs to Newton Investigations two steps at a time and rapped on the door.

"Come on in, Ustick," Newton said.

I entered and glanced around the old digs. My old desk was the same as the day I'd packed everything up and left.

Newton had put on a couple pounds, but that was normal when he was on a tough case. His next slow period would bring the return of the celery.

"I have news." I gasped for breath and stared at Newton. "A security guard at the Caldwell airport saw a woman drive a black caddy into the airport on the night of the murder. It sounds like it was Denise Waters."

Newton blinked. "It was."

I frowned. "How did you know?"

"Weston told me about it on the condition I not tell you."

I curled my fist. "Refresh my memory. Didn't Mr. Hernandez advise you to share everything with me?"

Newton put up his left hand. "If I hadn't promised not to share it, I would have told you. Besides, you found out eventually."

That didn't return my wasted time. I frowned. "So are they dropping the charges against Hernandez?"

Newton shook his head. "No, the county prosecutor thinks Denise was in on a conspiracy, working for Hernandez. Personally, I think the worm will drop the case right after the primary or once it's done enough political damage. Though, from what you texted me, if you've killed the sexual harassment story, that might force him to drop it earlier."

"Yeah and put our killers on the alert. Denise Waters tried to finish me off." I relayed my car's mysterious issue and eyed Newton. "You're looking pretty healthy."

Newton blinked. "What does that mean?"

"You're not within a mile of closing this case, but I am. If we play it your way, we'll most likely end up with no one being tried for either murder. How does Hernandez feel about his wife's murderer going unpunished?"

Newton frowned. "Calm down. Sometimes, these things take time."

"And sometimes murders end up unsolved. There's only one thing to do. I have to close this case before Thomas eats crow on the harassment case and our killers get even more desperate."

Newton said, "What are you going to do?"

"You'll find out." I turned headed to the door and then glassed back at Newton. "Eventually."

Chapter 21

I didn't actually know what I was going to do when I left, but there was only one way. Hit the weakest link in the conspiracy and hit her hard.

I sat in Diana King's waiting room.

"Mr. Philco," Diana King's mousy receptionist said.

I looked up through my glasses from the Sports Illustrated article on the Denver Nuggets playoff hopes at use of my alias. "Yes."

"Dr. King will see you."

The receptionist led me into a dimly lit office with matched blue leather chairs. Vanilla-scented candles burned behind the desk. I was wearing a gray tweed suit and had a gray tweed newsie cap on. I'd tucked my hair into my hat.

The receptionist said, "She'll be with you shortly."

I flopped in a blue leather chair and turned on the voice recorder on my smart phone. My fake mustache itched on my upper lip. I curled my lip. Yeah, right. Like that would help.

A petite, middle-aged woman with cropped brown hair entered in a dark blue top and black slacks. She extended her hand. "Mr. Philco, I'm Dr. King."

I smiled, stood, and extended my hand. "It's good to meet you."

She shook my hand and made her way to the other side of the desk. "So, what brought you here today?"

"I've been having disturbing dreams."

"Oh?" She pulled out a yellow legal pad and a green pen. "Tell me about them. What do you dream?."

"I dream . . . of murder."

She arched her right eyebrow. "Really? Do you remember any specifics?"

I nodded. "I receive a call from a woman saying someone was on to us. I get on an airplane and come out to Boise and go out to the North End to an apartment where loud music is playing, alternative rock, I think."

"Interesting."

"I kill a woman, an Amazonian she looked like, but the scene is a mess. I call the woman who called me in and tell her to come out immediately to clean up the crime scene."

The doctor stopped writing.

I continued. "The woman cleans the scene and takes away a baseball bat. I return to the airport. Next I see the woman give the Kirby away in a parking garage in Boise."

She dropped her pencil. It rolled across the floor. She glowered. "Who the hell are you?"

"Cole Ustick," I said as I ripped off the face rug. It pinched me a little while coming off. "I know everything."

She paled. "You're lying."

"The only legitimate degree you have is a Bachelor's in Sports Medicine. Your doctorate is from a diploma mill. Bart Bradley and Denise Waters hired you to give five women who'd been assaulted the suggestion that their assailant was Ignacio Hernandez. Only you made a mistake. After I visited Katrina, she called the campaign office, learned he was five-six, and realized that meant he was too short to be the assailant. She called you and left messages, scared out of her wits. When you heard her voice mails, you realized what danger you were in. That's when you called Bart Bradley."

She sneered. "You can't prove any of this."

"I can prove Katrina Robles called you like crazy. And I can prove you called Bart Bradley when we get your phone records." We needed to obtain them legally before they'd be admissible. "And I have the vacuum."

"Where is it?"

"Somewhere safe."

She smiled. "What would you ask to give it back?"

"What would you offer?"

"Five thousand."

I snickered. "No sale."

"Ten."

I shook my head.

"Fifteen. That's as much as I can pay."

I sighed. "Lady, do you know what your problem is? You accepted a bribe that required you to take advantage of six clients who'd trusted you. You assume everyone's willing to sell out and has no more ethics than you. By the way, did I mention I was recording our conversation?"

The remaining color in her face drained away. "Get out!"

"Sure, but somebody will be back, probably the police when they get done analyzing that vacuum and trace the serial number. Despite your best efforts, there's still proof it was used at the scene of the crime. And then I'll be glad to share a tape of you offering me $15,000 for a $2,000 vacuum cleaner."

She pointed at the door. "I said get out!"

I slapped a business card on the desk. "Let me know if you change your mind, and don't leave the county. I'll find out if you do."

I strolled out of her office.

The receptionist kept her gaze on her computer. "What happened?" She glanced up at me. "Where's your mustache?"

"What can I say? That meeting left me feeling like a whole new man."

That night, I sat at my house playing "Alexander's Ragtime Band" on the keyboard. Leah was singing along. I grabbed my handkerchief and wiped sweat from my forehead. "Let's take five, Leah. You can wear a guy out."

She rolled her glass of fake wine between her fingers. "Ustick, I'm simply testing your versatility as well as my own."

I chuckled. "For what future project? Are you going to record a country music album?"

She made a face like biting a raw onion. She grabbed from the end table a bowl of the Pasta Fazool I'd prepared and took a bite. "Just because I can sing country, doesn't mean I should sing country."

"You did a good job on 'Ring of Fire.'"

She raised her glass. "Johnny Cash was awesome no matter what genre he happened to be singing." She took a sip of fake wine. "If you don't want to play, you need to tell me something."

"What about?"

"That whole theatrical performance at King's office you told me about. How did you know she was the one with the vacuum?"

"Remember, based upon a call from Diana King, the killer drove to the murder scene in a car that Denise Waters dropped off for him. Did he take the vacuum cleaner himself?" I shook my head. "I think he landed an unexpected mess and he needed help. Who was he gonna call? Denise? No, she was at the airport and had no car to reach him. Besides, she owns a stick vac. Could it be some other person? Doubtful, why bring a new person into the conspiracy? No, the most obvious person was Diana King."

"You guessed."

I pointed the brim of my glass at her. "But I didn't guess at random."

The doorbell rang.

I looked through the peephole. Tara Burke. What was she doing here? What would she think of finding Leah here?

Why did I care? I took a deep breath, opened the door six inches, and peeked out. "Tara, what can I do for you?"

"Hi." She drummed her fingers on the side of my house. "I was thinking we could get Dutch Brothers and talk about the case."

I raised an eyebrow. Coming from any other woman, I'd think she was fishing for an excuse to go on a date. I put up my left hand. "Sorry, Tara. I've got to be stationed here in case our hypnotist makes a run for the sky."

She frowned. "Oh, okay."

Leah called out, "Ustick, who's at the door?"

Tara raised her eyebrows and folded her arms, leaning away from me.

I grimaced. What would she think of this, with the Don Juan reputation I had in her parish? I called over my shoulder, "It's Tara."

"Why don't you invite her in?"

Thanks, Leah. Now I can't win no matter what I do. Ugh. Why can't it be possible to simply go get the coffee? I gulped and glanced to Tara. "If you say hello to Leah real quick, then we can excuse ourselves to the kitchen. It's business. She'll understand."

Tara lowered her head. "No need to run off your guest, Mr. Ustick. Just email me later."

She trotted back to her car.

What could I say? Shoulders slumped, I returned to my living room and plopped on the couch.

Leah said, "Is she coming in?"

"No, she left."

Leah sighed. "A pity. I'd like to meet the woman who has captured Cole Ustick's heart."

"You sound like a cheesy Romantic Comedy."

Leah chuckled. "You two act like you're in one. It's obvious she's likes you, and you've wasted enough time on the insecure sort who want to scratch my eyes out because I'm beautiful, confident, and drawing the eye of a man they consider their property. If you don't swallow your fear of commitment and go after her, you'll be making the biggest mistake of your life."

I rolled my eyes and snorted. "Bigger than—"

"Yes, in my opinion, that would be bigger than any other mistake you've made." She turned her head from me. "I loved a man once, but he just wanted to have fun. That's what I'd agreed to, and it had made things easy for a time. Eventually, the feelings became too painful, so I pulled back. We managed to stay friends, but we took paths that were so different, we could never travel together as I'd once hoped. If you don't stop holding back your feelings with Tara and soon, you'll lose her forever. The clock's ticking, Ustick."

That sounded almost like her and I, except it couldn't be. I could always tell when my girlfriends developed such feelings for me: they got catty toward my other girlfriends. She never did.

She inhaled, glanced away from me, and wiped her eyes. "Think about it." She sipped her prenatal wine. "And if it still sounds hopelessly maudlin, blame it on the Martinelli's."

My cell phone buzzed. The text message read, "Subject heading East on 84. ETA at BOI airport=ten minutes."

"Gotta go." I dashed out to my rental SUV, pulled out of my drive, and headed onto Canal and up to Vista to the airport.

After following the looping road that led up to the airport, I turned into the short-term parking garage. A good spot lay in between a Miata and a Ford Caravan. I parked there, ran as fast as I could, and got to the terminal just as my phone buzzed.

The text said, "Turning into the airport now."

I took several deep breaths, pulled my hair out of its ponytail, and then retied it. I relaxed and popped in a stick of Juicy Fruit.

Three minutes later, Diana King walked up through the automatic door carrying a single carry on bag. She yelped and jumped.

I smiled. "I told you I'd have an eye on you."

"This is harassment."

I put my hands up. "Call the cops. I can play our little conversation for them, and you can tell me why you offered $15,000 for a $2,000 vacuum."

"And then they'd arrest you for extortion."

I shook my head. "Not when I declined your voluntary offers. That's not a crime."

She glared at me, did a one-eighty, and headed back to the parking area. I moved inside the doors near the ticket counter and waited five minutes. A text came through. "Subject headed West down I-84 toward home."

Hopefully, she'd stay there. I got in my car and checked my watch. Nine o'clock, eight o'clock Seattle time. I should probably get back to my guests. I sighed. Leah could entertain herself a little longer. I dialed Jensen's number.

That Friday morning, I sat in the spare bedroom. I glanced up at Jenson's superhero mural and chuckled. I paced and threw darts at a dartboard on the opposite wall. The way today was going, I probably shouldn't bill my clients.

I was one blockbuster piece of evidence away from busting this case wide open, but I needed something and it wasn't coming. I'd gotten King to make some incriminating statements and maybe the police could take my tape and get more out of it, but it wasn't enough. Not nearly enough.

Maybe I should give Newton and the cops another go at it. Yeah, after the way they'd snubbed me and made my job harder? That'd be great.

My cell phone rang. I answered. "Ustick."

"Hi, this is Doug Witherley. Word is Thomas is going to have a big story out on the case and that you gave it to him." He had a slight edge in his voice.

Reporters had big mouths. I sighed. "It was necessary to get information for my case."

"Do you have anything for me?" Witherley sounded like a kid asking for another ride at the fair.

To leak or not to leak. That was the question. I shook my head. "Sorry, I have multiple clients, and releasing everything publicly could hurt my case."

He loosed a massive sigh. "You got to do what you got to do."

"Yeah. I'll let you know if I get anything."

"I'm going to be driving up to Moscow for a debate later today. My cell reception may be sketchy in a few places."

"I'll keep that in mind." Not that I expected anything that day. I returned to playing darts.

Two rounds later, the phone rang again.

I picked it up. "Ustick."

"It's Diana King."

I sat on the bed. "What can I do for you?"

"Is this call being recorded?"

"No."

"I'd like to give you something."

"No amount of money's going to buy me off."

"I'm not offering money. I'm willing to give you Bart Bradley."

Now she had my attention. "How?"

"What else was missing from the crime scene other than a vacuum?"

"The softball bat."

"Do you have any guess as to why that might have disappeared?"

"It contained physical evidence."

"If I'd been dragged into this, I'd have gotten some protection. You can't trust someone who'd commit murder."

"Like you hypnotized a woman to go kill Tara and herself?"

She snorted. "Ustick, can you prove that?"

I bit my lip. "No."

"Good. Then I'm willing to give you evidence that incriminates Bradley in exchange for being left alone."

I frowned. "Police might have more to say about that than I do."

"All I'll ask is that you call off your goon squad and leave me alone. After that, if the police think they have a case, that's my problem. Just don't bring a cop with you. Come alone."

I smiled. I could leave the meeting with her and call the Weston and tell him she was a material witness afterwards. If Weston didn't listen? Not my problem. "When would you meet?"

"Tonight at six. Come alone."

"You said that."

"I'm saying it again. No one else, and you get your dogs off as soon as you show up."

"We'll play it your way. But be advised I'll be able to tell if you're giving me a fake. I saw the bat before the murder."

"Ustick, you're the master con artist. Meet me at my office."

I grinned. I was going to close this case and bring down the curtain without any help from Newton or the cops.

That afternoon, I sat in my car as I emailed Witherley a detailed report of my findings, save the sexual harassment report I'd given Thomas, and advised Witherley not to open it until eight o'clock. At that time, the debate would be over and Hernandez would be calling in to a conference line in his campaign headquarters to find out what his dollars had bought.

I sat in the car in the parking lot of the "Library!" and checked my email on my tablet.

There was an email from Mark Hearst:

Mr. Hernandez will be on the conference line at eight o'clock even if it means blowing off the press. Don't start without him. I told Denise that she, Tara, and Jared need to meet for a campaign conference call at HQ. They have no idea what it's really all about. Again, your discretion is appreciated, if at all possible, regarding that matter we discussed.

I frowned. I didn't have any need to disclose the affair, but Denise might. She was beyond our control.

Lieutenant Weston sent an email saying, "Ustick, this isn't an episode of *Poirot*. If you have evidence, give it to the police."

I emailed back, "I don't have the evidence yet. I hope to by 8. Come to the meeting."

Nothing from Newton yet. He would check it in time. If not, I'd call him at seven-thirty.

The only person who wouldn't be at the meeting was Bart Bradley, but I'm sure that it'd be just a matter of time before Bradley was brought here by the Boise constabulary.

I exited the parking lot and headed for King's office.

Parked outside King's office were a white SUV, a red new Bug, and a black Ford Taurus. Behind the last vehicle's wheel sat a detective from Sheryl Thompson and Associates. I waved him off, and he drove away. *Gotta hand it to Thompson. The bottom feeder has made money off this case from both sides.*

I entered the building. It had that eerie Friday quiet, like the apocalypse had hit and I was the last man on Earth. I strolled to number 107 and walked in. The secretary was gone and King's door was half-open.

"All right, let's have it," I said as I jogged inside her office as if I were an athlete taking a victory lap.

King was slumped forward onto her desk with blood pooled under her head. Beside the desk was a softball bat wrapped in newspaper.

"Freeze, Ustick!" a man said behind me.

I glanced back.

Tara and Denise stood in the corner, their hands in the air. Next to them, holding a .45 with a silencer, was Bart Bradley.

Chapter 22

No wonder pride was considered a deadly sin.

I turned and glanced at the man with the gun on me, Tara, and Denise. Bradley had acquired a pink scar that went halfway down his left/right cheek.

"Well, I wasn't expecting the whole gang!" I popped my gum. "My, what a big gun you have! And an illegal silencer to boot."

Bradley said, "Give me your gun, nice and slow."

"I left it in my other suit." My nose itched as I visualized my gun in its shoulder holster.

He pointed his gun at Tara. "Okay, wise guy, five seconds."

I slowly pulled my nine millimeter out and slid it across the floor.

Bradley turned the gun away from Tara and back to me. He pointed his free hand at the dead quack and then at a large garment bag. "Put her in there, and we'll get going."

I glanced at her, crossed myself, and closed her eyes. I lifted her waif-like body out of the chair. She would've needed to spend hours in the gym to keep so fit. What did it mean in the end?

That her corpse was easy to transport.

I lowered the body into the garment bag, set her hands so they wouldn't get caught in the zipper, and sealed the bag.

He picked up my gun. "All right, carry her out of here like you're carrying a suit."

"Did she plan this?" I asked.

"Do you really think she committed suicide?" Bradley laughed. "I told her the plan was for her to lure you here, and I'd take care of you. So she did. I had a change of plans. Having local accomplices is a pain. They had to go."

"What's Tara doing here?"

"I needed Ms. Waters to join our party, but they were going together to dinner, so I had to nab them both." He pointed at Denise. "You grab the bat."

Denise lowered her arms, grabbed her black handbag from behind her, picked up the bat, and held it upside down by her other hand.

He stuck his gun in his coat pocket and pointed with his finger. "To the door, nice and calm, and out into the parking lot. Ustick, you go first."

If Tara was out front, I could sacrifice myself to give her a chance to get away. "Ladies first."

He snarled. "You're lady-like enough for me. Go."

I sighed and walked with Denise right behind me and Tara bringing up the rear.

Bradley led me out to a late model Silver SUV. He used a remote to open the trunk. "Put the body and the bat in the back."

I did as he said and so did Denise.

He opened the doors. "Get in the back."

Anything but that, this was humiliating enough. I sighed. "You don't want me in the back."

"Do you want me to put a hole in your head right here?"

Maybe not anything. I put up my hands. "Okay, but don't say I didn't warn you."

I got in the back seat. Tara sat beside me and Denise sat by her. Tara was quietly praying. Her fingers were moving like she was holding an imaginary set of rosary beads. Denise clutched her handbag like it was a teddy bear.

Bradley started up the car.

At the first stop light, I tried the door handle.

Bradley chuckled. "Do you really think I'd be dumb enough not to lock the doors?"

Escape was out for now, but I could settle some accounts. I glanced at Tara. "I'm sorry for getting you into this mess, and I'm sorry for some of the awkwardness when we first met."

Tara smiled. "You're forgiven."

We turned down a bumpy stretch of road. The car lurched up and down, taking my stomach along with it.

"Ustick, are you okay?" Tara whispered.

My dinner threatened to revolt. I grimaced. "I'm getting sick. That's why I don't ride in the backseat."

She gasped. "Mr. Bradley, stop this car, or you'll regret it."

Bradley laughed. "Whatcha gonna do to me?"

My stomach's revolt came to fruition. I turned my head away from Tara and heaved up dinner all over the floorboard.

This was just not my night. Did I have to throw up in front of Tara? Tara sighed and put her hand on my shoulder. "It's okay."

Up front, Bradley growled and cursed. "Why did you do that?"

I snarled. "I get motion sickness. That's why you don't put me in the back seat."

"This is a rental! I'm going to have to clean it before I take it back!"

Tara said, "You could always turn yourself into the police and let them take care of it."

"Don't get smart!"

Tara said, "Denise, do you have any crackers?"

She said, "I've got some antacid. Will that help?"

Never take medicine from a poisoner. "Antacids don't help."

"Suit yourself."

I closed my eyes. "You know what the worst part about this is?"

"What?" Tara asked.

"I'm never going to see my son again."

She raised her left eyebrow. "I didn't know you had one."

"I don't talk about him much."

"Are you ashamed of him?"

"No, of myself. After a random hook up, the woman came to me, said I'd gotten her pregnant, and demanded money for an abortion. I insisted on taking her to Stanton Healthcare, and they showed her a free sonogram of Jensen. She decided to put him up for adoption. We made the mistake of telling our mothers about the plan. Each of them demanded we give the baby to a family member, if to anyone. Jensen's maternal grandmother in particular insisted she keep the baby."

"Why?"

"She wanted someone to leave the family business to and feared her daughter might never have another child. Anyway, when he was born, I held him and babysat on weekends. I fell in love with the little guy. I thought what I did couldn't have been bad because he was so precious." I wiped a tear from my eye. "Then Jensen's mother announced she was taking him and moving back to Washington so she could go to medical school. I wanted to keep him here and was willing to go to court to fight but . . ." I swallowed hard. "My mom said mothers knew best, that I wasn't ready to raise a child. She guilt-tripped me into letting him go. And now I see him one week a year. I talk to him every other night."

Tara rubbed her chin "Why didn't you move to Seattle?"

"For one, I can't get rid of my house. I owe too much, and I can't afford to maintain two residences. Sometimes, I think that's not the real reason."

Tara stroked her forearm. "Maybe, it's because everyone, including your mother, has told you that you're not needed or that you're harmful."

I sighed. That made sense. "Maybe you should switch to psychology."

She sent me a weak smile.

I frowned. That was assuming we made it out alive.

The sun was setting in an empty gravel parking lot. The SUV came to a stop at a wooden curb. "Stay seated until I unlock the door." Bradley opened his door and scooted out, stepped about ten feet back from the car and waved us out with the gun. He opened the back. "Ustick, grab the body."

I walked to the open back and scooped up Diana King's body.

Bradley pointed the gun toward a wooden curb. I ambled over to him.

He backed away, grabbed the bat, and pointed toward an overgrown path. "Ustick, you go first, then Denise and Ms. Burke."

After about a quarter of a mile of walking through the overgrown grass, he said, "Ustick, turn off to the side trail on the left."

I did so, and the other three followed. We'd slipped into a cemetery. On a worn down wooden arch at the front of the cemetery hung a sign. The top part was faded beyond recognition but the bottom said Methodist Cemetery. A little past us, a grave marker read simply, "Ida May Jones 1905-1982."

I eyed the dozens of unkempt graves. *That looks like the newest one.*

Bradley waved his gun. "Move, I don't have all night." He led us to a far corner of a cemetery where two fresh graves were dug. Two shovels stuck out of the mound of dirt. "Now drop Dr. King into one of the graves."

I placed the garment bag right side against the side of the grave and then jumped down inside.

Bradley shouted, "What do you think you're doing?"

"Lowering her in respectfully rather than throwing her in like trash."

Once I finished placing the body in the grave, I climbed up.

He sneered. "I'm not going to be so gentle with you." He lined Tara and I in front of one grave and put Denise in front of the grave that I'd put his other partner in and he took a few steps back from us.

So, this was it.

Bradley beamed like a farmer showing off his prize animals. "This was pretty clever of me. My aunt had me read Chesterton the one summer I was with her. I forgot most of it, but I remembered one story where the detective asked, 'Where does a wise man hide a leaf? In a forest. And where does a wise man hide a body? Where there are a bunch of other bodies.'"

Tara frowned. "I pity you if that's all you learned from Chesterton."

"You're the only one I regret killing. You weren't in the plan. Tonight, you disappear away from the face of the Earth. Nobody will find the bodies. All I have to do is fill in the hole."

"You have a choice. You can let us go, confess, and save your soul."

Bradley laughed. "Lady, I don't have a soul. Neither do you. Right now, you have a few minutes reprieve. Until I get bored with your boyfriend here."

I grimaced. No use showing fear. Time to keep talking and hope for a miracle. "I'll try and be more entertaining. I wish you'd found a good Catholic cemetery. I don't know what will bother Mom worse: that I died or that I was buried as a Methodist."

Bradley raised his fist like he would have decked me, if he wasn't ten feet away. "I don't want a standup act. What do you know about this case?"

"All I know is what I read in the papers."

He pointed his gun at Tara and rested his finger on the trigger. "You sure about that? She's what? Maybe 115 pounds. You know what a .45 would do to a woman her size?"

My stomach turned. Dear God. "I'll answer any question you have, but why do you want to know?"

"To see how much work I got to do to cover my tracks."

"Sure, I'll share, but get that gun off the lady and on to me."

He put the gun on me. "If you insist. Now talk."

On the bright side, it would buy us time. "It all began as a simple political mission for you. The Idaho Brotherhood of Labor didn't want Hernandez to get elected and brought you in from out of state to support the governor. You found the governor was in real trouble. Not only was he seen as out of touch, but people liked Ignacio Hernandez. So you hired private investigators. By the way, why'd you hire local guys?"

"Unions usually insist on it."

"Well, after Newton turned you down, you went to Sheryl Thompson and Associates, and they investigated him thoroughly and found there was less on him than on Miley Cyrus. During the course of your investigation, you met Denise Waters. The two of you conspired to get Diana King, a hypnotherapist, to plant the suggestion in the minds of three patients that Ignacio Hernandez was the man behind their assaults. Later, you deceived a couple more victims for good measure."

Tara broke in. "Denise, how could you have done this thing?"

Denise smiled. "Easy. Some people are meant to rule. I'm one of them."

I said, "The way I figure it, Denise planned to get rewarded for betraying Hernandez. The governor would appoint a legislator to some higher office in the state government, and Denise would take the legislator's vacated seat."

Tara glowered. "A legislative seat? You did all this for a legislative seat? All this pain, all these deaths?"

"Of course not, you twit." Denise laughed and sneered. "Once I get that seat, there's no limit to how high I'll rise." She bit her lip. "I guess I should say how far I could've risen."

Well, apparently she'd learned all the right lessons in self-esteem anyway.

Tara said, "I don't understand this. I thought you cared about—"

Bradley cut her off. "You care about issues. The saps at the Brotherhood of Labor office care about issues. I care about power. So does my ex-partner over there." He gestured towards Denise. "Now, let's skip the moral outrage and get on with it."

I said, "One thing I haven't been able to figure out. What is your angle in all this?"

"You don't know? Good. That's one thing I don't have to worry about then. Continue."

So he wasn't going to be a good sport and tell? No fair. "When King hypnotized them, she suggested telling the story in general terms with months and years without days. That way, Hernandez couldn't establish he had an alibi unless he had one for the whole month. You made it impossible for him to disprove the charge, and he had to do that. In the court of public opinion, it's guilty until proven innocent, the constitution be damned."

Fallen leaves crunched in the distance.

Was that a human or an animal? I spoke louder. "Dr. King made one mistake. She didn't take the physical dimensions of Hernandez into account. Katrina Robles was a tall woman, and the person who assaulted her towered over her. I made a mistake that cost her life when I hinted that Hernandez is a short man. She called the campaign office and found out Hernandez's height."

Tara gasped. "I remember that call! I thought it was odd."

I nodded. "As she headed to work, Katrina called and texted Diana King repeatedly. Likely, she suspected what had happened after King made no effort to return her call. She'd broken up a close friendship over her use of hypnosis. That night, she left a message apologizing to her alienated friend, and she told one of her bar patrons not to pursue hypnotherapy. She knew.

"What Katrina didn't know is that Diana King was also panicking. That's when she placed a call to you, Bradley. Or was it Denise?"

Bradley said, "Since it doesn't matter, it was to me."

It'd bought me a few more seconds and that mattered. "All three of you faced professional ruin if this came out. You assured King you'd handle it and talked to Denise. You then planned to kill Katrina Robles and frame Ignacio Hernandez for the act. To avoid your calls continuing to show up on her cell phone bill, Denise bought a pay-as-you-go cell phone over the Washington border while Hernandez was in Moscow. That new phone would allow you two to communicate on the night of murder without obviously giving away her alibi of being asleep the whole time. Of course, when purchase records for the phone are found, that alibi won't stand up well."

Denise grimaced as she clutched her open handbag by its handle.

I continued. "Denise, Hernandez, and Hearst spent the night in Caldwell. Denise made the reservations and got a second key to the Hernandez's room.

They all had cups of cocoa together. She broke open a couple of her sleeping pills and put them in both men's cocoa, ensuring they would not awake until morning." I took a breath, wetting my lips. "Later, she snuck into Hernandez's room, stole his keys, and drove out to the Caldwell airport."

I looked Bradley in the eyes. "Meanwhile, you had chartered a plane and had the pilot lie and say he had no passenger. She drove the Lincoln Town car to Caldwell and gave you Hernandez's keys as well as instructions on how to get into the gun room. You went to the Hernandez place, stole the gun, and then drove out to Katrina Robles' apartment. That's where you made another big mistake. You underestimated her. You weren't careful as you broke in, and she knew you were there and fought. That's how the baseball bat got blood on it. The blood is yours. Somehow, you did manage to shoot her eventually. The only thing that saved you from having the entire Boise PD there on the spot was that she had loud music playing. That drowned out the sound of the fight, and the neighbors had their own noise."

"I was lucky that way." Bradley sneered.

"But you made a mess in the process and needed to clean up. Otherwise, the police would've quickly eliminated Hernandez. Any remaining DNA traces will take longer to test. By that time, the primary will be over. Though, I don't know why you carelessly left your DNA all over a crime scene."

Bradley laughed. "The government doesn't have my DNA on file. I've been a good boy, mostly. The DNA might not match Hernandez's, but they wouldn't know who it did belong to."

A twig snapped somewhere in the forest.

Bradley glanced behind him from where the twig had snapped.

I jumped over the open grave.

Bradley turned back towards me, gun leveled at me.

I hit the ground.

Two bullets sailed past me right into his chest cavity.

Bradley turned toward Denise, his mouth agape and his eyes widening. He stumbled and fell down six inches from me.

Denise held a .22 in her hand. Her purse had an exit bullet hole ripped through it. She'd fired the gun while it was still in the purse.

She pointed the gun at us. "Tara, stay put. Ustick get back over to her."

I dusted myself off and walked back around the grave.

So much for that.

She strode to Bradley. Using a napkin, she reached into the inside pocket, and grabbed a letter out. She pried the .45 from Bradley's hands and put it in his coat pocket. She cackled. "Bart, you made the same fatal mistake twice: underestimating an Idaho woman."

Yeah, only a sexist amateur wouldn't think to search her purse. "Now what, Denise?"

"Continue. I want to know it all." She removed my 9 mm from Bradley's coat pocket, took the safety off, and deposited her gun back in her purse.

I gulped. "Well, with you getting your beauty rest, Bradley called King, and they cleaned up the crime scene at Katrina's. He then left incriminating evidence behind to the point the finger at Hernandez. A broken lamp was discarded where any cop could find it with a broken-off piece of the lamp-shade left inside the car, and the murder weapon was planted at Hernandez's house. Diana King got rid of the Kirby by giving it to a junk collector."

I shook my head. "And then there was the second murder. You got an old Tylenol bottle just like the one Mrs. Hernandez used for her sugar, and you mixed in the artificial sugar with poison. When we took our break, you went over to Mrs. Hernandez's purse and switched your bottle for her bottle. You put a relatively mild dose that would weaken her heart enough for a pack of bloodthirsty journalists to finish her off when they went into a feeding frenzy. While the rest of us were focused on her, you switched the bottles back, never realizing she'd spilled some of the tainted sweetener into her purse."

Denise frowned and glanced at Tara. "I wondered why they dropped the charges against you. Now I know."

Tara quivered and stared at Denise. "She was like a mother to us! How could you kill her?"

"It was business. It was supposed to drive Hernandez from the race and ensure the governor's re-election. If I'd known it wouldn't work, I wouldn't have taken the risk."

I glanced at Tara. Her mouth was agape as she stared like she'd seen a monster. Of course she had. I glanced at Denise.

Denise sneered. "Really, Tara, I didn't kill anyone. You did."

Tara gaped. "What?"

"Before one drop of blood was spilled, Hernandez was ready to quit, but you had to keep him going. You made us go to extreme measures. You and him." She pointed the gun at me. "Ustick the meddler, Ustick the busybody, this little scene is happening because you wouldn't leave well enough alone. By the way, how did you know it was me?"

I said, "It was the purple bag. You're a precise woman. Purse and shoes always match. If you're carrying a green purse, you're wearing green shoes. If you're carrying a red purse, you're wearing red shoes. If you're carrying an offbeat purse, you're wearing gray shoes. And another thing, you don't ever wear pink and purple. You carry small handbags, never over-the-shoulder bags. Your style choices are well document on Facebook. So, at this office meeting, you come in, and you're carrying a big purple bag with a shoulder strap and you're wearing green shoes."

I smiled. "I asked, 'why?' The answer was obvious. Your normal purses were much too small to hide Mrs. Hernandez's jumbo-sized Tylenol bottle.

You didn't realize that until you were going out the door, so you grabbed the purple purse. Which, by the way, is down at police headquarters. Killing us won't get you out of trouble."

Denise grimaced. "What else do you know?"

"Diana King hypnotized that woman to kill Tara Burke. It sounds like your idea."

"A pity she missed." Denise laughed.

Tara wept. "Why frame me for the murder of Mrs. Hernandez?"

"Why else? You're an annoying, little, self-righteous prick." She glanced at me. "And you denied me a man. He's less than nothing, but no one gets away with denying me anything."

She framed Tara for murder because I wouldn't go to bed with her and found Tara more attractive? Sheesh. This chick could challenge Norman Bates to a creepy contest.

Tara was sputtering. "I haven't been on a date since last summer."

Denise laughed. "Don't be so naive. I expect men to be cooperative prey. You spending your life in prison for murder and remembered as a man-crazy chick like Monica Lewinsky would be perfect irony. However, that wasn't the original plan. It'd be ruled death by natural causes and a grief-stricken Ignacio Hernandez would withdraw and the governor would be re-elected."

I said, "It would've worked, if Newton hadn't discovered the poison."

"What else?" Denise asked.

Branches crunched.

I looked through the trees and metal gleamed from somewhere. Could it be the cavalry, or an animal with a tag? I shrugged. "I know you tried to kill me by tampering with my car when I was parked outside the Brotherhood of Labor. I was still in the parking lot when it gave way."

She frowned. "I should've gone with the plan of breaking in your house and poisoning the milk."

"Why didn't you?"

"Home security system. I didn't want to set something off."

I laughed. "The sticker in the window came with the place. I don't have the system."

She grimaced. "I should've had one of those. Then you couldn't break into my apartment. A neighbor saw you leaving and reported it to me."

"I didn't break in. Someone gave me a key."

Her hand tightened around the gun. "That swine!"

Another crunch came from the forest.

Had to keep her distracted. "I know why you're keeping us alive."

She swiped the sweat from her brow with her free hand. "Enlighten me."

"You don't have a plan, and that is crippling. You improvise poorly."

"Shut up."

"You plan everything. You plan your outfits a week in advance. You plan murders down to the last details but when your plans are frustrated, what do you do? Even on our date, when I refused your advances, you were thrown off balance. You had to go and think of a new plan."

"What?" Tara squeaked. "You refused her?"

I looked in her eyes. "Who is the liar?" I whirled back to Denise. "You gave yourself away with the purse thing for the same reason you didn't poison me. It frustrated your plans."

Denise gaped.

"Your accomplices ruined your brilliant plans. They were inept fools, weren't they? King chose a woman who Hernandez couldn't have assaulted. Then Bradley storms in and makes a big mess."

Denise sneered. "They paid for their improvisations, but I won't."

"No, for lack of your own plan, you intend to stick to Bradley's plans, kill us, and bury all three of us. You're hesitating. Why? Problems nag you. Do you even know what they are?"

She laughed, her right eye twitching. "You tell me."

"How will you explain your absence from the after-debate meeting?"

"Good point. I'll have to think of something."

"Fine, look at those shovels and at Bradley's hands. Clear nail polish, freshly applied with a professional manicure, probably before he left Seattle. Who did he hire to dig those holes?" I raised my right hand.

"Likely, they were illegals who won't want the attention making trouble would get them."

That possibility wasn't nearly scary enough for my purposes. I waved my left hand. "A union man like him, hire undocumented, unorganized workers? No, they were mafia people. They'll know you killed one of their friends when they never hear from Bradley again, but you do show up. What do the grave-diggers know? Where are they? You don't know. It's no good."

She sneered. "It is no good—for you."

"Then you're going to use Bradley's gun to shoot us and put the gun in his hand. You tell the police that he held all of us at gunpoint, but he had to turn away from you to shoot us and then you shot him. You expect to be lauded as a hero who saved your own life and caught a killer. I bet you're already mentally writing your ad for the NRA."

She pointed the gun directly me. "Very perceptive, Ustick."

"You've still got problems. The police will wonder why he did it. The cops won't believe that Bradley decided to shoot two random Republicans, a private detective, and a phony doctor with no reason. I've already sent my report to a blogger covering the debate tonight. It's got all my suspicions and all my proof in it. Plus, there's that matter of angles, if you're planning on shooting us with Bradley's gun and hoping the police will think he shot us.

Police are very precise about that. Bradley's a full nine inches taller than you. You firing and him firing have entirely different trajectories, and the cops can trace all that. If you try and raise your hand higher to mess with the trajectory so it'll look like he shot us, that'll be awkward, and you might miss."

She relaxed her hold on the gun.

I spread my arms. "You have another option. You drop the gun. We all go back to the car and call the cops. We tell them our story. The whole thing. Now, they may believe us and charge you with murder, but you may get off. You're pretty clever at those things. If you get a good number of men on the jury, I'd bet on at least a hung jury. Plus the prosecutor really wants to stick this to Hernandez, so their political agenda may also get you off."

Over her shoulder, in the darkness, a man crept through the cemetery. He ducked behind headstones and moved forward at a deliberate pace. As he grew closer, I spotted that he wore a flannel shirt and had a gun drawn.

Newton. Our gazes met, and he put a finger to his lips.

I never thought I'd be so glad to see him.

Denise snapped her fingers, tightened her hold on the gun, and grinned at me. "Why don't I kill you, bury you, and leave? I'll drive his rented SUV as far as it will take me, buy myself a new wardrobe, and assume a new identity in Portland. I'll rebrand myself as a moderate Democrat, create a whole new look: hair, make-up everything. I'll use Bradley's credit card to pay for it. Back in Idaho, my disappearance will be considered a tragic mystery of state politics. The governor and Hernandez will issue statements about the tragedy of my disappearance and annual prayer vigils will be held in my memory."

"I don't like it."

She smirked. "Not nearly as much as I don't like it, but you've made a lot of trouble. You should've stayed out of my way. As your punishment, I'll kill your girlfriend first, slowly and painfully." She leveled the gun at Tara. "Once you've watched her die, I'll kill you."

A twig snapped.

Denise turned.

I swooped Tara into my arms, jumped into the grave, positioning my body between her and Denise.

Four nine millimeter rounds exploded overhead.

Tara quivered against my chest. "Christ, have mercy."

A body fell through the open grave.

Chapter 23

Denise Waters, would-be U.S. Senator, a woman born to rule, lay dead in a wide grave in the middle of nowhere. She was still clutching her purse.

Tara wrapped her arms around the body and wept.

I opened the purse, removed the paper Denise had taken from Bradley, and shoved it in my coat pocket.

Tara continued to sob.

Jerry Newton called down, "Ustick, Tara, are you okay?"

I called back, "Yeah!"

"You guys come on up. The sheriff's department will be there in a few minutes."

"Come on," I said to Tara.

She wiped her eyes. "No, I'll stay with the body until they come."

"You don't owe her anything. She wasn't your friend."

"But I was hers." Tara loosed a fresh round tears.

I patted her shoulder. "I'm sorry."

Newton extended his arm down and helped me out of the grave.

"How'd you find me?" I dusted off my suit.

Newton shrugged. "You left that GPS tracker on your phone and I tracked you here."

"Why did you do that?"

"I went up to Moscow because Denise had made a campaign visit there.

I found out she purchased some of the artificial sweetener Mrs. Hernandez had used at a GNC. Anyway, I stopped for dinner when I got back and read your email message while I was eating. Realized you were walking into a trap. I got here as soon as I could and called the sheriff when I arrived."

"Well, thanks."

Newton frowned. "You could have gotten yourself killed tonight, acting like a hotshot."

Why did he have to make a point of rubbing my face in this? I already knew I'd been an idiot. I clenched my teeth. "Maybe I wouldn't have had to go it alone, if you and the cops weren't so busy playin' footsie that you wouldn't let me in on anything."

Detective Weston emerged from the trail and strode toward us. "Jerry, what's going on?"

"We have three homicides. I saw Bart Bradley's death from the distance. He'd been holding hostage Denise Waters, Ustick, and Tara Burke. Waters shot Bradley and held the other two at gunpoint. She turned on me and we exchanged fire. Her shots went wide but mine found their mark. She dropped the gun after she was hit." Newton pointed to the left of the headstone. "It landed about five yards away."

I nodded. "I'll back him up on that. If he hadn't come here, we'd be dead. There's also the body of Diana King in the other unmarked grave. Next to her is Katrina Robles' softball bat. If you do a DNA test, you should find Bart Bradley's blood. That will place Bradley at the scene of the crime. He, Diana King, and Denise Waters were in it on together. You'll be able to close the case on Katrina Robles and Mrs. Hernandez."

Weston glowered. "So you decided to have your own little Shakespearean tragedy, and I'm Fortenbras coming to carry away the bodies with the help of the local sheriff's office."

"Fortenbras?"

"A Dutch nobleman who came on stage after everyone was already dead in *Hamlet*." Weston pointed his index finger at me. "No doubt the county prosecutor could come up with something to charge you with for tonight's charade. As it is, you're lucky. Everyone's gonna want this case to go away. But I suggest you not try this again."

I smirked. "Next homicide's all yours, Fortenbras."

"It'd better be." Weston walked over to the grave, knelt, and glanced down at Tara. "Ma'am, we need to get in there." He extended his hand.

He lifted Tara out of the grave and onto the ground.

"Thank you kindly, sir." She approached Newton, teary-eyed. "Thank you for saving our lives." She swallowed. "You did what was necessary."

Newton nodded. "I'd hoped to sneak up unnoticed and take her from behind. It didn't work out that way."

Weston patted Newton's shoulder. "There are a couple squad cars. Wait with the officers over in the parking. We'll get your statements in a little bit."

I nodded and Tara and I walked towards the parking lot.

Tara said, "Easter is coming in a few weeks. Have you ever given any thought to coming back to the Church?"

"I already have. The first day I nearly got you killed. Been attending mass the last two Sundays."

"Really? I haven't seen you."

I shrugged. "Been attending Saint Joan's in Eagle. From what you said that Saturday in the campaign office, it was clear I was a topic of gossip."

Gasping, she stopped. "Oh, Ustick, I'm sorry. Your mother knew my mother and they talked. That's all. You shouldn't be driving all the way out to Eagle. You should attend your home parish. If there is any further gossip about you, the gossipers will have me to answer to."

I glanced at my watch outside the Hernandez Campaign's office. It was eleven thirty.

Hearst met me at the door. "Ustick, Mr. Hernandez is waiting for you in my office."

"Fine," I said.

He touched my shoulder as if he were my father. "Did my relationship with Denise come out?"

I stared at him. "Seriously? Three human beings are dead, including your ex-lover, and you're worried about your affair coming out."

"So I'm self-absorbed and egotistical. I've earned the right to be with my expertise and my decades of service to my country. This has been like a sword of Damocles over me, and I have to know if it's still hanging."

I shook my head. "Tara heard me mention a friend of hers had given me a key, so the police questioned me about it. I told them I got a key from an ex-lover and I wouldn't reveal the name unless it was determined to be necessary. They're trying to wrap this up faster than a reality TV show makeover with only half an hour to go, so I doubt they'll ask."

Hearst let out a sigh. "Thank God. I decided that this primary campaign will be my last. I'm going to retire and really try and make up for lost time with my family. I owe that chance to you. Who knows what would have happened if it had come out?"

"If you don't mind, I have to settle up with Hernandez."

"Come on." Hearst led me into the office.

Hernandez sat behind the desk. There was more gray around his temple. He frowned. "Mr. Ustick, you had something new to report?"

"Yes, sir." I pulled the piece of paper out of my inside pocket and slid it across to Hernandez.

He read it and handed it to Hearst.

Hearst clucked his tongue and read the note. "'Provided Bart Bradley gives pivotal assistance in securing the re-nomination of Governor James Flanagan, I guarantee full and complete cooperation from the governor with any reasonable request. Signed Frederick Wexler, Campaign Manager' By God, he even wrote it on campaign stationery."

I said, "Sounds like a bribe to me."

Hearst nodded. "If Governor Flanagan honored this deal, it'd be worth millions in state contracts. If Bradley had used this to get political appointees into office, they'd have given him kickbacks, too. Whatever the case, it's the end of the governor."

"If it's made public," Hernandez said.

Hearst raised his right eyebrow. "What are you talking about?"

"Whatever his faults, do you really think the governor would give his consent to such a shady deal?"

"His campaign manager did."

Hernandez scowled. "You didn't answer the question, Hearst."

"It doesn't matter. He's responsible for those under him."

Hernandez grimaced. "On that score, neither of us are qualified."

Hearst smiled like a hungry lion. "Not at all. Denise was an operative for the governor. This all began with that worm Wexler signing a deal with big labor. They've made us suffer, now it's time to return the favor."

Hernandez leaned back in his office chair. "I got in this race because I thought we needed a new direction to make our state better: to get schools that served the interests of students, to create a tax code that will create an environment that will draw good jobs to the state. For the past month or so, I've been talking about sexual assault charges, murders, and had people suspecting everyone around me of crimes. I've lost my wife. I've been betrayed by and lost a young woman I'd treated like a daughter. We've been in a mud pit. The question I keep coming back to is, 'Where does it stop?' The answer is, 'It stops here with me.' Now."

Hearst sputtered. "But—"

"But if I win on the basis of this letter, will I have any mandate to do the things I care about?" Hernandez put his hands behind his head. "No, the people deserve a break from scandal. Mr. Ustick, keep the paper. If the police require it, hand it over. Otherwise I don't want it ever produced."

I shoved it in my pocket. "As you wish, sir."

"Sir, I better get going. I'm tired." Hearst crept out the door.

I started to follow him.

Hernandez said, "Mr. Ustick."

I turned to face him. "Yes, sir."

"We need a head of campaign security for the duration of the primary. Would you be interested in the job?"

"I'd consider it. What would the pay be?"

"Twenty dollars an hour. I suspect overtime would be included. It'd be for about two months."

I didn't have anything better to do. "Sure."

"Excellent. Start on Wednesday, after Denise's memorial service." He turned opened the blinds, and stared out into the dark night.

The phone rang.

I groaned and glanced at the clock. Six A.M. on Saturday no less. My black sleep mask lay discarded on the floor. I rubbed my eyes and picked up the phone.

A voice snapped, "This is Steve Danner at the Brotherhood of Labor."

"Is that a fact?"

"Yes, and I read the story published online by that blogger. You didn't withhold any information that would harm the brotherhood of Labor. You said you would!"

"I said I'd do my best and I did. That story didn't say that I suspect you of being accomplices in my attempted murder."

"What are you talking about?"

I groaned. "Whose idea was it to get our little soirée together?"

Silence.

Danner finally said, "Bart Bradley suggested it."

"When I got there, you stalled me long enough with fluffy chit chat to ensure Denise Waters had plenty of time to sabotage my car."

"I didn't know anything about any sabotage."

"And then there's the fact Bradley expected to wield a lot of power, and I bet he wasn't going to do it himself, from hundreds of miles away. I wouldn't be surprised if he hadn't mentioned some little, high-paying job he had for you after the election."

Silence.

I ran my hand through my messy hair. "At best, you were a useful idiot. At worst, you're an unindicted co-conspirator in the biggest scandal in state history. Either way, if I were you, I'd take my lumps and like it and pray the cops don't look too close at Bradley's correspondence. Now, if you'll excuse me, I have an appointment with the sandman."

Chapter 24

I wore a gold suit with a black tie as I stood by a dry eraser board sign that said, "Republican Primary Election Night Party."

Before me was the ballroom of a hotel almost overflowing with media people and party activists. Signs for hundreds of candidates hung on the walls. Flannigan and Hernandez each had dozens.

Jerry Newton strode into the room wearing a short-sleeved blue polo shirt and Khakis. "Ustick!"

I met him half way. "Newton, long time no see."

Newton nodded. "I haven't seen you since the inquest."

"I've been busy gallivanting across Idaho for the last seven weeks. It's a beautiful state. I'd never been much out of the Treasure Valley."

Newton pointed at my "I Voted" sticker. "I see you joined the ranks of responsible citizens."

Cheeks warm, I groaned. "Only to make Tara happy. With Jared Bach becoming Deputy Campaign Manager, Tara has been running the communications operations for the campaign. But today, she's been making phone calls since seven o'clock in the morning. When I left for the party tonight, she was still making calls up in the northern part of the state. I asked if I could do anything, and she gave me her spiel about voting. I told her I wasn't registered, and she said we had same day registration in Idaho. She'd worked so hard, I couldn't deny her. So, boom, I voted in the Republicans' primary and earned the right to drink their liquor and hit their snack tables."

Newton laughed. "So when is the Burke-Ustick wedding?"

Face blazing, I glared, waved both hands, and shook my head. "We're only seeing each other as friends. Even then, it's mainly to get something to eat after a long night at the office. Well, we also go to mass together, of course."

"Then you still have a full, active girlfriends roster?"

"No, actually. Two of them found permanent beaus rather than a nice date. And Leah, well, we're just friends, too."

"Interesting." Newton coughed, muttering something.

If the cough's mutter had sounded any closer to "love triangle," I'd have decked him.

Newton added, "So, how's your son?"

I beamed. "Hernandez went to bat for me! I'm going to get him for a month in the Summer and at Thanksgiving this year and Christmas next year. Before Hernandez called, Jenson's grandmother was going to visit Europe without him and send him to summer camp."

"I'm glad to hear it."

Hearst stepped out into the hall. "Newton, Ustick, Hernandez wants to see you up in his private suite."

I nodded. "We'll head up on up. How is it looking?"

Hearst bit his lip. "We're leading in all but five counties and Flannigan's lead in Canyon County is a lot less than it should be. But it's still early, and very little of Canyon or Ada is in. However, Mr. O'Dell's not fairing so well. He's losing 43 of 44 counties."

I frowned. "Does that surprise you?"

Hearst shook his head and lowered his voice. "No. He's not a good campaigner. I really was nervous about Hernandez's endorsement. It doesn't look like it'll drag us down though."

Hearst picked up the phone. "Jared, where are those results for Elmore County? They've been at three precincts for the past hour. What's going on down there? And I still don't have any results out of Benewah County. Call them, get them on the phone. I need this info and I need it now. This is the night where all the work pays off, and I can't wait for the Secretary of State's site to update. I need numbers before they get there."

I chuckled. Hearst was getting in some election night drama prior to retirement. I led Newton through the row of hotel rooms towards the stairway leading to the third floor.

Newton pointed at the "Bixby for Senate" signs outside of one hotel room door. "What's the set up with all these rooms? It looks like most of them have these signs."

"From what I gather, on election night, most Republican campaigns rent a room here and give free food to anyone who comes to their private party."

"Are the candidates here?"

I shrugged. "Earlier in the ballroom, Hearst pointed out a Congressman and Senator to me, but I really don't care."

"Typical." Newton laughed. "Let's go see Mr. Hernandez."

Fifteen minutes later, we finally reached Hernandez's door up on the third floor. David Gerber, my new assistant, stood at attention like he was in Afghanistan guarding a general's tent.

He stood at attention. "Evening, sir."

At least he didn't salute this time. "At ease, Soldier. I'm only here to see Mr. Hernandez." I knocked. "It's Ustick, I have Newton with me."

"Come in, gentleman," he said.

We ambled in. Hernandez sat alone on a standard issue blue hotel chair. The room had a queen sized bed with a loud orange bed spread and another chair on which Hernandez had draped his jacket. A yellow legal pad sat on the nightstand next to Hernandez's chair.

He muted the television. "Ustick, there are going to be changes in the campaign in the next few weeks, if we win the primary. Hearst is retiring, and we'll have a new campaign manager. Jared is also leaving us for missions work overseas. Tara will be with me a while longer, but I've insisted she go back and finish her law degree. Taking a year off with the campaign has been more than enough. If we win tonight, she'll be leaving in late August. That leaves you, and we may not need a private security detail. If the primary goes the way I hope, the campaign's going to be pretty low-key until August, and I may get some protection from the State Police when the campaign heats up."

I nodded. "I understand."

"Now, I don't know about investigations, but I do know about business, and the Valley can't support another private investigator business." Hernandez put one hand on my shoulder and another hand on Newton's shoulder. "You boys have had some differences. I'd suggest you patch them up."

Newton swallowed and looked me in the eye. "My attitude was wrong when I defended my actions of withholding information from you. I made you a commitment, and I should have owned up to it."

I nodded. "For my part, I should haven't been an idiot and played like I was Sherlock Holmes. And you deserved to know about my stunt with the Ford Fontaine way sooner."

Hernandez beamed. "I am glad to see you working things out. Newton needs your intuition, and you need his business sense."

"What do you mean?"

Hernandez laughed. "I've had cars that cost less than your expense account on that case."

I sighed. "I've been thinking about trying to move to Washington, but I still have a house I'd need to get rid of. So long as I'm here, I'd rather work for Newton than go it alone."

Hernandez nodded. "Work for me through the end of the week, and I'll give you a week's severance pay."

"So you can start on Monday." Newton added to Hernandez, "Thanks for your help."

Hernandez nodded. "Always glad to."

"Well, I'm going to visit the other campaigns' rooms." Newton glanced toward the hall.

"Boys, could you wait a moment?" Hernandez reached into his coat pocket. "Ustick, I had this for you and your son if you want it."

I glanced at it. Plane tickets to Philadelphia and a sight seeing brochure. I smiled and chuckled. Did I need a sightseeing guide to my own hometown? Then again, I knew Boiseans who hadn't seen the Capitol or the MK Nature center. Maybe I'd missed a few sights. "Thanks, Hernandez, but why?"

"Every year for the past decade, I've gone on one of these trips, but it's a trip you don't take alone. I already had the money budgeted for the trip and thought of you and your boy."

"I'd love to show him my old neighborhood. I'll have to work it out with Newton, of course, but I doubt that will be a problem." I grinned. "Thanks for everything,"

Hernandez dipped his head. "I'll see you in the ballroom, however the race turns out."

That was my cue to leave. "Okay, I'll see you then." I ambled down the halls back to the ballroom.

Tara stood by a large Hernandez for Governor sign while a TV reporter stood across from her and asked questions. Tara had changed into an elegant black dress that went to an inch above her knee.

I crab-walked through the maze of people until I was within earshot.

The reporter said, "So how are you feeling tonight?"

She grinned. "We're very encouraged by the early results."

"In recent weeks, some people have noted your boss seems to have lost a step. Doesn't he quite have the same energy?"

Tara blinked. "During this primary election season, every campaign has been grueling. We all are tired and deserve time to rest before the fall."

"Thank you for your time." The reporter glanced to the cameraman. "All right, that was Tara Burke, the Communications Director for the Hernandez campaign. And we're out."

Tara nodded. "Thank you." She removed her mic and joined me.

Newton came over with a plate full of crackers and cheese dip.

Tara leaned on my shoulder. "I am so exhausted, Cole!"

I smiled. *May I never give in and kiss you for being so affectionate.*

Newton raised his eyebrows, staring at me. "She calls you Cole?"

"Uh, yeah, that is my first name."

"Guys!" She put a finger to her lips and pointed at the big screen TV in the corner with Channel 7 on it. I looked up at it.

A guy in his early thirties with a professional haircut said, "Professor, tell us about this strong lead for Hernandez tonight. It's really surprising, given the scandals that engulfed this campaign two short months ago. They had him trailing by double digits."

A pudgy man with a graying beard and bald spot leaned in. "For a while, it looked bad for Hernandez. In the end, though, these scandals did the worst damage to the Flanagan campaign."

"How so?"

"Hernandez endured a great ordeal over allegations the evidence suggests are false. This has created a mass amount of sympathy for the challenger, at least from the Republican electorate. They already distrusted mainstream news organizations. Sympathy is not the best reason to choose a candidate, but it may not hurt in Idaho. The Democrats always face an uphill climb in the fall."

The camera cut to only the young anchor. He put down paper. "We have news from our decision desk in the Idaho Republican Primary. Tonight, the AP projects that Jim Flannigan will not serve a fifth term as Idaho's Governor. Ignacio Hernandez will be the Republican Nominee for Governor of Idaho."

A loud cheer went through the room.

On the TV screen, closed captions text read, "Hernandez leads 53-41% with 48% of precincts reporting."

Tara squeezed me. "Cole, we did it! We did it! Praise God, we did it."

I laughed. "You did it. I just made sure no one got to shoot him."

She released me. "This is fantastic. Let's have a drink to celebrate."

"Sounds good. I'll get a Strawberry Margarita."

"We'll make it two." She left and returned a couple minutes later with the drinks. She handed me mine and raised her glass. "Cheers."

I clicked glasses and took a sip. "So, when is Hernandez coming down?"

"Not until after Flannigan does."

"Why wait?"

"Good manners. When there are still votes being counted, it's not polite to claim victory. Right now, all we have is the AP's call. News organizations have been known to be wrong."

I nodded. "I recall the whole Bush-Gore flap when I was in fifth grade."

"Yeah, but they've not been wrong in Idaho." Tara grinned. "They know the state is very hard to call. When news organizations make a call fairly early like this, they're certain."

"Early? It's ten-thirty."

"The polls have only been closed ninety minutes in the northern part of the state. I wouldn't expect them to be done counting in Boise until two in the morning. So, this is early."

As I finished my latest sweep of the ball room for any hazards, Flannigan entered flanked by Idaho's first lady and his campaign manager, Frederick Wexler. The lines in the governor's face were deeper in the bright lights of the hotel. The man on the stage and the smiling cowboy on the campaign brochures I'd seen bore little resemblance to each other.

Beside him, Wexler spoke into a microphone. "Ladies and gentleman, it is my pleasure to introduce Jim Flanagan, the governor of Idaho."

Everyone stood to their feet and applauded. I glanced at Tara. She was clapping, too, so I joined in.

Flanagan traded positions with Wexler and extended his hands. "Thank you. Thank you very much. Tonight, the people spoke someone else's name. I accept that. I've called Ignacio Hernandez to congratulate him and wish him well as he represents the Republican Party in the Fall and seeks to lead our state for the next four years. Let me say that I'm so proud of our campaign team and the hard work they put in. And I'm also proud of what we've been able to accomplish in the last sixteen years."

A text messaged buzzed through from Marc Hearst. *Come to Suite.*

I slipped my phone back in my pocket.

Newton came up to me. "I volunteered to help on campaign security. Anything I can do?"

"I hadn't been notified." I frowned. "That's happened a few times. I've swept through this area plenty over the last couple hours, so just give one final check. When you see my assistant, David Gerber, help him with the crowd."

Newton nodded.

At another time, I might have tried to give my former boss a hard time, now that I was his boss for all of fifteen minutes, but I just didn't have time. I jogged down the hall over the route I would lead Hernandez down when it was his turn to speak.

I got to his campaign's room. Hernandez sat in the desk chair. His pen danced across a yellow legal pad. Tara and Hearst sat on the bed next to him.

Hearst said, "It'll be a few minutes. We keep getting interrupted."

Gerber entered, followed by a man with graying brown hair. "Sir, the Lieutenant Governor Charles Reuter."

Reuter had a big smile. "Ignacio."

Hernandez put down his legal pad and stood. "Charlie, good to see you."

Reuter shook his hand. "Congratulations on your victory. I'm excited to work with you in the campaign and, I hope, for the next four years."

Hernandez nodded. "Thank you, I'll be glad to have you on my team."

"How's your victory speech coming?"

"Slowly."

The Lieutenant Governor said, "If you'd like, I can deliver my victory speech while you write yours."

"Thank you, I appreciate it."

The incumbent Lieutenant Governor padded out of the room.

I scratched my head. "Isn't that guy the opposition?"

Hearst waved, laughing. "Pay attention. That ended thirty minutes ago. Now he's Hernandez's running mate."

Tara grinned.

Hernandez sighed. "I would've rather had O'Dell, but the voters have decreed Reuter and I must work together, and we're going to have a functional relationship."

I frowned. "Why are you talking like it's November?"

Newton chuckled. "Democrats haven't won the Idaho governorship since 1990. There hasn't been a democratic lieutenant governor since the seventies."

"Still seems a little premature, if you ask me."

Hernandez said, "Mr. Ustick, the only way I know how to do things is with confidence. I entered planning to win and I still plan to win. I don't plan for failure." He grunted. "I'm turning off my cell phone and finishing this speech. I don't want to be disturbed until it's done."

Gerber nodded. "Understood, sir."

Hernandez spent ten more minutes writing it and then passed it to Tara.

After she'd suggested a couple word changes, Hernandez made a couple quick edits and tore off the paper. "I'm ready to go."

I opened the door and said to Gerber, "Go on ahead of us, keep your eyes open, and text me if you run into anything."

He nodded. "Yes, sir."

Hearst said, "Tara, I think you should introduce our next Governor."

Tara blinked. "But this is your dream."

"You've been the heart of this campaign. We wouldn't be here without you. Besides, you've got a great future. I'd rather we celebrate this night with a sunrise rather than a sunset."

Hernandez beamed. "Exactly. Tara, you defeated Slime Incorporated."

Tara nodded. "All right then."

I cleared my throat. "Your public awaits."

"Lead on," Hernandez waved.

We reached the double doors leading to the ballroom.

Tara glanced to me. "I'll go first. You enter with Mr. Hernandez."

I nodded, stood at the doors, and listened.

After the party chairman introduced her, Tara stepped up to the microphone. "Ladies and gentlemen, it is my honor to introduce to you a successful businessman who sets an example of kindness and willingness to help others.

This great leader will take our state in a bold, new, conservative direction. I'm pleased to introduce our next governor, Ignacio Hernandez."

The crowd's cheering wasn't quite at the level of a Broncos game but it was still intense. Those who carried campaign signs waved them. Some people who I'd seen wearing Flanagan buttons earlier in the night were now waving Hernandez signs.

Hernandez came to the stage, patted Tara on the back, and smiled. Tara walked down to join me.

He spread his hands like he wanted to hug everyone in the room. "Ladies and gentlemen, my fellow Republicans, I want to begin by honoring Governor Jim Flanagan and his years of service to our state."

The audience stood and clapped.

"I wish him and his . . . " Hernandez swallowed and closed his eyes and then reopened them. "I wish him and his lovely wife all the best. Tonight, I'm honored and I'm humbled to accept my party's nomination to be the next Governor of the great state of Idaho."

The crowd roared with applause.

Hernandez's lip quivered. He tightened his fists. "I'd intended to share this night with my bride of forty-six years, but she is here only in spirit. We married poor and we shared everything: the toils and heartaches of those early years and the joy of success and service. We raised two daughters and buried them both. One died for her Lord and one died for her country."

The crowd clapped.

Hernandez said, "Knowing Liu has made me a better person. I miss her and am still adjusting to life alone. Those who are legally responsible have been dealt with, but many more are morally responsible."

The audience roared. I glanced around the room and spotted Gordon Thomas scribbling on a notebook. He looked peaked. Frederick Wexler, hung his head and stared into his drink.

"I've been asked at town hall meetings about my feelings about the press and others who played a part in my wife's death, and I've said that I felt like Andrew Jackson when he said, 'I freely forgive all my enemies,' but those who harmed his wife must 'look to God for mercy.'"

The crowd cheered like they'd been served red meat.

Slurred voices chanted, "Impeach Gordon Thomas!"

Drunks. Even I know you can't impeach a journalist.

Hernandez put up his hand. "Tonight, as I was watching the results, I thought about Liu and the type of man she would want me to be. I thought of my Lord and all He has forgiven me for, and I know what He wants me to do. Tonight, I have a declaration to make to everyone who has contributed to my wife's death due to a lust for power or a pursuit of big headlines. I'm holding nothing against you and will freely forgive any who ask."

The audience was still for a moment and then the applause began to sweep in the room as Hernandez wept at the podium.

He wiped his eyes. "Let us be clear, though. This campaign is about the future for the people of Idaho and our children." He spread his arms as if he was offering a hug to the whole room. "And the future starts here!"

I sat in my cubicle in the Hernandez for Governor office. A Rubbermaid box was almost full of personal papers while a cardboard box was half-full of campaign stuff. I crawled under the artificial desk and swept my hand across the floor and grabbed a stray pen. I dropped it into the campaign box.

Tara walked over. "Are you all set?"

I smiled. "Yeah, I've got it pretty well sorted."

"Did Marc Hearst talk to you before he left for the day?"

I nodded. "Yeah, he apologized for blowing up at me after the Robles murder."

"Did you forgive him?"

I laughed. "How could I not forgive after Hernandez's speech? Besides, I now have vouchers for ten Idaho Stampede basketball games next season."

Tara sighed. "I told him he didn't have to buy my forgiveness, but he insisted I accept it as a token of his esteem. So, I'm going to CPAC next year."

"CPAC? What's that?"

"It's a big conservative event in Washington, DC. I'll still have to pay the airfare, but he covered the whole event, including the banquet."

"You should hold out for him buying you a first class ticket and paying your hotel."

She frowned at me. "Cole!"

"Kidding." I leaned against my soon to be former desk. "Still, I wonder what good forgiveness does. If Hearst runs a campaign again, he'll be as big of a pain as he was on this one, and the media will still be irresponsible."

"Forgiveness doesn't change them. It changes us."

I shrugged. "So what are you doing with your week off?"

Tara said, "I'm going fishing on Snake River. It's not Alaska, but it'll do."

"That's a nice part of the state."

She peered at me. "Cole, have you ever thought about what Denise said about us being responsible for those deaths?"

"It was the ravings of a narcissistic sociopath trying to shift the blame."

She shook her head. "That's very clinical of you, but I've thought some times at night that, if I hadn't given that Slime Incorporated speech, six people would be alive who are dead now."

I placed my hand on her shoulder. "That's not your fault. You inspired Hernandez to stick things out. They chose to start the bloodbath."

She sat down in my chair. "Sometimes I wonder if I've got the stomach for this. I believe in being straightforward with people, and I expect the same in return. To be sure, I expected the other side to be out for blood. That didn't surprise me. But I never imagined anyone like Denise could be so treacherous, or that someone like Marc Hearst could be so ruthless, talking about me like I was a disease to be excised."

I smiled. "So you got an education on what politics is really like."

"So you still don't think someone like me should be in politics."

I leaned back. "It seems to me politics is so screwed up because there are less people like you and more people like them. You're a very special person, and I'd hate to see politics ruin you, but I think you're stronger than politics. I mean, you're even better than Helen of Troy."

She laughed. "What do you mean by that?"

"Helen of Troy got men to fight a war, but that was a small accomplishment in those times. You did something really hard. You got me to vote."

Tara cackled.

"I'm serious. I voted, not because I'm sold on the Republican Cause, but because I trusted you. I believe in you. I think you'll be the conqueror in your battle against political corruption."

She stroked my cheek. "That means a lot, Cole."

"It's been great working with you and getting to know you. "

She grinned. "And you can always get ten percent off a temporary tattoo from Evie."

I chuckled. How Tara had managed to talk me into doing that even once, I still didn't know. Then again, she also got Switzerland to vote to go to war because she was so adorable. I grabbed my Rubbermaid box and turned to leave. "I'll see you later."

She swallowed. "Well, yeah, I'll see you on Sunday."

I walked out the door onto the sidewalk. Who was I kidding? I'd see her at mass, maybe run into her around town, but we'd move on with our separate lives. That was the way these things went.

I stopped, put the box down on the pavement, and turned and strode back into the office. Tara was sitting by her desk at the front of the office.

She looked up. "Cole, did you forget something?"

"Yes, I did." I grabbed a chair from the vacant desk across from her and sat. "Over two months ago, I met the most remarkable and wonderful person in the world. I make a huge mistake. I never told her—let me start over." I gulped. "Tara, I never told you how much I admired you for your brains, your integrity, and your courage. You're beautiful inside and out."

She blushed. "Cole."

I put up my hand. "I'm in love with you. I'd like to see you, for us to see if we're right for each other. To be honest, I wrote off any chance of winning you when you lay dying in that hospital bed, the one I put you in."

She put up her hand. "You saved my life."

"It wouldn't have needed saving if not for me. I would totally understand you saying no. I've told myself no a hundred times because I figured I'd never be good enough for you."

She leaned toward me and took my hand in hers. "Don't put me on a pedestal. We've all done things we regret. I'm very fond of you, Cole, and I'd love to go out with you. Where are we going and when?"

My heart was leaping in my chest, and she wanted an itinerary? Now was not the time for a plan. "I'll call you."

She nodded. "That sounds great."

I squeezed her hand, stared into her green orbs, and smiled.

Author's Note

The events in the story are fictitious, but some actual events from Idaho history are referenced.

Ustick mentions someone "blowing up the governor" a hundred years ago. That was the assassination of former Idaho Governor Frank Steunenberg in 1905 by Harry Orchard. He was a paid assassin for the Western Federation of Miners. A monument to Governor Steunenberg sits across from the Idaho Capitol Building.

John McGee is a real former Idaho State Senator who was elected to that body at the age of 31 and became Chairman of the Canyon County Republican Party and later Chairman of the Senate Republican Caucus. He was discussed in the media frequently as a candidate for higher office until, in 2011-2012, a series of scandals put the brakes on his once-promising political career.

To my knowledge, no Idaho governor candidate has ever had allegations of sexual misconduct made against them. My fictional conspiracy was inspired by allegations made against a presidential candidate.

In late 2011, Herman Cain had been close to the top of most polls for the Republican nomination for president. The news media began to report a series of allegations of sexual misconduct against Cain that led Cain to end his campaign. The allegations were mostly anonymous and were often confirmed by sources that were equally anonymous. There were no specific dates; there was no independent corroborating of the evidence to support the claims.

Clearly media standards had declined since the sex scandals of the 1990s.

In the 1990s, political opponents might have whispered allegations with little evidence to support the claims. However, to have the scandal reported by mainstream news organizations required a lot more evidence.

Gennifer Flowers provided audio tapes that confirmed the existence of her affair with then-Governor Clinton. His accusers, such as Paula Jones and Kathleen Willey, provided precise dates, situations, information, and locations where they alleged harassment occurred.

In the case of the Cain allegations, the media pumped out endless days of anonymous allegations and speculation. After weeks of this, one woman finally went on the record, but her account still lacked the details and corroborating evidence that the press required in the 1990s before even reporting allegations.

This book does not provide any answers regarding the truth behind the allegations against Herman Cain. However, questions about the responsibility of the press in the Information Age emerged during the Cain campaign. Those questions certainly did play into how I approached this story.

Acknowledgements

Thanks to my wife Andrea for her editing and formatting assistance. She is an invaluable partner and a great help to me.

I also appreciate everyone who took a look at the early chapters and provided their feedback to help make this a better book.

Regarding my interest in politics, I'm indebted to the former Montana Senate President and former Montana Secretary of State Bob Brown. He is a true gentleman and public servant who spurred my interest in politics when I was thirteen. He was kind even though I thought I knew more than I did.

Rex Stout, Arthur Conan Doyle, G.K. Chesterton Raymond Chandler, William Link, and Richard Levinson and all the creators of beloved detectives from Sherlock Holmes, Nero Wolfe, and Father Brown to Columbo, the Rockford Files, and Monk. Their works encouraged my love of the genre. Without them, this book wouldn't exist.

About the Author

Adam Graham was a state coordinator for three different presidential campaigns. He has served two terms as a precinct committeeman, he is the former Secretary of Flathead County (Montana) Republican Party, and he was a delegate to the 2008 Idaho Republican State Convention. He is also a former candidate for the Idaho Legislature.

He has written articles on US and Idaho politics for a variety of sources, including PJMedia.com and CaffeinatedThoughts.com, and he formerly wrote a blog on politics for the Idaho Press-Tribune.

For the past seven years, he has hosted several old-time radio podcasts, most notably, *The Great Detectives of Old Time Radio*. Graham writes articles on mystery fiction at greatdetectives.net, and is author of the non-fiction ebook, *All I Needed to Know I Learned from Columbo*. The sequel *All I Need to Know I Learned from Dragnet* is in production.

Graham is also the author of *Tales of the Dim Knight* and the Adventures of Powerhouse series of Superhero comedy novels. He and his wife Andrea live in Boise, Idaho with their cat, Joybell.

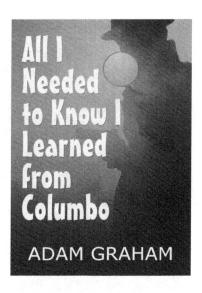

All I Needed to Know I Learned from Columbo

ADAM GRAHAM

> *"Murder mysteries are, among other things, our most moral form of entertainment."*
> *—Orson Welles*

Join podcaster Adam Graham on a fun journey through the mystery genre as he examines the histories and careers of seven of the greatest detectives from literature, radio, and television. Along the way, he stops to point to the sometimes surprising insights that these detectives teach, such as:

-How to avoid cluttering your brain from Sherlock Holmes.

-How to form valuable opinions from Nero Wolfe.

-How to find courage from Adrian Monk

These detectives will provide you with twelve, timeless life lessons in a fresh and entertaining way. *All I Needed to Know I Learned From Columbo* is a must-read for any fan of detective fiction.

Available for $2.99 in all major ebook formats. Also available as an audiobook in the Itunes story or through audible.com.

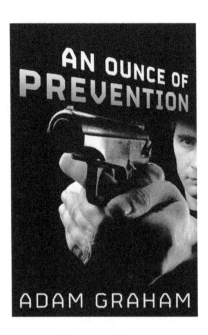

He thought it'd be a simple case that would pay the bills. Instead, a by-the-book detective faces the most difficult moral dilemma of his career.

A former cop turned private investigator, Jerry Newton agreed to protect a male teacher who had received threatening letters. He didn't know someone would bomb the teacher's car. He didn't expect to meet a mysterious woman who'd reveal the future. He didn't plan on coming to grips with his past. And he never expected to debate the merits of putting a bullet through his client's skull to prevent a series of heinous crimes.

Award-winning novelist Donna Fletcher Crow calls the novelette, *An Ounce of Prevention*, "Sam Spade meets Dr. Who."

Available for the Kindle and Kindle Reading Apps for 99 cents.

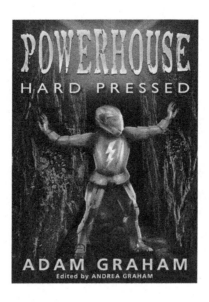

Dave Johnson's dreams have come true. He's taken Seattle by storm as Powerhouse, a metal-clad crime fighter. His awesome array of powers has the underworld on the run, his charitable efforts are successful, and his comic book is popular. When his publisher gets bought out, he's given every fan's dream: he's tasked with creating his own line of comic books. His biggest problem is his tendency to attract campy, wannabe "supervillains" who aren't worthy opponents.

Mitch "the Pharaoh" Farrow wants to turn Dave's dream into a nightmare. Mitch's job is to spread cynicism ahead of an interdimensional alien invasion. The aliens' king has promised to cure Mitch's dying daughter when he takes over and Mitch will do anything to save her. He uses every tool at his disposal, from a massive media smear machine to a force field bubble that crushes its victim into atoms.

With the help of new allies and old friends, Powerhouse strives to protect his family and the citizens of Seattle from the forces of cynicism.

Available in paperback ($10.99) or as an ebook or audiobook through audible.com.

Made in the USA
Coppell, TX
23 January 2022

72171024R00128